PLEASE

PLEASE

PLEASE

Renée Swindle

A Dell Book

Published by
Dell Publishing
Random House, Inc.
1540 Broadway
New York, New York 10036

Cover art by John Jinks

ISBN: 0-440-22376-8

Reprinted by arrangement with The Dial Press

Printed in the United States of America

Published simultaneously in Canada

June 2000

10   9

OPM

It was exactly 12:06 a.m. I know because I'd glanced at the clock and realized I had to go to work the next day and would certainly have a hangover. We were in the kitchen making coffee. We hadn't done anything except to kiss for a while on his couch, hold hands and talk, kiss some more. I was asking him where he kept his cups when I heard him come up behind me, his boots making a lovely sound against the kitchen floor.

He pressed his stomach into my back. "Don't move, okay? Just don't move."

I must have about died. He kissed the back of my neck and I let my head fall to the side. He kissed my cheek, smelled my hair. He lifted my blouse and I felt the cold tile from the counter against my belly. The cabinet above the counter was open, and before I closed my eyes, I noticed that I was staring directly into a bag of unbleached flour. I stood on my tiptoes because I wanted him to be able to hold on to my waist, my breasts, my ass. I held my breath as he tipped me over, raised a bare foot onto a boot one at a time then lifted my heels that much further. I didn't ever want to come down.

———

"It's very rare we cheer for those who admittedly do wrong. But Babysister's dazzling insight gives us a peek at how a man's words, actions and deeds are taken to heart, and shows how easy it really is to throw everything by the wayside—including friendship—when blinded by love."

—Franklin White, author of *Fed Up with the Fanny*

For my mother, Lucille Swindle, for
good friendship and advice

My father, James Swindle, for accepting me as I am

And my husband, Dennis Guikema, for constant
love and support

PLEASE

PLEASE

PLEASE

———

One

DON'T LET ANYONE tell you any different, sometimes love isn't about nothing but a crooked tooth, the curl of an eyebrow, the hairs on a wrist, a gold chain, or one small mole. For me, it's boots. Have you ever seen a black man in boots? Well, there you go. So when Darren sort of leaned into me and said my name, and I turned around to see his six-foot-three-inch body pressed firmly into two perfectly polished black boots, I'm sorry, but I was gone. Later. Goodbye. *Adiós*.

It wasn't like I'd never been with a man who wore boots before. But the thing with most of them was, once they took off their boots, they became that much shorter, that much fatter. At least that's the way it went with Greg and John and Roger too. No boots, no magic. Just like that, and they were reduced to this person walking around looking entirely lost. I tried. Believe me, I tried: Listen, baby, why don't you put your boots on. You look so *fine* in your boots. But sooner or later we had to go to bed, and poof, the magic was gone.

But not with Darren. Boots or no boots, he couldn't get on my nerves if he tried. Darren was it. The first time the combination was right: fine *and* intelligent. I've been out with fine men before but usually after two weeks it's like, Oh, you don't have a brain. Now why didn't I notice that before? Or the guy will be intelligent but get him in bed and he only knows one position: You on the bottom, him on top. A drop of sweat dripping in your ear every ten seconds. And don't even get me started on the pseudointelligent pro-black types. "My sister, my sister. Mother Africa, I see you have bought into the white man's lie. You must understand that it would be a mistake for me to go down on you. I refuse to partake in the white man's nasty habits. I can't believe that you would disrespect your man by asking him to do something like that."

Men are a mess. A complete mess. There's a communication problem going on that they don't want to discuss. So while he's going at it, you're left thinking, Hello??!! It sure would be nice if you kissed me on the lips now and then. Or, Hello??!! There is a thinking, feeling human being underneath you.

See, you touch a man anywhere and you've got a direct line to his dick. With a woman, a kiss on the ear might send a charge to her breast, kiss her breast and she feels something in her heart, suck her nipple and a dampness swells between her legs.

Let me put it this way: Have you ever seen a piano getting tuned? I was in the high school auditorium once and there was a man there tuning the piano. He'd barely tap a note, then he'd listen. Tap a note. Listen. Tap a note. Carefully. Gently. You could hear that piano loosen up just as nice. And that's the way it was with Darren.

He'd lick my earlobe. "Do you like that?"

Mmmm-hmm.

He'd hold the back of my neck in his hand and barely touch my breast. "Do you like that?"

Oh yes.

He wouldn't touch any harder until he felt my hip rise or until I pulled his head closer. "Do you like that?"

I'd moan and scream and sigh and after two, sometimes three orgasms I would just stare at the man in some kind of soap opera awe. "I've been reading the *Tao of Love and Sex*," he'd say. And I'd say, "I have no idea what that is, but you just keep on reading it."

Prince Charming, Superman, Superfly, all in one. I'm a believer because I have been there. Darren would reach down with his finger and move my panties aside, and I would be wet every time. *Every* time.

So what if the first time we met I was working at the bank, and when he said my name he was only asking me if I could make sure my best friend got the flowers he was leaving for her.

"Babysister? You're Babysister, right?" He had on boots, jeans, and a soft white shirt that I would have loved to unbutton. He had thick black hair cut short and neat, deep brown eyes, and a warm generous smile that made you feel that you were the only woman on the entire planet.

"Yeah."

"Well listen, would you do me a big favor and make sure Deborah gets these flowers? I sort of want them to be the first thing she sees when she gets here."

You are the finest, most drop-dead-gorgeous motherfucker I have seen in a long, very long time, and would you please prop me up on this counter, brush the pens aside, and do whatever it is you want to do?

But "Uh-huh" was all I said. "No problem."

Then he said, "Deborah said you were nice."

And I watched him jerk his keys, put on his sunglasses, push open the door with one elegant hand, and walk out.

When all that was left of him was the faint smell of Afro Sheen, I took a peek at the card.

> Deborah—
> *Thank you for a marvelous dinner.*
> *—Darren*

I thought again about how he said my name. Baby-sister, he said, and just like that, my name sounded as familiar as two dimes hitting the floor. *Ting. Ting.*

Two

I ALWAYS GET what I want. My father spoiled me as a child because I lost my mother. She died when I was four. We had just been to the store and she was carrying a large bag of groceries. We were headed to our car, which was parked across the street in front of a Baskin-Robbins. My mother took my hand before she stepped off the curb. I remember she cried out "Oh" just as an orange car pushed into her side and made her body fold like the flap on an envelope. "Oh" was all she said. I remember the hood of the car was shaped like the mouth of a shark, a large silver tooth near each front tire. I remember she said at the stoplight, "Maybe we should treat ourselves to a couple of ice-cream cones."

I hit the ground too, but as soon as I started to stand up, some woman screamed, "Somebody take the baby! Take the baby! She shouldn't ought to see this!" A man picked me up and took me to the corner. "Are you all right?" He squeezed my arms to make sure my bones were straight.

You'd think it would be a complete tragedy to see your mother die, but sometimes it doesn't seem like I was there at all. The accident happened so long ago it's become more like a dream. I consider myself lucky that I was so young when it happened. I mean, even though my mother pushed me out of the crosswalk and died under a car, all I have left from the accident really is a dark-brown scar on my right knee shaped like a bow on a gift.

I am my father's baby girl. I have an older brother named Malcolm, but I'll be honest with you, he doesn't get nearly as much attention as I do. I get so much attention not only because Malcolm gets on everyone's nerves, but because I was there when my mother died. It seems to me like the day after the funeral I started getting whatever I wanted. I mean, I had so much shit. My yellow skateboard with red wheels, my Flip Wilson doll with Flip Wilson on one side and Geraldine on the other—pull the string and he'd say, The devil made me do it! My Betty Crocker You-Can-Bake! Oven that made chocolate cake— only with the help of Mom, but who cared because it tasted nasty anyway; my pink bicycle, my red wagon, my skates that looked like tennis shoes with wheels. Later I had Barbie dolls. Barbie dolls everywhere. Barbie town house, Barbie mobile home, Barbie Corvette, swimming pool, beauty salon, and horse. Black Barbies, white Barbies. I got a VW Bug for my sixteenth birthday and after I wrecked it, a used Toyota. After the Toyota broke down I got a Honda Civic. I went with the finest man in high school to the senior prom and was named homecoming queen. Remember tag and having to decide who was it? Stuff like one potato, two potato, and Johnny ate a booger and it tasted like sugar, you're it? Well, this might sound a bit strange, but I never had to be it. I made sure that I wouldn't have to be it even if it meant holding my breath until I might pass out.

All I'm trying to say is this: I don't remember a time when I didn't get what I wanted. And I wanted Darren like nobody's business.

I waited until Deborah finished with a customer before going over to her desk. She had recently been promoted to loan officer, so unlike the rest of us lowly tellers who had to stand behind the bulletproof protection glass speaking into a microphone all day, Deborah had the interesting job of helping people with loans and mortgages, a name plate that said *Deborah Michelle Moore* in cursive letters, and even her own desk and a chair that leaned back and swiveled. Her desk was right beneath the poster of a black couple with their young son and new baby wrapped in a yellow blanket. They stood in front of a two-story house. The wife was almost as light as Deborah and they all had perfect smiles and perfect teeth and perfect clothes. In other words, they looked nothing like the people who came into our bank. The bottom of the poster read *Let us work for you.*

I knocked twice on Deborah's desk. She had turned her coffee mug into a small vase and was busy gazing at her new bouquet, which leaned heavily to the right and forced her to lean her head as well. I caught myself tilting my head a bit too, but straightened up when I asked her why she hadn't told me about Darren. Not a word.

Still gazing at her flowers, she hid her smile behind two small fists. "I don't know. I've been meaning to."

"Well, how long have you been seeing him?"

"It's been about two months now."

"Two months! I'm surprised you haven't said anything."

"Well . . ."

I picked up a freesia and took a whiff. "So how did you meet?"

"A blind date," she giggled. "Can you believe it?"

Blind date my ass, I thought. For one thing you don't meet men like Darren on blind dates. And for another, I knew everyone Deborah knew and couldn't imagine any one of our friends wanting to share him, whether she was single or not.

"Who set this blind date up? And why didn't they tell me about him first?" I said as if I were joking around.

"Because my mother set it up. See, Darren's the son of a woman my mom met at our church's anniversary a few months back. Darren's mother sang in the visiting choir. It was one of the best anniversaries we've had in a long old time. I told you to come. Sister Wilma tore up 'Take My Hand, Precious Lord.' You should have seen all the people walking up to the altar. Last year our own choir sang. It was okay, but this time felt like a real celebration. Darren's mother is an alto by the way, just like my mother. And did I tell you about the dinner the scholarship committee put together?"

I tried my best to pay attention as she jumped from one subject to another. That was the thing about Deborah, a simple noun or name could send her off on some totally different story. She'd hear the magic word, and somewhere, way back somewhere in her head, something clicked or gonged or beeped and off she went on an entirely new subject. You had to let her return to the point at hand on her own, otherwise it was a lot of "Hold on, hold on. I'm getting to that." She had been like this since we were girls.

". . . So anyway, when my mother mentioned her friend's son, I honestly didn't know if I should go or not!

I'd never been on a blind date before. Never!" She let her head fall into her hands. The part in her hair was perfectly straight. A frail line of skin surrounded by thick black hair. "Should I go? Should I not go?" She ran her fingers straight through the top and the part disappeared.

There was a time when I would have done anything to have hair like Deborah's. When we were girls, she would come out of the bathtub and sit on the floor between her mother's legs. Wisps of wet hair would stick to her face and her mother would simply glide the comb straight down her back. One continuous slow pull and then another. After a few minutes Deborah's hair was braided into two long, shiny plaits with one perfectly straight part. I, on the other hand, had to get my hair pressed every other week. After Momma died, our neighbor Mrs. Davis started fixing it. She'd come by every other Friday to wash and press it. My hair was so nappy, it had to be handled in sections. Mrs. Davis's thick fingers pushed at my temples, moving my head down and to the side, cocked and turned just so to the left. Hold your head still, girl! and then the sizzle of the comb touching the grease and the smell of burnt hair.

". . . and so we finally hooked up." Deborah's face brightened, satisfied with the ending of her story. "I'm sorry I didn't say anything. I don't want to jinx it is all. I want to move real slow with this one."

I wanted to wrap my hands around her bony neck. I put the freesia back and pulled out a chrysanthemum. Interesting that he thought to buy something besides roses. I decided I liked this bouquet better. It showed originality.

"With all this slow movement there must be something wrong with the man. Don't tell me he doesn't have a job."

"Oh, he has a job all right."

I watched her eyebrows rise, her eyes widen, and her burgundy-painted lips shape each word. She looked around the bank as though we were discussing a robbery.

"Girl, he's an architect. An *architect*, Babysister."

"Get outta here. How old is he?"

"Thirty-two."

"Married?"

"No."

"Kids?"

"No."

"Gay?" I whispered.

"No." She whispered.

"Single?"

"Single."

I looked around for our boss, Ms. Hodges. When I didn't see her, I plopped half of my ass on Deborah's desk, bumping against the picture she had of the two of us in a brass frame. We wore identical peach-colored dresses in the photo, our arms wrapped around each other's waists. The picture was about three years old. A friend from high school was getting married and we were bridesmaids. We hated the dresses because they made us look twice our size. I had said something about the bride wanting everyone to look as fat as she is, and Deborah's mother took the picture right as we started laughing, right as our mouths fell open and our bodies leaned toward each other. The photo was taken at a time when we were truly the best of friends, before Deborah found religion and could still laugh at a good joke. And while I knew she still believed us to be as close, lately I had begun to wonder if there was much more to our friendship than the fact that we had known each other for so long and hung out with the same group of people.

I watched her pick up a pencil, put it down, pick it up again. "He sounds too good," I said.

"I know. That's why I want to take it slow. If I play it right, who knows?"

"Well, be careful. You might've gone and got yourself hooked up with a player."

"I don't think so, Babysister. He's real nice. That's why I had him over for dinner. Twice."

"Girl, you need to quit. I thought you said you wanted to take it slow."

I lifted the chrysanthemum I was holding as if to say, may I please have it? She smiled and nodded yes.

"So what do you think?" she asked.

"About what?"

"About me and Darren."

I give it two more weeks. Tops.

"You're a lucky woman," I said, giving my flower a twirl. "It sounds too good to be true."

He grew up in none other than Baldwin Hills. Graduated from UCLA. You hear me? UUUU . . . SEEE . . . LLLL . . . AAEEE. He owned a condo and drove a BMW. Wanted kids, marriage. Listened only to jazz and sometimes even classical. And get this, according to Deborah, he had no hang-ups whatsoever about spending money on a woman, had already bought her a small hand-carved jewelry box he found in an African gift shop.

It was time to throw a dinner party.

Nine days after Darren had walked into the bank, I found myself making dinner for six in his honor—not that anyone would know this but me. I set the party for Saturday evening. I decided to invite Byron from work who, like Deborah, was also a loan officer. He had been feeling depressed since his wife left him for a garbage collector who wrote poetry. I have to admit that it didn't hurt that Byron knew a lot about jazz music. I hadn't talked to Cynthia Woods since she'd quit the bank eight months earlier after marrying a rich man who owned ten video stores, but I thought she and her husband would make perfect guests because while her new husband hadn't gone to UCLA he *had* attended USC and I figured what's the difference; not to mention, Cynthia played piano and knew about classical music. It would be perfect. I'd find out from Deborah what kind of food Darren liked and serve his favorite dish with a gracious smile; I'd light candles and place them in the center of the table next to a bouquet of flowers, I'd play classical music and jazz and nod my head as he talked with Cynthia and Byron about his favorite musicians.

There was only one problem with my plan. I didn't want to invite my boyfriend of the past three and a half months. I mean, how was I going to get to know Darren with Rob sitting next to me, holding my hand and carrying on? In the end, I told Rob I was having a friend over from work. I made up some sad story about how she had recently been dumped and was two months pregnant. It was easy as hell to get rid of him. Besides, I only needed him away for one night.

I met Rob at the grocery store, a place where I happened to meet men on a regular basis. Even when I purposely went to the store in sweats and without makeup, men made passes, asked for my number. Most of them weren't worth the time—"Hey, baby, you lookin' good in them sweats. I oughtta get your number"—but a few of them were pretty nice. Rob, in fact, was the best of the grocery store men. He wasn't much taller than me and had a football player's build and cute round Santa Claus cheeks that gave him a boyish look. When he saw me reaching for a head of iceberg lettuce he said, "You should use romaine or red leaf. They're healthier." I would have told him to mind his own business if his body hadn't looked so good stuffed in those blue shorts and that cutoff black T-shirt with the missing sleeves. He told me he repaired computers. "Do you have a computer? 'Cause if you ever have any trouble, I could help you out." There was no way I was going to stop this one from following me around the grocery store.

Turns out, there was more than physical attraction going on, too. I genuinely enjoyed hanging out with Rob. He loved video games as much as a kid, and taught me how to play a few. He had all the popular games at his apartment: Mortal Kombat, NFL Game Day, Killer Instinct, Bushido Blade. We could play for hours. I liked to play primarily because playing video games got him excited for some reason. We'd be playing a game, and the next thing I knew, he'd have me on the floor in front of the TV, crazy cartoon sounds or action music blaring in my ear as we kissed and moaned. We liked to eat Chinese food and watch old movies, too, and once in a while we'd go out dancing. Yeah, it was a nice, easy relationship. The only problem, really, was that before long, old Rob started feeling more like a buddy than a lover. He hated to hear me say this, but it was true. By the third week, I was greeting him at the door in my sweats. By the second month I knew everything about him. Details only a wife would appreciate. I knew he carried sandwiches to work on Tuesday and Thursday, salads Monday, microwave lunches Wednesday and Friday. I knew what days he swam, what days he ran. Precisely how much milk he put in his coffee. That he manicured his damn nails every other day. How he folded his underwear.

What was worse was how everything turned routine in bed. He was like a robot, a sensual robot, but still a robot. I often thought that certain moves had been programmed into his brain by an ex-girlfriend. Or maybe he had read one of those how-to books like *How to Please a Woman in Ten Easy Steps*. When he was about to go down on me, for instance, he'd go through the same series of moves like a trained animal. He'd kiss each side of my neck then he'd kiss one breast while giving the other an obligatory squeeze; he'd wiggle his tongue over my belly button as he fingered me; and right before he found the spot he had been looking for all along, he'd kiss my inner thighs. The same thing always and forever. When I mentioned this to him he got all hurt. "No one else has ever complained before." He'd try to break the routine for a while, but it was no time at all before we were back to the same four-step dance. Neck, breasts, belly button, thighs.

I don't mean to make Rob out to be as pathetic as he might sound. Like I said, he was my buddy, and even though sex wasn't the greatest, I liked hanging out with him. I liked walking down the street with my arm wrapped around one of those huge biceps. I liked sitting in bed with him and eating Chinese food. I liked his goofy jokes. Who knows how long we would have lasted if Darren hadn't entered the picture.

My dinner party was a success, but I have to admit that I couldn't stop thinking about Darren. I couldn't stop thinking about all the things I really wanted to say:

Thank you for coming to my dinner party tonight, Darren. I wish I could talk to you more, but Byron won't shut up and I don't want to look like I'm not interested in my guests, even though I'm not. You look so handsome. Who taught you how to eat like that anyway? Scooting the food with your knife instead of bread? Look how elegantly your fingers curve around your fork. I can't begin to tell you how glad I am you came tonight. By the way, just ignore Cynthia, she's not really my friend any more. Sorry about the way she's going on and on about her new house. Money changes people. I knew you would like the dinner, though. Deborah mentioned you liked soul food. Black-eyed peas with okra, turnip greens, roast beef, candied yams. Bet you haven't eaten like this in a while and Lord knows Deborah can't cook.

Have you noticed the music? It's "Chi . . . cow . . . ski." I made the guy at the record store repeat the name over and over until I got it right. Later, after we eat the peach cobbler, I'll play some Miles Davis. You can talk to Byron about him. He knows a lot about jazz.

Listen, Darren, don't think I'm weird or anything, but I could seriously just look at you all night. Move the furniture, sit you in the middle of the room, and just stare. You'll be my TV, my centerpiece, my fireplace. Forget Deborah. Forget her. I mean, look how dingy she's been acting all night. Doesn't all that giggling get on your nerves?

One more thing: you're looking mighty mighty, but would you please take off your boots before I scream?

Not ten minutes after everyone had gone, I sat on my couch sucking the fork Darren had used to put peach cobbler into his mouth. I repeated Darren Forrest Wilson, Darren Forrest Wilson, Darren Forrest Wilson, until his name blurred into a three-beat rhythm, a waltz inside my head. He had impressed me more than once during dinner, so I knew my attraction was based on more than the fact that he looked good and had money. He was confident but not arrogant. He never tried to dominate the conversation like men often do, helped me clear the table before dessert, held his own against Cynthia's husband who believed that affirmative action should be abolished. Basically, he seemed like the type of man who knew how to take care of himself, which of course is a very rare thing.

I went back and forth between he likes me, he likes me not. As far as I could tell, I had three things going for me: 1. He had said he loved the meal. 2. He had given me a kiss on the cheek on his way out, and 3. I had caught him looking at my breasts exactly four times. Problem was, I had also watched him put his hand on Deborah's knee, lean in and give her a kiss, and before he had taken a sip of his coffee with sugar but no cream, he had wrapped a lock of Deborah's hair around his finger as though it were a satin ribbon. I tried to think of something that could top a hand on a knee and a kiss, but who was I trying to fool? If I was going to get Darren to notice me, I'd have to do more than throw a damn party.

I should say right now that my attraction to one of Deborah's boyfriends was a first. We never competed for a man because we never had to. Deborah usually went for the type of guy who enjoyed a good glass of milk, worked on his lawn every chance he could, still did the Shuffle at parties while encouraging everyone to join in, and dreamt of owning a Winnebago someday. So basically, while I went after the kind of man you might find in a smooth malt liquor ad, Deborah went for the type of guy you see in bank advertisements, like the one that hung over her head at work. I should also add that I always knew I could trust Deborah with my boyfriends because she's not the competing type. But God only knew if I could trust any of my boyfriends with her. I asked an ex once if he could choose between me or Deborah, who would he choose and why. I can't remember his name for some reason— Justin? Calvin? Chris? But I do remember he had the habit of playing with his nose when he got nervous. He'd pinch, sometimes start to dig. Naturally as soon as I asked, his hand went straight for the top of his nostrils and began stroking. "Well, you're sexy. You're cool, see. You have a way of walking, of acting, that can get any man going." He pinched the sides of each nostril between his index finger and thumb. "Deborah, on the other hand, is beautiful. But she's *too* beautiful, see. Dating someone like Deborah would be a huge headache." He blew out air like his nose was too dry and needed snot, pinched again. "Besides, baby, thing is, who has the better body? You do! Hands down. I'd rather have a fine together woman like you any day. And that's the God's honest truth."

I took off my shoes and stretched out my legs. I had on tight pants and a blouse held together by as few buttons as possible. My brown breasts sat up in my bra like the heads of twin infants, round and hopeful, waiting patiently for attention. I sighed. Well Chris or Justin or whatever your name is, my body wasn't much of an asset tonight.

I tapped Darren's fork against my hand and began to wonder if he was at Deborah's place or not. Deborah was too religious for her own good, but she was a woman, after all. He's probably with her right now, I thought, burying his head in her hair, nibbling on one of her big ears, telling her how beautiful he thinks she is. Shit.

I drank the last bit of wine from one of the open bottles sitting on the coffee table and told myself moping wasn't going to accomplish anything so I might as well clean up. I scraped dishes, put away the leftovers and even swept the living room floor. And that is when I found them. Leaning against the coffee table leg, acting as though they belonged, were Darren Forrest Wilson's sunglasses.

I held the glasses close to my chest then put them on and watched the room go dark. It was almost midnight, but I picked up the phone and dialed Deborah's number anyway. After a few rings, I heard Deborah's dreamy "Hello?" and started right in.

"Hey girl, you alone?"

"Huh?"

"Well, the way Darren was looking at you tonight, I thought that you guys might be going at it right now." I imagined her barely holding the phone, sitting on top of Darren and swaying her hips, staring straight into her print of a black Jesus talking to a group of rainbow children.

She let out a heavy sigh, or maybe it was a yawn. "Yeah, he was pretty sweet. Thanks again for having us over. Too bad Rob couldn't make it. It was nice of you to invite Byron, though. Poor thing, doesn't eat well since Myra left him. Did you notice how much cobbler he had? And I know you noticed how Cynthia was bragging about that new house. I think she's changed since she got married, don't you? She never calls me anymore."

I took off the sunglasses and tried to smell them. Nothing. "He didn't even stay over for a drink?"

"Who?"

"Darren."

"Nope. No excitement tonight. It's just me and Noodles." She began speaking in that disgusting voice pet owners use. "Poor thing. Him has dry skin and it irritates him. Him needs to go to the vet."

"It's always you and Noodles. I've never known a black woman to love a cat so much."

"Babysister, I don't mean to be rude, but do you realize it's almost twelve?"

"It's a Saturday night, Deborah. You used to stay up past three on Saturday nights."

"Well those days are gone." I heard a long yawn, which grew loud enough so that I had to hold the phone away from my ear. "I'm going to church tomorrow so I need to get to sleep."

"You going with Darren?"

"No, Babysister. I told you, we're taking it slow."

"Damn, you're cranky when you're sleepy. You've always been a crank when you don't get your rest. And you were always the first to fall asleep at slumber parties, remember that?" I was trying my best to sound sweet.

"Baby, what do you want?"

"Darren left his sunglasses."

"And?"

"And so what should I do with them?"

"Bring them to work Monday and I'll give them to Darren the next time I see him."

"Well, I thought maybe I'd call him and let him know I have his glasses and then what I could do is . . ." I tried to think up the lie as I went along, something I have talent for. All you have to do is stay calm. ". . . while I have Darren on the phone, I could try and find out a little more about what he thinks about you. What do you think of that idea?"

"I don't know."

"Don't you want to know what he thinks?"

"I don't know. Maybe I don't. Maybe he doesn't really like me. Sometimes I get the feeling that he doesn't want to take things so slow. Maybe he's getting impatient."

"Well, you won't know what he wants unless I do a little spying for you."

Long silence.

Finally she spoke up. "Well, I guess a little spying won't hurt anything. You got a pen?"

Deborah's family had moved into the neighborhood when we were both in preschool, and I swear she hadn't changed much over time. Deborah was one of the most naive people I ever met. I remember a particular instance a few months after I started working at the bank and we were walking out to our cars. The bank was closed by then so the parking lot was fairly empty. This guy drove up in this seriously tacky car. The car was barely off the ground because it was sitting on those wheels that were half the size they were supposed to be. It was painted purple with gold trim and had red lights going around and around the YOBABYO license plate. Music was blaring all over the place.

Deborah and I were saying our goodbyes and getting ready to get in our cars when the guy pulled over near the entrance, rolled down his window, and motioned toward Deborah as if to say, This is your lucky day. Negro had gold chains *and* a Jheri curl. I kid you not. The man had loser written all over his nasty-looking self. He took off his sunglasses. "Hey." (Yeah, he was real smooth.) Deborah looked over and was all smiles and giggles. "I need to talk to you 'bout some bank b'iness."

Instead of getting in her car like any sane woman, or certainly any woman who grew up in our neighborhood, Little Miss Debbie shook her head like, Oh awl right, I'll talk to you, and actually walked over to the fool, who could have had a gun or a knife or somebody hiding in his backseat prepared to grab her. She was a few feet away when I told her straight out, "Deborah, get over here. You don't need to be talking to him. If he needs to talk to you about bank business, tell him the bank opens at nine." Deborah looked at me like you're so right, Babysister, shrugged her shoulders toward him as if to apologize, and walked away. He pulled his shades down. "Oh, so it's like that?"

"Yeah, it's like that," I yelled.

When he drove off, Deborah wondered if he would come to the bank. "Not in this lifetime," I told her. "That fool has probably never written a check before."

So what's my point? Close your eyes and think of a deer walking in a forest nibbling at leaves or whatever it is they eat. Think of bunny rabbits or those white furry seals with the big eyes that get clubbed. That was Deborah. If Deborah were an animal, she'd be like the kind you see in Disney cartoons. Bambi, Thumper, Dumbo. Take your pick.

I figured, by going after Darren, I was merely doing her a favor. I was saving her from the heartbreak he was sure to inflict after he ultimately saw through her good looks, saw through her dimples and her smooth skin that still showed the remains of several white ancestors, and her long hair that fell naturally into loose curls well beyond her shoulders. Sooner or later, Darren would realize who he was dating. Her birdlike laugh would become annoying, her need to go to church three times a week obsessive. But most of all, he'd get tired of bringing up serious issues involving things like sex or politics only to be met by a faraway look, which lately appeared all too often when things got too "worldly" for her—the sort of look that only hints at something deeper, like a cloud that threatens rain but never delivers.

I called Darren the next morning while Deborah was at church. I actually felt nervous before dialing his number so I told myself to play it cool, get a grip. Breathe. I reminded myself that he was a man after all, nothing new. He picked up the phone after four rings. It surprised me that he knew who I was right away and immediately began thanking me and going on and on about my cooking. His voice sounded as though his vocal chords had been dipped in something hot and rich, like caramel or fudge right before you pour it on vanilla ice cream. As I sat there listening, I imagined this voice pouring into the phone and through the phone lines that stretched all the way from his house straight into the curly cord that led directly into my ear.

After I told Darren about the sunglasses, we fell into an easy conversation mainly because Darren did most of the talking. He told me about his hobbies—reading, collecting old blues and jazz albums—and about his job.

We had talked for a good forty minutes when he said, "Listen, why don't we finish this conversation face to face? Why don't you bring my sunglasses out to my place and

I'll take you out to lunch? You wouldn't mind driving out here, would you?"

HA!

He lived way out near Westwood ". . . toward the end of the block. The blue and beige condos on the left. But hey, why don't you meet me at this Thai place I know first? I'm starving. You mind Thai food?"

I wondered what the hell kind of food Thai food was and hoped that it didn't involve goat meat or insects. I wore my black mini, my white rayon blouse that dips in the front, and my white sandals. Tied my hair up in a scarf, perfume, gold earrings, and oh yes, black silk panties with matching bra because you just never know.

Three

WE ARRIVED AT the restaurant sometime after noon. The place was empty except for three white people sitting at a table in the back. Darren and I sat in the front with a window all to ourselves, and when we weren't talking, we'd casually watch people walking by. I didn't have to worry about what I should eat because Darren ordered all of the food. "You don't mind?" And I said, "No no, go ahead."

I couldn't believe how delicious the food was. I like to consider myself a good cook, but for the life of me I couldn't figure out what some of the seasonings were and kept bugging the waitress with, What do you put in this? And what kind of noodle is that? I mean, the most exotic food I had ever eaten was China Kingdom all-you-can-eat buffet, five ninety-nine Monday through Friday. My tongue did not know what to do with all those new textures and flavors. I won't lie either, all that Thai beer made me burp, but it was worth it. Not to mention it was completely free. The bill came to thirty-four dollars and eighty-nine cents, but all Darren did was ask if I wanted anything else, and when I said no, he took out his gold card and casually placed it on the table like having your very own gold card was no big deal at all.

As I sat there scraping my spoon against the last bit of my fried ice cream, I realized that no matter how old I'd become someday, I'd be able to look back on this date with Darren and feel complete happiness. I pictured myself at seventy or eighty, still able to vividly remember sitting in the wood chair with the burgundy cushions and gazing at the thin line of light cutting across Darren's right eye and down his cheek. Even at eighty, I'd remember the gold statue directly behind him, a woman wearing a pointed red hat standing with one leg bent in midair, her fingers curved so that it looked as if she were holding a tiny piece of lint. I'd remember the gurgle of the fish tank in the middle of the restaurant and the huge colorful fish watching us eat. I'd remember the odd, intoxicating smells coming from the kitchen and the sound of Darren's wrist-watch hitting the glass tabletop every now and then. One day, I'd be sitting in my rocker on the porch of an old-age home—or better yet, on the porch of the house Darren and I had owned for some forty years—playing with my tongue in my mouth as my head nods lower and lower. I might look like I'm dozing off, but actually I'll be feeling my body getting warmer and my long thin breasts swelling as my clitoris perks up. I'll be thinking about that lunch with Darren where I felt as though I had left Los Angeles altogether, spent a few hours in an exotic place, and that's when I'll lift my lips over my huge false teeth and stretch them out into a smile.

I was reaching for his sunglasses when he asked me if I wanted to see his condo. "It's not far from here. We could walk over."

I was screaming inside, jumping up and down like a

kid, but I managed to stay calm. "Sure," I said. "Why not?"

First thing he said when we entered his condo was "Sit down, I have a surprise for you." Then he disappeared into the kitchen.

I pressed one ass cheek at a time against his leather couch over and over. The left cheek; the right cheek. It felt so good. He had several paintings on the walls: black children dancing, a framed picture of a group of jazz musicians, several African masks. Large art books sat on the coffee table and there was a variety of plants in colorful flower pots. I felt like I should have been sitting in high heels and a sleeveless black dress—tight with no back—and at any moment Darren would step out in a dinner jacket and tie holding two fat glasses of cognac.

When he returned from the kitchen, he shouted, "Thai beer!" then held up four sixteen-ounce bottles in each hand like bouquets. "You're not in any rush to go home are you?"

Darren kept offering more beer until I noticed that it was close to eight o'clock, but there he was standing at the bottom of the staircase in his living room, suggesting we go up and sit on the deck. The view was so nice up there we didn't bother talking much. We simply looked out over all the palm and magnolia trees and what seemed like all of Westwood.

Next door, a white man came out into his backyard. Since we were upstairs, we could see his entire backyard. The man wore these green gym shorts that no longer fit—like he hadn't realized he'd gained twenty pounds. While he searched for the perfect spot to put his sprinkler, Darren started asking me questions about where I grew up and what was my family like. When I told him about my mother's death, his expression turned sympathetic. It usually gets on my nerves when I see even a hint of pity in someone's eyes, but Darren seemed genuinely interested. I told him that my mother was a seamstress who had started her own business and described all the outfits she made for me when I was a girl. I even found myself telling him about the day she died, how we were going to buy ice cream, and then just like that, she was gone. I told him about my father as well. How he was sort of known in our neighborhood as the widower who raised two children on his own. "I know he feels bad about me growing up without my mother," I said. "He tried to make up for it by giving me things. He worked at the post office when we were growing up and when I was a little girl, he'd bring these packages for me. He'd tell me that people never wrapped their packages right and that he hated to do it, but had to bring home whatever it was, then he'd tell me to go on and open it. And that's how I'd end up with a new doll or whatever. I don't know why he didn't just say he bought me a gift, but it was sweet."

"He sounds like a good man."

"He is."

I put my feet up on the ledge of the balcony and sipped my beer. I couldn't remember the last time I'd talked about my family so much. I felt so comfortable sitting there I almost forgot how fine Darren looked. The thought occurred to me that I could spend the rest of my life hanging out with Darren, talking, drinking beer, not doing much more than enjoying his smile.

We watched Mr. Gym Shorts come out again. He walked over to the side of his yard and moved the best he could until he was on his knees. He looked like he was about to do some weeding or something, problem was, as soon as he bent over, his shorts began to slip down until we had a perfect view of his pink behind. Darren and I looked at each other with raised eyebrows and squished-up noses. "Would you like to see a picture of my parents?" He laughed. I told him anything would be better than looking at his neighbor's ass, and we went back downstairs where we sat on the floor with our backs to the couch.

He showed me a picture of his parents sitting in lawn chairs with fruity drinks in their hands. His father was heavier than Darren but Darren had his father's nose and high cheekbones. His mother wore a straw hat and sunglasses but from what I could tell she had given Darren his perfect lips. Both his parents had on these tacky flowered shirts and beige shorts.

"This was taken on a cruise we all took in Greece last year to celebrate my father's sixtieth birthday."

"What do they do?"

"My dad's a lawyer. My mother studied history in college. She married my father after she graduated and had me. She's really involved in her church. She does a lot of volunteer work."

I studied the picture again.

"They're really nice people," he said.

They're really *rich* people, is more like it, I thought.

Besides the picture of his parents, I saw him standing on the Golden Gate Bridge making a peace sign; somewhere in Arizona—a brown spot in between two rocks as white as clouds; a picture of him as a boy with a huge Afro. In the last picture he showed me, he was holding a woman's hand at a dinner table. They were too busy staring at each other to notice someone was taking their picture.

"Ex-girlfriend."

She was almost the same complexion as Deborah. Big eyes that looked sad and strong at the same time and a very short brown Afro.

"Her name's Angela. I guess you'd say she was my first love."

Darren and Angela met at a UCLA Black Student Union open poetry reading. Later, when he called her, they stayed up talking literally all night. They were both pretty lonely and had a lot in common. "I know that's why we lasted so long," he said. "At the time I hadn't met too many sisters who were into hanging out at museums." They browsed through used-book stores, drank espressos at night, saw foreign films. After making love, Angela would recite poems by Maya Angelou and Nikki Giovanni while feeding him grapes. Well, he didn't say that exactly, but he might as well have. I mean, by the way he talked about their relationship, you would've thought it was straight out of a black romance novel and not anyone's actual life.

"We're still friends. We were together almost three years, but after graduation, she went off to grad school at Berkeley. That made it too hard. It fizzled out. She's married now, but is still one of my best friends. She teaches high school and her husband teaches at Stanford."

He thumbed through a couple stacks of pictures finally pulling out a recent picture of Angela and her husband, who turned out to be white, standing in front of their house in Oakland, California. The house looked pretty big, too, from what I could tell. Angela still had the short

Afro and was wearing a floral skirt and long earrings. Her husband had his arm around her. He had long brown hair and a goatee. He looked like he probably enjoyed things like rock climbing and hiking.

Darren pushed his beer across the coffee table with two fingers. It wasn't until he placed his elbow on the couch that I noticed he was sitting so close I could see the thin hairs coming in over his lips. I wondered if he planned on letting a mustache grow in. "How 'bout you. Who was your first love?"

"That Mustang convertible sitting out in front of your house. I was with my father when I saw it. The car lot was next door to the restaurant where we had eaten breakfast. My Mustang was up on a platform. The sun was shining down on the red paint and gold trim like a spotlight. I heard angels singing, swear to God."

"Be serious!"

"I am serious. I was never a believer in love at first sight until that day. My father helped me with the down payment and me and my car have been together ever since."

"Okay. Okay. Who was the first *human* you ever loved?"

"Love? As in, I think I want to spend the rest of my life with this person?"

"Yes."

I knew I should have had a name to give him as many men as I had dated over the years, but I didn't. I went down my list anyway, all the way back to seventh grade. "I don't think I've ever been in love," I said. "I've been in like. I've been in lust. But I don't think I've ever been in love. I don't think I have."

He let his arm reach across the back of the couch and

looked at me as though it was the first time he had actually seen me. "I'm surprised," he said. "You're a very pretty woman."

I widened my big, dark-brown eyes and raised my perfectly arched eyebrow. "I never said men haven't fallen in love with *me*."

"Being in love is a wonderful experience," he said.

"It's not like I've never had wonderful experiences," I said. I thought about the three men who had proposed, not with flimsy promises of marriage, but each on his knee, with diamond ring in hand.

I'd had plenty, *plenty* of opportunities to fall in love and if I hadn't completely fallen in love with a man before, I surely loved certain things about each one I'd been with, certain things they did or said, certain touches or smells. Derrick was a mechanic but had the softest hands you'd ever want to touch. His skin always made me think of a baby who had been powdered and changed. Mark was a manager at Sears and maybe it was because, like me, he was on his feet most of the day, but he had a serious thing about giving me foot massages. Whenever I put my feet up, there he was explaining the importance of taking care of your feet while giving me a lengthy massage. Several were good at helping me fix things around my apartment or helping me with a bill or two. I mean, I loved all kinds of things about my men. I couldn't help it if I had to break something off because I had grown bored or because I'd inevitably want more.

The thing is, whenever I thought about falling in love, I always imagined a certain feeling taking me over, the kind of feeling that makes you want to cover your mouth because you might cry out. Let me explain it this way. I saw a documentary on James Brown a few years back. I was so moved by watching that man sing, I immediately ordered the documentary through PBS. I've lost count of how many times I watched it; I can still watch it and be amazed. Something magical happens to James Brown when he's performing. I love how he'll jerk his shoulder when a certain note on the bass guitar is struck, move a hip right before the drummer bangs the cymbal. That was what I wanted when I fell in love. I wanted whatever feeling James Brown had when he was onstage back in the sixties, when he'd run his fingers along the length of the microphone's long silver frame as if caressing the outline of a woman's body, when he'd press his pelvis into the mike before suddenly dropping to his knee—almost, just almost—letting the microphone fall to the ground. I don't know if it was crazy for me to want so much, but I was prepared to wait until I found someone who made me feel whatever James Brown felt as the sweat poured down his face and he pleaded "I'll Go Crazy" or "Try Me" or "I Want You So Bad" or "Please Please Please."

I decided to let Darren think whatever he was going to think, though, and we sat in silence for a while drinking our beer. I scanned the titles on his bookshelf and tried to remember the last time I'd read a book. I had to have been in high school because I knew for a fact that I hadn't read one since. Magazines yes, but not a single book. Thing is, I had enjoyed reading while I was in school. I'd worked hard on all my assignments and had graduated with a 3.4. But I was fast, way too fast. My progress reports said things like "Has a lot of potential, if she'd only *apply* herself." "Talks back. Must realize her role as *student*." "Continually talks when teacher is talking." When the time came to apply to college, I figured I'd had enough of school. After graduation, I'd work for a while before going back, save some money, have some fun. I eventually started taking night courses at Los Angeles Southwest College. I'd start classes at the beginning of each semester, but would inevitably drop out. I found that after working all day selling clothes at Nordstroms, the last thing I wanted to do was go to school at night. My father suggested I try a different school, so I went to Compton Community College for a year. I managed to complete two math classes and a speech class, but after I got my job at the bank, I became less interested and soon stopped going altogether. Sure I had moments of guilt for not following through with college, and have to admit that sitting in Darren's living room looking at all his books didn't help matters. I told myself I should at least start reading again. You want an intelligent man like Darren, you have to start acting intelligent. God help you if he wants to start talking about literature or something.

I stared down at my bottle and began pulling off the label. That's when he said something that hurt so much, he might as well have told me to take my black butt home.

"So tell me," he said, "do you think I have a chance with Deborah?"

I pulled again at the label on the beer bottle, tore off an entire word. Shit.

"That depends."

"On?"

"Do you like going to church?"

He smiled for a second but then bit his lower lip and shook his head. "Yeah, she is into church. But I like that about her, you know? There's something about her that seems different from most women I meet. She's not impressed with the material or financial stuff for starters. She's a special, special woman. She's not the type you want to jump into bed with—not that we haven't come close."

"So if she's so special, what's the problem?"

"Something about her makes me nervous. I actually find myself feeling like a teenager. Has she said much about me? I can't tell if she really likes me or not."

I knew for a fact that Deborah was serious about Darren, mainly because she *hadn't* talked about him all that much. Usually she told me everything about a new boyfriend and I'd end up giving her advice or teasing her about her taste in men. But she kept her feelings about Darren pretty much to herself like he was too precious to be analyzed or discussed. Yeah, she was serious about him all right. But what I told Darren was this: "To be honest, Deborah wants a churchgoing man. I asked her, too. I said, 'So what's up with you and Darren? He seems nice. You like him or what?' And she said, 'My eyes are on the Lord, and they'll stay there until I get a *marriage* proposal.' "

"*Marriage proposal?*"

"Marriage proposal. I kid you not. She said she thought you were good-looking, but seemed too 'worldly.' She wants to save herself until marriage. She calls herself a born-again virgin or something. Marriage or nothing. Don't tell her I told you this, but she told me about those times you two came close. She says she'd break up with you if you ever come close again. She's serious, too."

The more I lied, the more the lies felt like truth, which

of course is the best way to lie. The way I see it, you've got to believe in what you're saying whether it's the truth or not.

He sighed. "I guess it's good she can stay so strong. I'm not into any bed-hopping myself, and I've enjoyed going slow. We're developing a good solid friendship, and I think if you're serious about someone, that's important." He paused for a second or so then said, "Waiting until marriage, though, seems extreme, don't you think?"

"Hmmph. There's no way in hell I'd give up sex to wait for marriage. Marry some guy who's only into kinky shit or one position, or only likes it once a month. No thank you. I like sex too much to wait anyway. I love to feel a man's body next to mine. There's nothing like it in the world."

I straightened out my back so that my two greatest assets appeared even greater, gazed out into space just to give him an opportunity to stare. Take it all in, I thought, get a *good* look.

"It's been a long time since I met a woman like Deborah," he whispered. "But I don't think I'm ready for the kind of commitment she wants."

I gazed into his brown eyes and let out a quiet breath. I wanted to wrap my thighs around his body and pull him right to me.

"You can wait for Deborah," I said, "but why give up your own personal pleasure while you're waiting?" And then, I said, "You don't mind if I use your rest room do you?"

I went to the bathroom and closed my eyes. Dear Lord, please, if there is any chance, let Darren like me. He looks so good sitting there in his boots and jeans, the top of his shirt unbuttoned exposing that one vein I want to set free and suck.

When I returned, he was still on the floor, blowing into a beer bottle. I sat next to him, made myself comfortable. His lips had a soft sheen like maybe he had put on some Chap Stick.

"I know I keep saying this," he said, "but I like hanging out with you. I haven't had this much fun in a while. It feels nice." He bumped my shoulder lightly.

I bumped his right back. "Same here."

"So you and Deborah have been friends for how long?"

"Since preschool. But we're not close, we've just known each other for a long time. It's not like we're best friends or anything."

"She seems to think you are."

"What?"

"Best friends."

"It's sad, but we've grown apart."

"You two ever fight over men?"

"Never."

He rested an elbow on the couch, took a sip of beer. "Can I ask you a question?"

"Sure."

"Never mind."

"Don't do that. I hate it when people do that. Ask me."

"Well, I don't know. I've really been having a nice time today. I feel comfortable with you. Reminds me of Angela a little." He snapped his fingers. "An immediate connection. Know what I mean?"

"Yes, I do. But what's your question?"

"I don't want you to take offense."

"I won't."

"I don't want to cause any trouble between you and Deborah."

"You won't."

"What do you think about me?"

"Is that your question?"

"No, but I'll ask the question depending on your answer."

"I like you. I like you a lot."

He drank the last bit of beer from the bottle. He tensed his jaw and looked out through the patio doors and into the dark night. "May I kiss you?"

Before he could back out of it, I let my fingernail follow the side of his face and leaned in. I don't swim, but I imagine it would be like kissing Darren. His tongue went into my mouth and mine in his, and I was pushed under water where I was weightless, kicking my legs against all that blue silence.

It was exactly 12:06 a.m. I know because I'd glanced at the clock and realized I had to go to work the next day and would certainly have a hangover. We were in the kitchen making coffee. We hadn't done anything except to kiss for a while on his couch, hold hands and talk, kiss some more. I was asking him where he kept his cups when I heard him come up behind me, his boots making a lovely sound against the kitchen floor.

He pressed his stomach into my back. "Don't move, okay? Just don't move."

I must have about died. He kissed the back of my neck and I let my head fall to the side. He kissed my cheek, smelled my hair. He lifted my blouse and I felt the cold tile from the counter against my belly. The cabinet above the counter was open, and before I closed my eyes, I noticed that I was staring directly into a bag of unbleached flour. I stood on my tiptoes because I wanted him to be able to hold on to my waist, my breasts, my ass. I held my breath as he tipped me over, raised a bare foot onto a boot one at a time then lifted my heels that much further. I didn't ever want to come down.

Four

I LIVED IN Inglewood, about ten miles from LAX. And unlike most people in L.A. County, I actually lived in the same city as I worked. Century Bank of Los Angeles was located on Century Boulevard and Figueroa. We all called it the Bank of the 'Hood because it was a few miles from Watts, in an area that had far more check-cashing stores and pawnshops than legitimate financial institutions. The bank was a small no-frills place, and by no frills I mean you wouldn't come in and find things like mahogany desks or velvet ropes where people stood in line. There were a few posters on the walls, a cheap blue love seat and coffee table in the corner next to a vase of plastic flowers. Someone had carved the words *Fuck Poverty* into the coffee table. The two desks where Byron and Deborah worked sat in a carpeted area near the windows. The area that wasn't carpeted was often covered with deposit slips. Once in a while our manager, Mrs. Hodges, hired her nephew to come out and paint things on the window in bright neon colors, like *Consumer Loans* and *Investment Services!* or *Credit Card fees with low 5.8% Intro. Rate!* You'd think we were a car dealership the paint jobs were so tacky.

At any rate, I liked working at the bank well enough and was one of the best tellers there, but that Monday I couldn't stop making mistakes. I couldn't concentrate to save my life. No matter who spoke to me, all I saw or heard was Darren. A customer would say, "I'd like to make a withdrawal," but I'd hear Darren's voice whispering in my ear: "That was wonderful. You're incredibly sexy, you know that?" Another customer would ask to have a check deposited in her savings account, but I'd be thinking about how Darren had insisted on walking me to my car even though I had left his place at four in the morning. "No regrets, right?" he'd said after closing my car door. "You can't fight a powerful connection, right?" I'd start typing an account number into the computer. "Did you say savings or checking?" And the person would get all pissed. "*Savings.* I've told you two times now."

As soon as I walked through the door that morning, Deborah was on my heels. She had left four messages on my machine the night before asking me what had happened with Darren, but I never returned her calls. She started in with the same questions as I headed for the break room. Had I talked to Darren? How long had we talked? What had he said? I still had sunglasses on my head because even the dull lights in the bank made my brain throb, but in order to get her to drop it, I took them off and told her that yes, I had spoken to Darren. We had met briefly at a cafe near his condo. I was too hung over and too sleepy to come up with anything else so I told her I'd give her all the glorious details over lunch.

"That sounds good," she said, then looked at me oddly.

"Somebody looks like she didn't get enough sleep last night."

"Yeah, I made the mistake of going out with Rob on a Sunday night. I didn't get in until two."

She put an arm around me and gave me a light shake. "No wonder you didn't return my calls. Well, I'll go see if anyone put the coffee on yet. We don't want you abusing the customers."

"Thanks."

We went to Ramiro's Taco Shop, a restaurant across the street from the bank, for lunch. I ordered six rolled tacos with everything, refried beans, rice, and a large coffee. I was starving. As usual, the place was packed. Deborah and I were forced to sit in the back next to the out-of-order jukebox. Ramiro's was one of the few places in the area that Mexicans and blacks visited in equal numbers. I mean, we lived near each other, went to the same schools, but might as well have been as separate as blacks and whites. My brother was known for talking about how Mexicans and Koreans were taking over the country, but the way I saw it, nobody was taking over much of anything anytime soon. Type in most of the account numbers at the bank, and whether the person was black, Mexican, or Korean, you could bet that he was just as broke as the next person in line.

Deborah took a bite of her tostada and started right in. "So what did he say?"

"Well, pretty much what you thought he'd say. He does like you, but he's not ready for the type of commitment you want. He says he feels he's at a time in his life where he still wants to see other people."

Deborah ran a flat hand over her head. *"Other people?"*

"Yeah."

"Well, what else did he say?"

"That's it."

"*That's it?*"

"Pretty much."

"You didn't let on that you'd be talking to me did you?"

"Of course not."

She took a tiny bite from her tostada and looked as if she had to remind herself to chew. "Sorry I got you involved. This is like the stuff we pulled in high school."

"Well, at least now you know." I chowed down on my food while watching her twirl her fork around in her beans.

"I don't get it, Babysister. He treats me so well. He says things to me. He says I'm special. He says he can see sharing his life with someone like me! I can tell he's sincere. I don't understand what happened." She stared out at the restaurant as though lost in a vast desert with nothing but a lonely palm tree in the distance. "*Other women? I can't believe it. Are you sure you understood him?*"

"I ain't no fool, Deborah. He's being a man, girl. That's the way they are." I sweetened my voice when I saw I hadn't convinced her. "I'm sure he likes you, and he does seem very nice. Sincere and all that. He paid for my coffee at the cafe. Pulled out my chair. Men don't do that shit anymore. But you should face it, Deborah, he's a player. I mean, it's the whole fear of commitment thing. He probably feels close to you, but he's scared. Men aren't as mature as women."

Deborah scooted her plate toward me. I wondered if she was going to eat her tostada. No sense wasting it.

"You know," she said, "I should probably go on and sleep with him. It's not like I don't want him. I want him bad, Babysister." She let out a deep moan while hugging herself. "Real bad."

My eyes went big. I hadn't heard Deborah talk about wanting anything that much since she first saw her cat, Noodles, curled up in his cage at the pound. He was a pathetic spotted thing with sickly yellow eyes, but Deborah saw another animal entirely. "Isn't he precious, Babysister? Isn't he beautiful?"

She said, "Stop looking at me like that. I'm no saint. Far from it." She leaned over the table. "We've come close, you know. How do you think I know he enjoys . . ." And then she whispered the words *oral sex* like a schoolgirl.

"Deborah!"

She covered her dimples with her hands. "I know I shouldn't have let him, but he was *so* good. He is *so* good, Babysister."

I know, I thought. Believe me, I *know*.

"Maybe I should. He probably wants to see other women because he can't get anywhere with me. He probably thinks I'm a prude. Sometimes I think this whole idea that I have to wait is ridiculous. What woman in her right mind would make a man like Darren wait? And what am I waiting on anyway?"

"Commitment, Deborah. I thought you said you wanted to develop something based on commitment and trust. I thought you wanted to develop a relationship based on friendship. You've only known Darren for two months. That's nothing, girl, and you know it. You can't possibly know what he's really like after two months. You're always saying how you want things to be different, more spiritual or whatever. What happened to all that?"

"I've never been tempted like this before. I don't want

to lose him." She paused then, and gave me a funny look, like maybe I had something on my face but she couldn't figure out exactly what it was. "Since when do you care if I go to bed with somebody or not? It's not like you of all people to be pushing celibacy on a person. You're usually telling me to lighten up."

Good point.

"Yeah, but I know you, Deborah, better than almost anyone. I know if you start having sex with Darren, you'll start feeling like shit, then you'll start complaining to me about how come I didn't talk you out of it. I know if you give in, you'll never forgive yourself."

"Yeah, I guess you're right." She nibbled at her tostada then said, "You know, I was reading from Romans the other night, you wouldn't believe how the chapter I was reading ties into what I'm going through right now."

When she mentioned the Bible, I knew to prepare myself for a lecture on what she had read as well as any other subject that might flash across her religion-soaked brain. Sure enough, she went on and on about various sins, miracles of the Old Testament, why people back then lived to be over two hundred, something about slaughtering goats. I couldn't figure out what any of it had to do with sleeping with Darren or not, but I thought, if having to listen to her ramble on about the Bible helped her make a decision in my favor, so be it. Amen.

Deborah hadn't always been so committed to living the moral life. Naive, yes. Too sweet for her own good, yes, but she wasn't always the black Mother Teresa, either. Back in junior high, it was *her* idea to egg our math teacher's brand-new Cadillac. And when we were in high school, she was the one who talked liquor store employees into letting us buy beer and cigarettes. She was never into skipping school, but at the same time, I rarely had trouble convincing her to join me. Now those were some good days. Sometimes we'd drive out to Venice Beach or Santa Monica pier. We'd flirt with men twice our age, play video games, eat chili-cheese fries. If I had any weed, we'd find a park, hide out in my car, and pass the joint back and forth. Once we were good and high, we'd race out to the swings or the monkey bars and play around like we were kids again. Afterward, we'd lie on the grass and talk about what our lives would be like after high school. I wanted a life full of men and money. All she wanted was three kids and a husband who could afford to support them all on a single paycheck. There was a time when Deborah would go out dancing with me and not want to get off the floor until closing time. There was a time when she could have a conversation without bringing up a single Bible verse. There was a time when Deborah could say the words *oral sex* without acting like it was as bad as bestiality.

I'd say her *transformation* had begun almost two years earlier. We had been out dancing all night at a club with a great reggae band. Everything seemed fine until I turned to see Deborah standing in the middle of the dance floor hardly moving. When I asked what was wrong, she said she was tired and ready to go home. When we met for breakfast the next morning, she had her hair in two plaits and was dressed in enough black to make you wonder who had died. Her voice was gruff from all the cigarettes we had smoked. "I'm getting too old for all this," she had said.

"Getting too old for what?"

"Going out every weekend. It's making me depressed. I need a change."

"Oh, please, Deborah. Worry about making a change

when you hit thirty. You're supposed to enjoy your twenties."

"I don't think I'm enjoying myself anymore."

"Lighten up, girl. As hard as we work all week, we deserve to go out Friday night."

She took off her sunglasses. The bags under her eyes were pinkish gray and round as seashells. "I'm not happy, Babysister."

When I called her the next day to see if she wanted to check out a matinee, she wasn't home. "I went to church," she said when I finally reached her. "And you know what, Babysister? It was so nice I might even go again."

And that was pretty much the last I saw of the Deborah I grew up with. And while a part of me was still hoping for her return, the other part was trying to get used to the woman left in her place.

I watched as she took a sip of her soda. "So what do you think?"

I had no idea what she was talking about.

She tapped the table with her fingernail. "It all comes down to that single verse." She gave me that you-have-something-on-your-face look again. "Were you listening?"

"Of course I was listening. I was just thinking maybe Bible verses don't matter. Maybe you should follow your heart. I mean, do you want to be with a man who wants to be with other women? I know Darren might be a temptation for you, but you're strong. Now is the time to prove to yourself and God just how strong you are."

She gave my hand a squeeze from across the table, her brown eyes now big and shiny and filled with—thank goodness—newly found determination. "You're right." When she smiled, I thought about the year she wore braces, even with all that silver in her mouth and all the chunks of food caught in the wires, she still had a great smile. "It means a lot to me to know you've got my back. It really helps to know that you understand where I'm coming from, what I'm trying to do with my life. Thank you, Babysister, really."

"Sure," I said. Then I pointed to her tostada. "So you gonna eat that or what?"

I lived on the top floor of a two-story apartment building. I had a view of the houses across the street and the liquor store at the corner. The building itself was pretty basic. It was painted beige with brown trim and had a small stairway out front that led to the downstairs entrance. There was usually a group of four sisters playing double Dutch or hopscotch out front. Their mother constantly yelled at them about keeping the front steps clean. She had one of those big-booming I-sing-in-the-church-choir voices and could be heard throughout the entire complex. "You girls better get on out here and pick up these crayons. This is not the Beverly Hilton and I ain't no maid!" A man who looked to be in his mid-fifties lived across the hall from me. I had the impression that he thought he was living in England or something because he always wore a plaid wool hat and bow tie and used a cane with a silver handle when he took his morning stroll. He'd look startled whenever he saw me coming out of my apartment. I don't think he ever realized I actually lived there. The neighborhood itself wasn't the best that I had seen in Inglewood, but it also wasn't among the worst. The apartment complexes on either side of my building were in need of paint jobs, the liquor store at the corner was covered in its share of graffiti, and most of the houses had bars on the windows. But I liked my street well enough, crime was low, and except for the occasional person who drove by blasting music or the occasional police helicopter circling overhead, it was quiet enough.

When I got home from work, Guess Who was sitting on my porch, all grins. Unfortunately, Guess Who wasn't Darren, but Rob.

"What are you doing here?"

"We had a date remember? Chinese food and a movie. Six o'clock."

I noticed the plastic bags from China Kingdom by his side and a video in his hand. "Oh, yeah." I glanced at my watch. "You're early."

"I missed you. I wanted to be here right when you pulled up. I called last night to wish you sweet dreams. Where were you?"

"Yeah, I got your message. I made the mistake of going out with Lisette. I didn't get in until one." I rested my head against his chest while faking a yawn. "I'm pretty beat. I don't know if I'm up for a movie. In fact, I was going to call and cancel."

"But I already have the food. Come on. We'll go inside. I'll open up a bottle of wine."

"Really, baby, I'm cranky. I should probably go on up to bed."

He put one of his thick hands on the back of my neck. "Come on now, let me take care of you. I want to. I'll feed you, clean up the kitchen. I'm not driving back home until I know you're feeling better." He took hold of my wrist, started leading me up the stairs. "What you need first, young lady, is a long hot bath."

What I really needed was to call Darren. But how could I do that with Rob sitting around eating Chinese food, acting like he was somebody's husband?

As soon as we entered my apartment, I went straight for my answering machine. Two messages. The machine was in the kitchen so there'd be no way I could listen to the messages without Rob, who was busy getting things ready for dinner, listening in as well.

"Hey, Rob?"

"Yeah?"

"Would you mind running down to my car and seeing if you can find my Sade tape? I think I'll take that bath after all. I'd like to listen to some music."

"No problem. I'll be right back."

As soon as he was out the door I pressed Play:

"Babysister? This is your father. I'm gonna need that pot you borrowed this weekend if we're having spaghetti. Make sure you bring it. Okay. Bye."

Daddy hated answering machines. Unless he absolutely had to leave a message, he wouldn't say a word; he would just breathe into the receiver. My brother and I always knew it was Daddy when we heard the sound of the television going and a man's low breath.

I wanted to scream when I heard message number two:

"Babysister, it's Darren. So yeah. I had a nice time last night. I'd like to see you again, that is, if you're comfortable with that. But, um, if you feel like it wouldn't be best, I'll understand. It would be nice to see you again, though. Well, okay. *Ciao.*"

"*Ciao,*" I said out loud while clutching my blouse. *Ciao.* I was still clutching when Rob walked in.

"I couldn't find it," he said. "You sure you left it in the car?"

I didn't own any Sade tapes, only CDs. "Maybe I left it in my headphones. Oh well. Thanks anyway. I got a message from Deborah. She's having man troubles."

"She's seeing somebody?"

"You know Deborah. Who knows what'll happen. I'm gonna give her a quick call. You sure you don't mind taking care of everything?"

"I don't mind at all. Now go on and get in that tub."

I took the glass of wine, grabbed my cordless phone, and headed for the bathroom. I didn't call until I had a few sips of my drink and was immersed in bubbles. "Darren? It's Babysister."

"Hey, I was wondering if you'd call. It's nice to hear your voice. For the record, last night was incredible."

By the end of the conversation, I had melted so far into the water, the phone was about to get soaked. We made a date for Thursday night.

Rob walked in right after I had hung up. I couldn't believe my timing. "Refill?"

"Yeah," I said, lifting my wineglass. He set the phone on the sink. After pouring the wine, he held the glass to my lips so that I wouldn't have to lift a single finger.

"Can I join you in there?"

"Nope," I teased. "But you can massage my shoulders."

While he pressed his fingers into my shoulders, I thought about how nice he was. No Darren, but very nice.

"How's Deborah?"

"Oh, she'll be all right."

"How are you doing? Feeling better?"

"Baby, I feel great. You were right about this bath."

He got on his knees then and turned my face toward his. His kiss hardly registered, though, because I was already trying to figure out what I was going to wear on my date with Darren.

———

We went to see a French movie that Thursday. It was one of the most boring movies I had seen in my entire life, but before it began, as we stood in the aisle trying to decide where to sit, he had lifted his leather bag from across his shoulder and whispered, "Let's sit in the back because I brought a bottle of wine." I had to stop myself from crying out to everyone in the theater, "Can you believe it? He brought a bottle of wine!" And after we sat down, he began pulling things from his bag like a magician: two wineglasses, corkscrew, fancy slices of cheese in a plastic bag, expensive crackers. I was truly impressed. Most men think it's romantic if they pay for the popcorn or pull out a bottle of rum and offer to spike the Cokes. I mean, if Rob showed up at a movie with cheese and wine, I would have been like, *Negro please*, who are you trying to be? But Darren made wine and a foreign film seem natural. And as he handed me my glass with a kiss on the cheek—"Are you comfortable? Do you need anything else?"—I realized that what set him apart was more than his looks or his style. No, what made him stand out from all the rest, what made me shake my head at my luck, was how special he made me feel.

After the movie, we went to a Japanese restaurant that seemed made out of paper and about four beams of wood. The room was so light and so airy I kept waiting for the big bad wolf to come by and blow the place down. Everything about our time at the restaurant was pretty, from the irises placed on every table to the tea leaves swirling around my cup. Darren looked pretty balancing clumps of rice between his chopsticks. I looked pretty when I finally gave up on the chopsticks and used a fork. And I have to admit that while the food was very pretty, if Darren had been anyone else, I would have told him it was far too bland to get excited about, like it needed a few good pinches of salt or even better, a side of fried chicken so you could actually get full. But you know when he asked me if I liked it, I simply stabbed another piece of raw fish with my fork and told him it was delicious.

"Glad to hear it," he said. "I can't believe you haven't had sushi before or Thai for that matter. We'll have to try Ethiopian next time."

Next time echoed in my head. I'd eat all the raw fish in the world for you, baby.

He told me all about his trips to Europe and Mexico, how he was planning a trip to Belize. When he asked me where I'd been, I lied and said whatever came to mind. I made up a funny story about a family trip to the Grand Canyon in which I had thrown up in my brother Malcolm's lap; a trip to Atlanta to visit an imaginary friend; a romantic trip to New Orleans with an imaginary boyfriend who had lots of imaginary money. I purposely stuck to places in America because telling him I'd been somewhere like Africa would have been too risky. Considering I had never been out of Los Angeles County, I was lying enough.

We had finished eating when he eased his leg out from under the table and leaned forward. I thought he might be flirting, but the expression on his face was too serious. "So I thought we should probably talk about what's going on."

"What's going on?"

"You, me . . . Deborah."

"Haven't we talked about that already?"

"Have you said anything to her?"

Of course I hadn't, what would I have said? Hey, Deborah, guess what I did over the weekend.

"No, I haven't, have you?"

"No. To be honest I still don't think we should say anything." He picked up a chopstick, started scooting it around his plate. "But I did want to talk about what's going on with us, if you don't mind. I don't want you expecting anything because I don't know what's going to happen. Just because I'm here with you, doesn't mean I don't have feelings for Deborah. I still have feelings for her."

I was feeling too confident to let his comment effect me much. The way I saw it, if he was so sure about his feelings for Deborah, Sunday night never would've happened. I watched him make a few squiggly marks on his plate with his chopstick. His jaw was tense and the lighting in the restaurant made his face seem even more angular, more chiseled. "Damn, you look good," I said.

He turned away embarrassed. "You trying to change the subject or something?"

"Yes," I said, reaching for his hand.

"I had fun tonight," he said.

"Me too."

I felt his boot tap lightly against my calf. One, two, three, four. Finally, he put his elbows on the table and leaned in. "Listen, I know it's getting late, but do you think you'd be up for some company tonight?"

See what I mean?

Five

WE WERE A SMALL GROUP of people at Bank of the
'Hood. There were six tellers: Marsha, Vicky, Danisha,
Tonya, Carol, and myself. As tellers we did most of the
grunt work for the least amount of pay. We had our own
key to our cash box and our own station where we liked
to stand, but not much more. Danisha had a little more
responsibility than the rest of us. You'd think she was the
president of Bank of America just because she had the
glamorous job of doling out our money every morning
and leading customers to their safe-deposit boxes.

Danisha, Carol, and Vicky spent most of their free time
together. They were a female version of the Three Stooges,
only mean. Danisha wore high heels that made her stand
five one at best. She also wore bright suits with tight short
skirts. Carol wasn't much taller than Danisha and was fine
from the front, but had an extremely wide butt and tiny
feet we were always managing to step on. Vicky was about
five eleven and big-boned. She wore blond extensions and
green contacts that made her look demon-possessed. I
called them the evil stepsisters because they were a perfect
reminder of what Cinderella had to put up with. Deborah

and Byron, as I've mentioned, handled things like mortgages, consumer loans, lines of credit. Mrs. Hodges had a small office in the back next to the room where we kept our things and took our breaks. She was a typical boss: oblivious to the fact that everyone disliked her.

We worked by two basic rules at the bank: You had to expect to be talked about, and you had to dish out if you knew anything. The only one who refused to participate was Marsha and as a result no one liked her. She usually wore these homely-looking dresses that fell to her knees and made you think of old-time missionaries or spinsters. She chose to work at the far end of teller's row, window eleven. You could see her acting friendly enough to the customers, but for whatever reason, she hardly said much to the rest of us. If we played like we didn't care about what was going on in Marsha's life, we certainly knew everything about each other's. Vicky and her husband, Phil, were seriously behind on their bills and close to losing their house. Tonya had beautiful brown eyes and a great figure, but was clearly unstable. We could never figure out if she was born crazy or if working at the bank drove her that way. She could get so dark sometimes we half expected her to come in with a gun one day and go off. Danisha had herpes. Rumor had it that she had given the disease to the last security guard who worked at the bank. We were almost certain that Carol was sleeping with Martin, the new security guard, but we needed more evidence than all the flirting that went on between them to come right out and say it. We all knew the details of Byron's separation. I was the one who had advised him to go through his wife's things. "How will you ever know for sure that she's cheating unless you do a personal investigation?" I told him. He got drunk one night after work and showed Tonya one of the poems the garbage man had written. Tonya later told us the poem was written in calligraphy on purple and lavender stationery. She had memorized a couple of lines from the poem and by the end of the week we all had them memorized as well. "My heart flutters when we are together. Birds dance wing to wing on my soul." We were all surprised that a garbage man could be so sensitive. Danisha had said, "I don't blame his wife for leaving him. Besides the fact that garbage men make a decent living, this one really knows how to appreciate a woman." We all agreed.

At any rate, three weeks after my first date with Darren, Deborah underwent what I came to refer to as her "little depression." You would have thought the earth was coming to an end the way everyone at the bank reacted. Just because she hadn't smiled for two weeks straight, just because she had stopped wearing makeup and fixing her hair, didn't bring doughnuts in for everyone on Friday, and ate her lunch alone in her car while listening to Christian radio, everyone began acting as if the girl was going to kill herself. Vicky came up to me as I was processing a money order: "What's wrong with Deborah, Babysister? Is she sick?" Carol worked at the window next to mine and would look from me to Deborah: "What happened to Deborah, Babysister? Why does she keep staring out the window like that?" All day I'd have to put up with people asking me about Deborah in hushed voices as if it weren't possible for someone so perfect to be upset. I didn't say anything to anyone, of course, but I knew perfectly well why she was depressed. She and Darren were over. Finished. *Finito.* It was perfectly normal for her to be sad. She needed time, that was all.

One night, close to the second week of her little

depression, Deborah stopped by my apartment. I must say, the girl was not looking too well at all. She must have changed after work because she had on jeans and an old tie-dyed T-shirt. Her eyes were thick and red as if she had been crying for hours, pieces of grass of all things were tangled in her hair.

I pulled her into my apartment before anyone could see her. "What happened?"

"I was at the park."

"At the park doing what?" I started picking thin blades of grass out of her hair.

"Nothing. I think I might have fallen asleep."

Rob was on the couch watching TV. I still hadn't figured out what I was going to do with him. I knew we needed to break up, but life was getting complicated enough without having to deal with that. Besides, on the nights Darren and I weren't together, I still enjoyed hanging out with Rob, playing a few video games, relaxing.

He waved to Deborah from the couch. "Hey, Deborah, you want to join us? We were about to watch *Blazing Saddles*."

Before she could say anything, I took her hand and started leading her to my bedroom. "I think she needs to talk. Go on and enjoy the movie."

I sat across from Deborah on my bed. For a moment, it almost felt like we were girls again and she was spending the night. I gently tucked a few strands of wild hair behind her ear. "What's wrong?"

"He hasn't called in three weeks. I don't know how many messages I've left."

"I thought you decided he wasn't what you wanted, that you could do better."

"I know, I know. I miss him is all. I didn't think I'd

miss him this much." She fell against my shoulder and started crying. I quietly put my arms around her as she sobbed.

I don't remember much about my mother's funeral, but I do remember sitting with Deborah in the front pew and how we both held on to each other because neither of us could stop crying. I remember Daddy saying something to Deborah's mother then scooping the two of us up with one arm and taking us out of the church. Everyone in the church broke out into tears when they saw us in his arms like that.

I reached for my box of tissues and gave her a small handful. "It'll be okay," I said.

She blew her nose. "I wanted to talk to him about what I was feeling, but didn't get a chance. He stopped calling right out of the blue. And he won't return my messages." She stared down into her hands and bit her lower lip, but tears swelled in her eyes anyway. "I guess he was serious about wanting to see other people. I know he met someone. It's the only way to explain why he won't return my messages. I loved him, Babysister, but now it's too late. I messed it all up."

"It'll be okay," I said, wiping a few tears from her cheek.

The phone started to ring in the other room, but I didn't think anything of it until I looked at the clock and saw that it was six forty-five. Darren was supposed to call when he got back from visiting his parents—sometime around seven. Then I remembered Rob in the other room. Shit.

I handed Deborah more tissues. "Listen, sweetie, I'll be right back, okay? I'm expecting an important call from Malcolm. I'll be *right back*."

She managed a nod and I rushed off to the phone. Once again, I was blessed with perfect timing: Rob was just about to pick up the receiver.

"I'll get that," I said. "You go watch your movie."

"Is Deborah okay?"

"Oh, yeah. Bad day at work. I'll take this in the bathroom so I won't bother you."

"You won't bother me none. Problem with watching a movie on TV is that there are too many damn commercials." He went into the kitchen and opened the fridge.

So that's how I ended up talking to Darren right in front of Rob, with Deborah crying in my bedroom. Having to talk to everyone at once wasn't as uncomfortable as you might think. Rob didn't have a clue as to who I was talking to because I kept my answers nice and brief: How did it go? Oh really? Yes. No. Deborah couldn't hear anything so she wasn't a problem either. When Darren had asked if he could stop by, I told him it would be easier if I met him at his place. "I'm looking forward to having you in my arms," he said. And since Rob was sitting right there I didn't flirt or anything, I simply told him that I'd see him in an hour.

After I hung up, I went over to the couch and took Rob's hand. "That was Malcolm. I need to go over there tonight. We're planning a surprise party for my father's birthday and Malcolm is making a mess of everything. We need to finalize who's doing what so that the party turns out okay."

It wasn't the best lie in the world. A surprise party for Daddy? First of all, we weren't a surprise party type of family. And second, Daddy's birthday wasn't for another six months.

"You have to go over there *tonight*?"

Though I was fond of Rob, it will probably come as no surprise that he was growing less and less attractive since I had started seeing Darren. His head, for instance, seemed to shrink in size every time I saw him. Why I hadn't noticed that it was way too small for his body before, I don't know. I also realized he was more stocky and short than well built. And why did he have to manicure his nails every other minute? He had big ears, too. Way too big for his little bitty head.

"I hardly ever see you anymore," he whined.

"It's only been a few days since we last saw each other, Rob."

"It's been eight *long* days. I miss you, girl. I miss *being* with you too. We hardly ever fool around anymore."

I had had sex with Rob twice since I had started seeing Darren. The first time was a few days after Darren had taken me to see the French movie. The second was the last time I had seen him, eight days before, and I had told myself then that I should stop sleeping with him altogether.

I slid my tongue around his ear. When I felt his body relax, I pulled down his zipper and began fondling with the only area on his body that hadn't changed much over the past weeks. I heard a long, guttural moan.

"I have to make sure Deborah's okay," I said, removing my hand. "And listen, baby, you might as well go home. I probably won't get back from Malcolm's until late."

"But what about this?" He pointed to his erection, which at the moment was pushing his underwear up through his pants with all its horny strength.

"I swear I'll make it up to you. Think of all the anticipation we're building. Besides, we can't do anything with Deborah in the other room."

"I could wait for you."

"You know how it is when I get together with my brother. We'll probably be arguing all night about what needs to be done for Daddy's party. I'll make it up to you. We'll spend tomorrow night together. I'll cook dinner. I'll be all yours." I kissed the top of his little bitty head and stood up. "I have to check on Deborah."

"Okay, I'll take off. You're mine tomorrow, though." He started zipping up his pants.

"All yours."

I found Deborah wrapped up in one of my quilts and hugging one of my pillows. My father had given me most of the quilts my mother had made as well as the sheets and pillowcases she had decorated with hand-sewn flowers. The stitching she used to spell out her name, Althea, was so thick that if you closed your eyes, you could easily figure out the letters. Sometimes I caught myself running my fingers over her name as though I were reading Braille. I also owned her cedar chest and the two Tiffany-style lamps that once belonged to her mother. I kept my rocker in the corner. I rarely sat in it but it looked good. My bedroom was the complete opposite of my living room, which was decorated with contemporary everything, forest-green couch and love seat, slick black tables and shelves. I had charged the furniture on one of my first credit cards, and was still paying it off. None of my things were as fancy as Darren's, but considering I didn't have as much money as he did, my apartment looked just fine.

Deborah fell back on my bed all distraught when she saw me, and as I watched her bury her face in my pillow, I decided that I needed to help her get over Darren once and for all. For one thing, she was beginning to make me feel more than a little guilty. And for another, I figured if she got on with her life, she would inevitably meet someone else, someone more suited for her, maybe a religious man who could quote Bible verses with her. And who knows? Maybe one day we'd all go on a double date and laugh at how complicated everything was in the beginning. None of these things were going to happen, though, unless she came to her senses and realized that Darren was all wrong for her, that they would have broken up sooner or later so she might as well forget him. At least that's what I told myself at the time.

I put my hands on my hips and stood over her like a mother. "Listen, girl. Enough okay? You are better than this. How long have I known you? Practically your entire damn life, that's how long. And this one thing I do know: We have never, ever allowed men to bring us down. I have never seen you act like this over a man. It's not right. I thought it was important to be faithful in the hard times. What are you saying to everyone at work by dressing like a war victim every day? You've been crying over that man long enough, Deborah." I grabbed her by the wrists and pulled her up from the bed. When this didn't get a reaction, I sat down next to her and said as softly and gently as I could, "Come on, Deborah, you need to stop this. No more, okay?"

She slumped over so that her hair fell down over her head. I held her and we sat together listening to the quiet of my apartment and the noise coming from the street when finally, *finally*, I heard a faint "Okay" coming from somewhere behind all that hair. I put my arm around her and asked if she wanted a cup of tea. I still had time, after all.

We drank our tea at my small dining room table. I tried to cheer her up by telling her what everyone was saying at the bank, how the gossip was getting more and more out-rageous. Danisha thought she was smoking pot. Vicky thought she was pregnant. When I told her that Marsha had told me that Tonya was going after Byron, she mum-bled, "That'll never work," then resumed drinking in silence. If things had been different, if the man she was trying to get over wasn't Darren, if I wasn't meeting Dar-ren that same evening, I would have asked Deborah to spend the night. She and I still had sleepovers every now and then. We would put on our pj's, make these gigantic sundaes, and pig out in front of the TV or play cutthroat games of backgammon.

Anyway, I was about to start hinting that it was getting late when she said, "You know what? I'm getting sick of being depressed anyway. It takes up too much energy."

I smiled and shook my head. "It does, doesn't it?"

"And I miss taking showers," she sighed, then started cracking up when she saw the surprise on my face. "I'm kidding," she said. "I wasn't that depressed."

She gave me a long hug before leaving. "I love you, girl," she said.

"I love you, too."

I did love her. Like I said, we weren't as close as we had been, but that hadn't changed my overall attitude toward her. I couldn't help but feel somewhat sorry for her. It would be awful to have a man like Darren dump you and I certainly wasn't about to add to her pain by telling her the truth.

Six

I WENT TO VISIT my father on the following Saturday. He lived in Lynwood in one of those neighborhoods where people raised their children and stayed put. A few of the houses on our street were run-down, but the lawns were neat and everyone spoke to each other. Our house—the same house I grew up in—was one of the better-looking on the block. It stood on the corner and had an elm tree near the front entrance and was painted a soft yellow with an off-white trim. The only thing that made our house stand out in any way was that the front window was made up of clear diamond-shaped panes. The same design was used for the window in the front door, but those panes were made with colored glass so when you looked out to see who was at the door, the person could be any color from purple to green, depending on where you stood.

I tried to have dinner with my father at least twice a month. Between Malcolm and me, he didn't have to worry too much about being alone, not that he needed our company to keep him busy. He stayed on the go. He went to Vegas so much we told him he might as well move there.

He loved playing cards and dominoes with his friends, and even had a girlfriend named Melvina who would show up at the house wearing red suits like Daddy had told her red was his favorite color.

Daddy had started bringing Melvina around the house my senior year in high school. She was a big woman with a large behind and strong calves shaped like upside-down bowling pins. She had the habit of throwing her hands in the air whenever Daddy told a joke, kicking up those big calves like Daddy was the funniest man alive. I didn't care for her at all, to be honest. For one thing, she had the annoying habit of talking to me like I was a three-year-old. It also got on my nerves that she was constantly dropping hints that she wanted to live with the three of us. "Sugar, you know how I feel about your daddy, right? And you know how good I am for him, right? Well, don't you think your daddy needs a woman in the house?" It wasn't until Malcolm and I had both moved out that Daddy started suggesting that he was actually considering letting Melvina move in. I made it clear that I would never accept her. "I'm happy for you, Daddy, but I just don't think I'd be able to come around as much if you let her live here. She makes me uncomfortable, Daddy, you know that. I want you to be happy, but why bring her here?" And I guess he got my point, because he soon started going over to Melvina's house more often while she only showed up at our house on the occasional holiday.

I found Daddy stretched out in front of the TV Malcolm and I had bought for his sixtieth birthday. Daddy was always quick to buy something for me, but rarely treated himself to anything new. He had bought the last TV while I was still in junior high school. No remote control. You had to use pliers on the missing volume button.

I wasn't surprised at all to find Malcolm there sitting on the couch and yelling at the TV. When he wasn't with his girlfriend, Sharice, you could usually find him leeching off Daddy's food and complaining. First thing out of his mouth was, "Jesus, girl, don't you think those pants are too tight? Who you trying to impress?"

"Not you, so why don't you mind your own business."

Daddy said, "Don't start up now, you two."

Malcolm had decided at the age of three, when Momma gently pulled the tiny pink blanket away from my face and told him to say hello to his new sister, that he would never ever like me and would spend the rest of his life proving it. Whenever Momma and Daddy weren't around, or were simply not looking, he loved to torture me. Relentless torture. He'd trip, shove, punch, mimic, chase, tease. He was dedicated to the idea of making me miserable.

I gave my father a kiss, showed him that I had remembered to return his pot. It was the same pot I had used to make the turnip greens for the dinner party with Darren and Deborah. The same iron pot Darren had pretended was too heavy to lift after he had offered to help me take the food out to the table. "Now *this* is a pot. My grandmother owned one just like it."

I stood behind Daddy's chair and he gave my hand a pat. "You still want spaghetti, baby girl?"

"Spaghetti sounds fine to me."

Malcolm said, "I guess nobody cares if I want spaghetti or not. I guess nobody cares that Sharice and I had spaghetti yesterday."

Daddy and I were silent.

Malcolm sighed. "So how are you preparing it, Pops?"

"Same way I always do. Hamburger meat, tomato

sauce. It's already made. All we need to do is heat the sauce and boil the noodles."

"I don't eat meat anymore, remember?" Malcolm sat up in his chair as if we had asked him a question he had been waiting on for hours. "I feel great. It's been months now, you know. I can't even stand the smell of the stuff. My relationship with Sharice has really helped me to appreciate my body as a temple. You guys realize how much water and grain it takes to feed cows? There would be more food to go around if we stopped making beef our number one priority."

Daddy said, "I guess that means more sauce for me and your sister."

Malcolm pushed the recliner he was sitting in forward then pointed from me to Daddy. "Humans don't need meat. It's unhealthy."

I said, "I bet as soon as you and Sharice break up, you'll go right back to eating roast beef, hamburgers and all the rest of it."

"*When* we break up? Excuse me, but I have no intention of breaking up with Sharice, ever. She's a very special woman and we have a very special bond, something you clearly know nothing about."

"Daddy, did you hear that?"

"Watch your mouth Malcolm," Daddy said, but I had the feeling he had no idea why he was saying it. "I don't know what you want to do about your dinner, Malcolm. I was going to say you could have some leftover fried chicken, but I don't guess you'd want that. There's some tomato paste in there. You could mix it with water and pour it over your spaghetti noodles."

"Is it organic?"

I had to laugh. "Jesus, Malcolm, give it a rest."

"I'm serious. All those pesticides and insecticides they use cause cancer!"

Two things changed about Malcolm after he started seeing Sharice. First of all, he gave up eating meat and everything he ate had to be organic this or organic that. Tell him that a meal was made with chicken stock or bacon grease and he'd complain like rat poison had been used. And second: He started talking about Africa like if he didn't go there soon, he'd die of shame or something. He even started wearing African shirts with beaded necklaces and bracelets. He tried to grow dreadlocks and even though that experiment had lasted about half a minute, he still had the nerve to lecture me on the fact that I used "too many murderous chemicals" in my hair. Said our African ancestors cried out from the grave each time I went to the beauty shop.

Every time Malcolm fell for a new woman, he'd end up changing in some way or another. He was like a chameleon, became the male version of whoever he was dating regardless of what the woman was into. He started meditating after seeing Lonnie, staring off into space and chanting like he was deep or something. He joined the Nation of Islam while dating Tessa. Those were the days of the white man this, the white man that. After Jacey knocked on his door one Saturday morning, he became a Jehovah's Witness. He even had the nerve to come knocking on my door one Saturday. And you know I treated him like all the rest of them. No thank you. No thank you. No not today. I wouldn't open the door too far. He got all pissed. "You're not even going to let me come in? I'm your brother! You should at least hear me out! Jesus Christ!"

We all went into the kitchen to help Daddy with dinner. After asking me to start the water for the pasta,

Daddy said, "When am I going to meet that boyfriend of yours, Babysister?"

It took me a second to realize he was talking about Rob and not Darren. He and Rob still hadn't met, but then again, at the rate I was going it didn't matter.

Malcolm put his hand on Daddy's shoulders. "No offense Pops, but have you noticed how you're always more interested in who Babysister is seeing than who I'm with. I've been with Sharice for six months and you hardly ever ask how she's doing."

"I don't need to ask about your friends because you're either talking about them or bringing them over." He opened the fridge. "You want a salad, baby girl?"

"That sounds good."

Malcolm leaned against the counter and crossed his arms. "I guess no one wants to know if I want salad."

He turned his head slightly and put his fist under his chin as though he were bored. For a moment he looked like a model posing for a picture. Every so often, when Malcolm moved a certain way or was coming toward me from a distance, I would be struck by the fact that he was actually good-looking. Personally I could care less about his looks because he was my brother, but everyone else has always talked about how handsome he is. When we were growing up the girls were constantly calling. Is Malcolm there? Heeheeheeheehee. He wasn't so much a player as someone who couldn't settle down. He had lived with countless women and had probably broken as many hearts as I had. After high school graduation, he worked as a model for a while. He was on the cover of a calendar called "Black Men/Black Love." He was Mr. March and wore a lime-green thong while standing under a waterfall somewhere in Jamaica. After he started working for UPS, he modeled for a "Men in Uniform" calendar. He was the UPS man. He wore his UPS uniform with the shirt opened and falling off one shoulder. He lifted a cardboard box high above his head and showed off his perfect model face —a face I had seen him practice in the mirror when we were little. Big grin. One eyebrow raised way up into his forehead.

The two of us look nothing alike except for the fact that we both have Momma's short nose and high cheekbones. And while I might have her large round eyes, dark brown skin, and big wide gorgeous smile, Malcolm has Daddy's cleft chin and thick eyelashes and a combination of both their mouths, which gives his lips a nice full shape.

Malcolm crossed his legs and rolled his eyes. "So no one cares whether I want salad or what?"

Daddy said, "Malcolm, don't start up now, hear? I assumed you would want some salad. You don't eat meat anymore, remember?" He buried his head back into the refrigerator. "I wasn't planning on letting you starve."

I was Daddy's favorite, no doubt about that. I'm not trying to say he didn't love Malcolm, I just think parents can't help but have favorites. Maybe it's because they have an easier time with a particular child, but it seems only natural that they're going to feel slightly closer to one child versus another. Daddy probably couldn't help but choose me as his favorite because not only was I the youngest, but as I've said, I looked the most like Momma.

I learned early on that Daddy couldn't say no to me. One day I was sitting in my room crying because Malcolm wouldn't let me go to the movies with him and his friend Jason. I had no business asking if I could tag along, of course, but I cried just the same when Malcolm told me I couldn't go. It had to have been at least two years after

Momma's death, but for some reason, when Daddy found me in my room sobbing into my stuffed animal, he had assumed I was crying about Momma. He tried his best to console me. "Stop your crying now. Everything will be okay. Momma's in heaven, remember?"

I started crying more when he mentioned Momma. By that time, I had turned my mother into someone who had never said no to me, a fifties mom who wore fancy aprons and greeted me from school with all sorts of elaborate treats. "If Momma were here," I said, "she would have *made* Malcolm take me. I miss Momma!" I cried out. "I want my momma!"

Daddy tried to explain again that she was an angel in heaven. She missed me too, but one day we'd all be together.

I cried and cried.

When he realized he wasn't helping any by talking about heaven and my dead mother, he tried another route. You want a glass of milk? I shook my head no. Juice? No. Soda? No. What about some toast with that strawberry jam you like? I cried harder. What about a scoop of ice cream? I lifted my head to see if he was serious. I loved ice cream.

His voice rose like he was talking to a deaf mute and had finally figured out what she was trying to communicate. "You want me to bring you some ice cream? Is that what you want?"

I managed a feeble nod.

"All right. Stop your crying and I'll get you ice cream."

"Can I have two scoops, Daddy?"

I was even more surprised when he didn't make me go into the kitchen to eat it. I mean, my father, Mr. Take-that-on-into-the-kitchen, you-know-better-than-to-eat-food-in-here, actually told me that I could eat the ice cream in the bed with the covers pulled up. I felt like my friend Donna must have when she had had her tonsils taken out and everyone treated her like royalty.

Hmmmm.

The next day, Daddy found me moping on the couch, my head slumped up against my fist, my legs tucked beneath me.

"What's wrong?"

"Nothing." I stared down at the floor. Who knows what I was sad about, probably not much. Either way, if he assumed it was about Momma again, who was I to stop him?

He started going down his food list. Soda? Water? Toast? Sandwich?

I said no to them all. I kept my eyes fixed solemnly on the floor, when tears came I turned to him. "If I could have a Baby Alive doll, it wouldn't be so hard being the only girl. I wouldn't have to feel so lonely when none of my friends can't play or because I don't have a sister or because Momma's in heaven. I wouldn't have to be so bored so much. You can feed a Baby Alive. And you can change her diapers."

I got my doll over the weekend. And let me tell you, there was no turning back after that. "If I had a three-speed, I could go faster." "If I had a skateboard, I could get more exercise." "If I had a moped, I could get to school faster and come home faster." Clothes, new bedroom furniture, the latest toys, I had it all. At Christmas Malcolm would throw a fit when he saw my pile of presents under the tree. "Why does she get so much? Another bike! She just got a bike last year!" I would have felt sorry for him if he hadn't been so mean.

The conversation over dinner was typical. Daddy and Malcolm talked about Malcolm's job at UPS. Daddy had retired from the post office, but still got a kick out of hearing about all the people Malcolm ran into while making deliveries. They also talked about sports, sports, and more sports. Daddy and I talked about my job, my car, a movie we had both seen on cable. When Daddy mentioned that he'd be going to Vegas at the end of the month, Malcolm turned his mouth down and started cradling his chin. "Have you ever thought about going somewhere out of the country? Sharice and I are thinking about going to Africa. She's been there before, you know. She's been to Nigeria."

"I don't need to go to Africa. If I want to see black folks, I can look out my window."

I looked down at my watch. "I was wondering when you were going to start talking about Africa. Running a little late, aren't you?"

"It's important for us as a people to go back to the motherland."

"You only started talking about Africa after you met Sharice, before that all you ever talked about was going to Atlanta."

"Wouldn't you want to go to Africa? All kidding aside. If you could afford it, wouldn't you want to go to Africa?"

"Heck yeah, I would want to go."

"Maybe we could all go as a family sometime. That would be nice, huh Pops?"

"Vegas is good enough for me. Don't need to go a thousand miles away to have a good time."

Daddy could be amazingly stubborn and set in his ways. For a while, Malcolm and I would buy him more stylish clothes for gifts, more expensive alcohol, and we also tried to get him to go out to see a movie instead of watching cable all the time. But he wanted nothing to do with all that and we soon gave up.

Malcolm said, "Well, I'm going to Africa one day. I'm going to see some lions and I'm going to hang out with some of our African brothers."

"Well I hope you have a good time," Daddy said. "Feel free to bring me a souvenir."

After dinner, Daddy and I went to watch TV while Malcolm cleaned the kitchen. ("Pops, it's about time you got a dishwasher. You need to come on into the modern age." "What I need a dishwasher for when I got you?")

Daddy settled into the recliner we bought him a few years back and began watching a boxing match. He'd yell at one of the boxers now and then. Sports was about the only thing that could get Daddy riled up. I watched him put a fist in the air and move around in his recliner. "Use your left, man! Your left!"

We have a few pictures of Daddy when he was younger. He was heavier, but still had thick eyebrows, thick eyelashes, and a high forehead. He almost always had a hat on his head—so that wasn't new, but from the looks of the pictures, Daddy wore suits more often back then and even wore a ring on his pinky. In a couple of the pictures, he stood in front of his best friend's brand-new 1966 Cadillac with a drink in his hand. In my favorite picture my mother is standing next to the car like a model on a game show as my father waves from the window. I like the pictures with the Cadillac because you can see my father once had a silly side, like he had taken advantage of the fact that he was young and in love. He had grown thinner since the photos were taken, but there were no bags under his eyes or wrinkles under his chin or neck.

You wouldn't know he was in his sixties if it weren't for the gray scattered about his head like spilt salt.

Boxing bores the hell out of me, but I watched for another ten minutes or so because one of the boxers was pretty cute. Malcolm came in from the kitchen complaining about the dish soap Daddy used then started yelling at the screen like he knew what the hell he was yelling about. Daddy made them both a couple of drinks then settled back into his recliner. When I told them I was going into the kitchen, I got absolutely no response. What is it about men and sports? Can someone explain it to me, please? Why do they have to pull that zombie shit whenever a game is on? And why do they act like games are so damn important? I mean, a team loses and suddenly the world is about to end or something. *Who cares?* Which reminds me of yet another wonderful thing about Darren: He didn't like sports. Said he enjoyed watching basketball now and then, but that was it.

Until I turned fourteen and discovered my love for boys, I would find myself getting pretty depressed while Malcolm and Daddy watched one of their beloved games. I'd find myself wondering how things would have been different if my mother were around. I mean, I would have enjoyed convincing her to go shopping or to a movie while everyone was into whatever game was on TV. She would have come into the kitchen and say something like "Hey, why don't we girls find something fun to do while they're watching that dumb football game?" And of course it would have been nice if she had been around to help me with just about everything having to do with puberty. I had to rely on a saleslady to help me pick out my first bra and she had had the nerve to flirt with my father the entire time. "So you're a widow, huh? Why that's too bad." I had a hard time with my hair. Getting it washed and pressed took all day. During the week I had to wear my hair in two ponytails because that's all Daddy knew how to do. I wore two fucking ponytails for *years*. Sometimes low, sometimes high, but that was all he could manage so that's what I put up with until I could finally fix it myself. But I don't want to make it seem traumatic or anything, and to be honest, the only time I truly missed having my mother around was when my period started. I don't want to dwell on the subject of my period for too long, but the story of how I told my father sums up my father and brother pretty well, so you'll just have to excuse me.

I found the brown stain on my panties one night after being awakened by what I thought might be the flu. I was twelve years old and remember sitting on the toilet and holding my underwear in my hands like I had never seen blood before. I even held my panties under my nose so as to be sure it was blood. I had imagined that blood would be gushing out, nonstop, enough blood to fill a pad in a few short minutes, but the stain on my underwear had been the size of a quarter and it had been a rusty brown, not at all like when you prick your finger and the blood's ruby red. I didn't have any pads or tampons so I hid my dirty underwear in the trash, found another pair, then carefully rolled several pieces of toilet paper together and stuck it between my legs the best I could.

The next day I stuffed more toilet paper between my legs and walked to a drugstore far enough away so I wouldn't have to worry about running into anybody I knew. I started hiding the tampons I had used in a brown paper bag. I kept the bag under my bed until it was full, then tossed it in a Dumpster behind one of the liquor stores I passed on my way to school. I was prepared to do this month after month until I turned eighteen and left home. I hadn't counted on Malcolm's nosy self going through my things, though, and a few months after my first period had started, I came home from school to find him sitting on the living room couch spinning a (thank God) *unused* tampon high above his head. Turns out the fool had hidden my tampons everywhere. I had to find them all before Daddy got home. I opened the refrigerator and found a tampon sitting in front of the milk like a tiny white mouse, I found one in the *TV Guide,* the washing machine, between the cushions of Daddy's old recliner. Malcolm had me running all over the damn house. I found the last two—one in the potted plant in the living room, the other in one of the coats Daddy kept in the front closet—while Malcolm was helping Daddy with dinner.

After we ate, we all went into the den to watch TV. I watched a smile slowly make its way across Malcolm's face as he watched Daddy untie his shoes.

I said, "Daddy, Malcolm's smiling at me."

Daddy kept his eyes on the TV. "Stop smiling at your sister, boy. Hand me those slippers so I can take these shoes off."

I looked from the slippers to my demon of a brother who could hardly keep from laughing. Daddy wiggled his foot around in the slipper, as if it had suddenly grown too small and he couldn't get his feet to fit inside. "Somethin' is in this here . . ." He held the tampon in the air as though it were a white turd. "What is this?"

By this time Malcolm was rolling around on the floor laughing. "It's not mine!" he yelled.

Daddy walked over to the trash can next to the TV and

tossed it in. "I guess it's yours then, Babysister?" The tone of his voice pleaded, Say it's not yours. Please say it's not yours.

I thought I might as well tell him. "Yeah, they're mine. Malcolm was teasing me with them."

Daddy finished off his drink in a couple of fast gulps then said, "Malcolm, I want you to take your little conniving butt on into your room. I told you about getting into Babysister's things. And don't ask me about going to that game Sunday either."

"But—"

"Get on in that room."

Daddy went to Malcolm's room about five minutes later after taking off his belt with a tired sigh. I rushed over as soon as I knew it was safe then pressed my ear against the door so I could better hear the *swoosh* of Daddy's belt and the sound of Malcolm's beautiful wails.

The next day, Daddy put a lock on my door. The day after that, he returned from work with two large bags. "Babysister, take these on into your room." Inside the bags were enough boxes of tampons and Kotex to last me a good six months. There was also a book called *Becoming a Woman: Everything You Need to Know,* and two giant-size bags of peanut M&Ms. My favorite.

While Daddy and Malcolm argued over the fight, I made a cup of tea and called Darren's answering machine. I knew he was seeing a concert with a couple of friends and wouldn't be home, but I called anyway. I called twice actually, just so I could hear his voice, so I could hear him say *ciao.* I called my own machine next. There was a message from Rob begging me to stop by after I left my father's house. A message from my friend Lisette: "Girl! I just saw Deborah. She looks amazing, girl. She's back to her old self. She told me all about how you helped her. You're an amazing woman, okay? We're going to the Beverly Center tomorrow. We were wondering if you wanted to come with us. Let's go out, okay?"

Deborah and I had originally met Lisette at work and she became one of our closest friends. She had left the bank almost two years before to work as a secretary for a lawyer who handled sexual harassment suits. Lisette Seda called herself many things: feminist, womanist, woman of color, moon daughter, divine African-Puerto Rican princess, and Nubian goddess. As soon as she opened her mouth, you thought about cop shows set in New York, hot dog stands, Central Park, loud taxicab drivers. As soon as you heard her, you wanted to say, You're from New York, right? She wore thick makeup because she had a scar that ran from the side of her mouth all the way up to her ear. Her ex-boyfriend had gone off on her one night then told her if he ever saw her again, he'd kill her. So as soon as she was well enough, she moved to L.A. She also had these huge guppy eyes and lips that puckered and drooped. She looked like a human fish to me, even had a way of getting in your face like when fish get up close to the glass of the tank.

Both her parents were Puerto Rican: one white, one black. She had a thing about people assuming she was black, when actually she was mixed. "I am a MIXED person, okay? What you think? Just because people might assume I'm black I should deny my Spanish heritage? I cannot define myself as both? I have *Spanish* blood; I have *African* blood. What don't you understand about this? I spoke Spanish until my mother sent me to school, okay? You think it was easy for me to learn English? I got teased every day at school 'cause of the way I talk and 'cause I have dark skin. It was hard. I am a MIXED BILINGUAL person, okay? I am a living breathing image of this fucking country!" When Mexican people who didn't know English well came in the bank and Lisette broke out in Spanish, you could see their nervous bodies ease up and soon Lisette would have them rambling away. Everyone loved Lisette.

I made another cup of tea and called her back. I hardly said hello before she interrupted me.

"Listen, Deborah told me how you talked to her and got her to come to her senses. I knew if anyone could straighten her out it would be you. So why do you think she had it so bad for that dog anyway? I don't care how special she thought he was, I can't see getting that depressed over someone who would stop calling without an explanation. Why don't they ever have an explanation, Babysister? Can you explain this to me, please? So what did you say to make her feel better anyhow?"

"I basically told her she had cried long enough and what's over is over."

"That's all you said? I could've told her that. Let me tell you something. My problem is that I am no good at comforting people. I told Deborah she should go to that dog's house and cuss him out something good, and then she should slash the tires of his BMW, and then she should scratch *fuck you* across his car with a key."

"You're being a little extreme aren't you?"

"I think Deborah needs to learn to get angry once in a while. Women need to empower themselves, okay? We shouldn't get *depressed* because some jerk doesn't call, we should get *angry*. We should get angry and let them know they have no manners. Women act like they can't enjoy

life without a man, but let me tell you, we can have a good
life with or without them, it's about love of oneself and
the planet. So are you going shopping with us tomorrow
or what?"

"Yeah, Lisette, what time?"

"How's eleven? Shopping is empowerment. Capitalism
is evil, but it still makes you feel good."

"That's for sure. And maybe we can have an early
dinner."

"Food is empowerment."

I laughed and told her I'd see her tomorrow.

I called Rob afterward. I didn't want to be alone and
figured as long as I didn't have sex with him, there was
nothing wrong with a friend asking another friend for a
massage.

"Can I still come over?"

"Of course you can."

"You'll give me a massage?"

"Full-body massage with wine and with candles. How
does that sound?"

"And you'll make breakfast for me in the morning?"

"I'll even serve it to you in bed."

"Okay, I'll be right there."

"I'll be waiting."

The fight was still on when I went to say goodbye.
Malcolm barely managed a wave. Daddy gave me a hug,
but I had a feeling his eyes were on the fight the entire
time.

Men.

Seven

TRUE TO HIS WORD, Rob massaged me from head to toe. It wasn't one of those massages men usually give where they focus on your shoulders for two minutes and your breasts for twenty, or where he starts to massage your back but as soon as he's aroused starts begging for sex. He was in no hurry at all, took his time as though he had never touched my body before and wanted to savor it. He dug his thumbs into my calf muscles, kneaded his fingers in the curve of my spine, worked his palms over my shoulder blades. I felt his breath against my skin when he came in close, inhaled his cologne as he cradled my neck. I thought, hell, if I had known he was going to be this appreciative of my body, I would've stopped having sex with him sooner.

When my massage was over, I rewarded him with such a slow, sensual handjob, he couldn't stop muttering, "My God, my God, I can't wait. Oh, baby, I can't wait," which was exactly the point, of course.

The next morning I awoke a little after nine to find a lumpy bowl of oatmeal, a sliced orange, and two hand-picked roses next to the bed. Rob appeared in the doorway with a cup of coffee and plate of toast just as I realized the breakfast was for me.

"This is so sweet, Rob. I didn't expect you to do all this." I took the toast and juice then pulled him down close.

"I said I would," he beamed. "I want to start showing more of my romantic side." He nuzzled his face against my cheek then traced his finger along the length of my arm. I turned my head so I could kiss the inside of his palm. When I felt his other hand move to the flat area right above my breasts, I caught myself moaning. I mean, a way to a woman's heart is to make her a meal; whether the food turns out good or bad, believe me, she's yours. As we kissed, I began to feel like we were in the earlier days of our relationship when things were easy and fun and not so damn predictable. I was surprised to find I was so wet when I felt his finger slide inside me. I pushed his hand aside and untied his robe, helped to slide his underwear off with my foot in one long motion that began close to his hips and ended somewhere near his ankles. Then I pulled down on those huge biceps and wrapped my legs around his waist.

I didn't start feeling guilty until after we made love and Rob held me from behind. There was something about the way he was trying to get me to play itsy-bitsy spider with him that made me feel awful. He was acting so sweet, yet the whole time we were making love I couldn't stop thinking about Darren. I had no business having sex with Rob, I thought. And later, as he fed me lumpy spoonfuls of oatmeal with his dopey love-struck smile and little bitty head, I swore to myself—*swore*—romantic side or no romantic side, I would not have sex with him ever again. Period. A handjob is one thing, but it simply was not my style to sleep with two men.

Rob tried to convince me not to go shopping with Lisette and Deborah and to spend the rest of the day with him. "We could go somewhere ourselves," he had said. "We could go somewhere fun. Venice Beach or something." But I told him I was looking forward to hanging out with my girlfriends for a change. Besides, it had been weeks since I had been shopping. At any rate, I said goodbye to Rob and drove to my place. Deborah and Lisette were meeting me there so we could drive together in my Mustang. We wanted to hit the smoggy freeways with the top down. Lisette brought her Chaka Khan tape and we sang along to "Sweet Thing" in loud voices with our arms stretched out in the air like we were in a music video.

Lisette was right about Deborah's being back to her old self. She laughed and smiled, looked great in this short blue dress with a sky-blue scarf and blue sandals. She looked like an actress from the fifties on her way to get her hands and feet mashed into wet cement. Before stepping into my car, she had positioned her hand over her heart and stared solemnly at me then at Lisette. "I will *never* let a man get me down like that again. Never. And if by chance I do, I give you both permission to slap me."

We shopped for hours. Deborah was having one of those days when everything the girl tried on was perfect for her—pants, shoes, dresses, it was just a matter of deciding what she wanted most. Lisette was all over the place, trying on things half her size, things she could never afford. "Oooh, look at this. Oooh, come here, look at this." We tried to keep up with her. "Oooh, come touch this blouse. Oooh, I have to have this purse. All these mannequins should be a size twelve. You know anyone this skinny? It's ridiculous. Oooh, look at that over there. Pretty, huh?"

Our last stop was one of those beauty stores where all the products are made from things you can eat. I didn't want to go in myself. "Why should I pay twenty dollars for banana conditioner?" I told them. "If I want to wash my hair with bananas I can go to the store and buy a bunch for less than two bucks," but Deborah and Lisette insisted.

Lisette shoved a bottle under my nose. "Oooh, Babysister, smell this shampoo. It smells like vanilla ice cream."

"Yeah, it does, but who wants their hair to smell like ice cream?"

"What? You have something against ice cream? It smells good."

I took another whiff, realized I was hungry. "I thought we were going to have an early din—"

Lisette tapped my stomach with the back of her hand. "Look over there."

I turned and saw Deborah talking to a man in his late thirties, early forties, not much taller, with a beard, glasses, gray pants, gray tie, and a briefcase. He was definitely her type. They looked like a living breathing advertisement for a home loan. I saw the words *Let Us Work for You* written above their heads. Lisette and I followed them around the store, doing our best to eavesdrop. Deborah played with the ends of her hair. The man rocked back and forth on his loafers. Deborah laughed. He laughed. Finally he gave her a business card and they shook hands. After he waved goodbye, we rushed over.

"Girrrl," Lisette said, "who was that? He likes you, I can tell these things, okay?"

"Calm down, Lisette. That man goes to my church. He's married. I know his wife *and* his three children. One of his daughters plays the piano. The girl is amazing. She plays once in a while for the youth choir. Carl and his wife are starting a book club, that's what we were talking about. I'm thinking about joining."

"He seems nice," Lisette said. "Too bad he's married."

We watched Carl take his change and leave the store. Too bad he had such a flat ass, I thought.

Deborah pretended to sulk. "It's probably all over for me the way my love life has been."

"Not with this face," Lisette said, pinching Deborah's cheek. She was only three years older than Deborah and me but tended to act like she had a good twenty years on us sometimes. "You have to make a list of what you want. Make a list then you gotta visualize it, okay? What you think? Your dream man is gonna fall out of the sky like a fucking comet?"

Deborah smiled at me. "Remember how much time we spent talking about our dream man? What our lives would be like? Remember how we wanted to have a double wedding?"

"Yeah," I said, and suddenly felt so much guilt all I could do was stare at my feet. There was something about seeing her with Carl. I know I've said she was one of the most naive people I ever met, but to be honest, she was also one of the kindest. If anyone deserved to meet someone like Carl, have three kids including a daughter who played piano, it was Deborah. I picked up a bottle of kiwi-lime lotion, pretended to read the ingredients. *What the hell was I doing?*

Lisette said, "You goddesses hungry or what?"

"I'm hungry enough to eat this lotion," I sighed, and as I returned the bottle to the shelf, actually considered canceling my date with Darren that next night.

We went to a restaurant in Century City Lisette had heard about. We were walking toward the entrance of the place when two teenagers walked by, staring at us like our sole purpose on the planet was to give them something to look at. The one with cornrows winked at Deborah and said to his buddy, "I like that real light-skinned one in the dress." Deborah rolled her eyes and went inside, but Lisette glared at them over her shoulder. Maybe it was because they were young, but she didn't get nearly as loud as she normally would have. "Way to internalize racism," she said to Cornrows with a smirk. "And women are not objects to be stared at. You treat us with respect, okay?" Cornrows gave her the finger and the two boys headed down the street. She began mumbling in Spanish as we walked through the door. I caught the words *dick* and *objectification*. Then she turned to me and said, "Jesus fucking Christ I'm hungry."

We pigged out, too. I guess I had just needed to eat, because the more I ate, the quicker the guilt seemed to vanish along with the food on my plate. I mean, it wasn't a perfect situation, but things would work out. Things always worked out for me.

Before dessert was served, Lisette pulled out a paperback from her pocketbook, and plopped it down in the middle of the table. The book was called *10 Ways to Love Yourself*. "National Best Seller!" screamed from the top of the page. "Over 1 Million Copies Sold!" "Before you say a word," she said to Deborah, "I personally want you to take this here book. Read it cover to cover. Don't say no. It's a gift from me to you, okay? I was worried about you. All that crying over that dog was no good. This book here is about women and self-esteem. You beat that, that esteem shit, and your whole life will turn around. You won't even let a man like that come near you again. I don't care how fine he is." She turned to me. "Huh, girlfriend? Am I speaking the truth or what?"

I picked up the book. "Oh, yeah. That's definitely the truth."

"Like I told you, you gotta make a list, and you gotta visualize." She pointed to her eyes. "You gotta know what you want to get what you want, okay?"

"She's right," I said. "Sometimes you have to tinker with certain situations, but it doesn't have to be difficult to get what you want out of life."

Deborah said, "I just want to say thank you to the both of you. Thank you, Lisette, for the book, and thank you again, Babysister, for all the talks you gave me."

Lisette lifted her glass. "To goddesses of color across the world." Deborah and I clinked our glasses with hers. "We need to stick together, you know? All we have is each other, okay? Look at any fucking country on this planet and who has it the worst? The women. Women and the kids too, you know? I am a stronger woman because of this book. It's for empowerment, you know? Just in case you get the urge to call that ignorant ass. That night I visited you in your apartment. I never seen you so sad. Not the same at all. I say to myself, What happened to the Deborah I know and love? Where is she at?" She pointed to the scar on her face. "Listen, let me tell you something. After this here happened, I'm lying in the hospital bed and

I'm thinking to myself, Lisette, if it's one thing you need to learn in this life, it's that men are fucking animals. Animals everyone of them. That's when I started reading more about feminism and empowerment. Now I realize, of course, that all men aren't dogs. Some are like the one that did this here, but not all. But the thing is, the thing to remember is, you can live without a man just like you can live without a dog. Right, Babysister?"

"Damn straight," I said, and lifted my glass.

Deborah lifted her glass. "Damn straight," she said, then broke out laughing.

Five weeks later, while I was at work and pouring myself a strong cup of coffee (Darren and I had gone to hear a salsa band in Long Beach and didn't get in until after three) Danisha came right up to me and pointed her finger in my face. "People around here are beginning to talk about you." It was doughnut Friday, the only time you could expect Danisha to show up early. The girl could put away some doughnuts, even had the nerve to complain if Deborah forgot to buy enough ("Well, it's not like we don't chip in!"). She licked a blob of strawberry filling from the tip of her fingernail.

I glanced over her face and arms. I had developed a habit of checking over Danisha's skin for rashes ever since I heard she had herpes. "What?"

"You seem awfully happy these days." Even when Danisha's mouth was empty, her cheeks puffed out as though she was playing a trumpet. She was darker than the coffee she was drinking, but had the nerve to wear a super-bright yellow suit with matching yellow shoes. "So what's up? I don't see a ring on your finger, but word has it you're getting married."

"*Married?*"

"Vicky thinks you're planning on quitting. Carol thinks you're pregnant."

"*Pregnant?*"

She sipped her coffee. "Something's gotta be up. You've been acting different lately. Can't help but notice how nice you've been to the customers."

"I'm always nice to the customers."

Not true. Sometimes I wouldn't even look at them. I'd keep my eye on the computer and the money.

Byron came over. We didn't bother telling him he had a couple of chocolate sprinkles in his mustache. "Who's pregnant?"

Jesus.

"We're having a private discussion," Danisha said.

Byron pointed toward Deborah with his thumb. "Is Deborah pregnant?" he whispered.

"Nobody's pregnant that I know of," Danisha said. "We were discussing why Babysister has been so nice lately."

"Yeah, what's up with that?"

Instead of bringing up his wife and the garbage collector like I could have, I simply tossed my napkin in the trash. "It is time to get to work. And I don't care what the gossip is, I've been no happier than usual."

Also not true. I had never been happier in my life. Sounds dramatic I know, but seems like after my afternoon with Deborah and Lisette, the following weeks fell into this seamless happy groove. Some evenings I fixed dinner while Darren played jazz or classical music. Sometimes he'd come up from behind and wrap his arms around me while I cooked and we'd end up on the couch, on a table, on the floor. He made dinner for me as well.

He'd take out these big, heavy cookbooks and move around the kitchen with a towel draped across his shoulder and a glass of wine in his hand. Malcolm would've loved his cooking. He made things like stuffed bell peppers with wild rice, or spicy shrimp with garlic and olive oil. In the morning he'd hand me my driver's mug with a sweet kiss on the cheek then I'd patiently sit in bumper-to-bumper traffic, drinking my coffee, letting cars who wanted to get in my lane cut in front of me without a beep of my horn or a single cussword. You want to cut in front of my car? Sure, go ahead. Have a nice day! You want to drive fifty in the fast lane? No problem! Then I'd arrive at work and greet everyone with a friendly hello. It was a beautiful five weeks. On the nights when we weren't cooking for each other Darren and I would explore L.A.: restaurants, museums, concerts. And let me tell you, there is nothing like a man who likes to get out and do things, who isn't content with sitting in front of the damn TV all the time.

Speaking of which, I told Rob that I was feeling smothered and needed space two weeks after Darren and I began seeing each other more often. I gave him the old line about absence making the heart grow fonder, but it didn't go over too well. "Babysister, I'm fond of you enough as it is. I can't get any fonder!" I told him I was feeling distracted and a little space would bring the spark back into the relationship. "We don't need sparks," he'd said, "we just need each other. We're doing fine." We went back and forth, but in the end he told me he'd always be there for me and if I needed space, he'd give it to me.

Deborah and I had lunch together when we could, and thank goodness, she soon stopped talking about Darren altogether and resumed her role as the black Mother Teresa.

The one and only glitch during those weeks was when Darren's mother stopped by one night while he was still at work. How such a nasty woman had managed to have such a beautiful son was beyond me. I was in the kitchen making dinner when I heard her knock.

"You must be Deborah," she said, extending her hand. "I'm so delighted to finally meet you. My son has told me such wonderful things about you!"

When I told her that, No, I actually wasn't Deborah, she looked me over sharply. I'm sure she didn't miss the fact that I was making myself awfully cozy in her son's UCLA T-shirt and UCLA shorts.

"From what my son told me, he was dating a young Christian woman named Deborah."

I'm young! I wanted to say, but I kept my mouth shut. Her hair was cut short and highlighted brown. Her makeup was flawless and made her small eyes bigger and her thin lips fuller. The only problem I saw with Mrs. Wilson's appearance was the outfit she had on, which looked like something the captain of the Love Boat would wear, navy blue pants with a matching navy blue jacket that stopped at her waist, shoulder pads, and a huge gold pin shaped like an anchor. Ahoy, mates.

I should have known better than to tell her that Deborah and I worked together and were friends. As soon as the words tumbled out of my mouth, her nose practically brushed up against the ceiling.

"So let me get this straight. Darren and Deborah are no longer dating and now *you're* seeing my son?"

I nodded yes, but she didn't say anything. She simply

turned away and began looking around the place as if she had lost something, or more likely was making sure I hadn't stolen anything. She even had the nerve to walk upstairs to Darren's bedroom where my robe and nightgown were still lying across the unmade bed. When she returned from her surveillance check, she sat on the barstool in front of the kitchen and waved her hand toward the skillets and pots. "Don't let me interrupt you."

I could not only smell Mrs. Wilson's expensive perfume as she sat there eyeing me, but felt as if I was able to get a good strong whiff of her entire privileged ancestry. From the house slave who never had to work the fields and served his master's food in white gloves, all the way down to her upper-class relatives who lived in large houses with white servants and brought their children up on piano and vocal lessons, and who discussed the Negro problem as though they weren't.

I put a couple of catfish in the sizzling oil, began checking on the other pots. I told her Darren had called but said he'd be late. When I asked her if she wanted something to drink, her eyes seemed to say, Really now, who do you think you are playing hostess in my son's home? She said, No thank you, then stared at me as if she was trying to figure out how in the world I had wiggled my *un*educated, *un*rich, *dark*-skinned self into Darren's life.

"I haven't smelled a meal like that since I was a girl. What *are* you making?"

I pointed to each pot. "Fried catfish, skillet yams, string beans. I'm about to start fixing the corn bread. Would you like to join us for dinner?"

Please say no!

"Good heavens, child, and have a heart attack? A meal

like that is loaded with fat and salt. We as a people *must* start watching what we eat." She shifted her weight on the barstool, a look of concern on her face. "My son hasn't been eating these meals often, has he?"

I had a very strong urge to go off on the woman, but reminded myself that I was in Darren's home. As much as I wanted to, it wouldn't be right. "No, Mrs. Wilson," I said, "not often at all." I hit the spoon against the pot of string beans.

She shifted her weight on the barstool again, asked where I was born, where I grew up, where I was living now, what college I had attended. Not a single answer met with her approval, but she smiled anyway, that same distant smile I gave to customers at the bank. Needless to say, I was all too happy when, without any warning, she got up to leave. "Tell Darren I stopped by and to give me a call." She took my hand. "Well . . ." she began, holding her smile as she waited for the right words to come to mind. She said it again, "Well . . ." as if surely this time she could think of the appropriate words to say to the young woman practically shacking up with her son. When the words didn't come, she squeezed my hand and pushed the corners of her mouth up even higher.

After opening the door, I looked at her as warmly as I could. "It was nice meeting you." She rushed off toward her Mercedes, and since she waved goodbye without turning, and had no way of seeing me, I gave her the finger without thinking twice.

Hours later, after Darren and I had gone to bed, I found that I was too excited to sleep, and so without making too much noise I went outside and stood on his deck. Over dinner I complained that if I'd been introduced to his mother, she might not have acted so negatively. And instead of getting defensive, Darren apologized and said, "You know what? I think we should have our families over for dinner soon. I'd love to meet your father. And once my mother gets to know you, I'm sure you'll win her over." I got up from the table and jumped into his lap when he said that. I mean, the fact that he wanted our families to meet suggested that I was as important to him as he was to me.

I walked to the edge of the deck and stared at the moon, imagining the big dinner I'd make when our parents came over. My father would tell funny stories about my childhood and Darren would laugh as he hugged me to his waist. Even Malcolm wouldn't be able to find anything wrong with him.

I smiled and walked back inside. Darren was still fast asleep. I began tracing his ear with my fingertips, thinking about how perfect the past weeks had been. I know you're supposed to be all shy and sappy when you're about to tell someone you love them for the first time, but I didn't feel that way at all. I didn't have an ounce of fear or embarrassment. I was so excited, in fact, I didn't stop to think and gave his body a few strong shakes.

"What? What's wrong?"

"I wanted to tell you that I love you," I said.

He lifted himself up and dug his fingers through his hair. "Wow, that's really nice. It's extremely sweet of you to tell me that. Thank you." He gave me a long hug then kissed me on the cheek and pulled me down onto the bed so we could go back to sleep, but all I could do was stare at the back of his head in disbelief. I thought about shaking him again, Excuse me, I just told you that I *love* you, but I stopped when I felt him reach for my hand. I told myself that I should be content with the fact that he wanted to get our families together. That such a wonderful man cared about me and made me feel so special. And then to stop myself from worrying, I simply wrapped my arms around him and pressed my body into his.

Eight

IF I WERE ever to make a list of all the men I'd been with I'd have to write their names under two headings: "Men I Almost Loved" and "Men Who Have Gotten on My Nerves." The list under men who have gotten on my nerves would be endless.

Before I started dating Rob, I was in a relationship with a man named David. David had read *The Autobiography of Malcolm X* twenty-one times and was working on a one-man play based on the book titled *Malcolm*. He liked to carry his play around with him wherever he went because he never knew when an idea might come. Sometimes we'd be sitting in a nice restaurant having a conversation and he'd suddenly whip out his notebook and start scribbling words and forget that I was there altogether. When I complained, he said this was what you have to expect when you're dating a serious playwright. Sometimes he'd read Malcolm X's autobiography to me in bed. Sometimes he'd act out scenes from his play, using the bed as a stage when he was really into it. He'd imitate Malcolm's voice and recite speeches about self-respect. This was all cute at first, but I got nervous when he grew a goatee and kept doing his Malcolm imitation even when he wasn't working on his play. I was out of there when he asked me to start wearing scarves over my head like a Muslim woman and wanted me to call him Malcolm even when we were out in public.

Before David was Kenneth. Kenneth was one of the grocery store men. Even though Kenneth was twenty-nine years old, he still dreamt of becoming a rap star. He couldn't rap to save his life, but all he ever talked about was how he was going to be a rich rap star. He was constantly trying to rhyme words together. He couldn't even hold a normal conversation without trying to turn it into a rap. "Babysister is fine, but she hates my rhyme. A niggah needs a woman who can put in the time, support her man on a spiritual basis. It's the real thing, girl. You should never forsake this."

Diondre had a drinking problem. I don't want to have anything to do with a man who drinks vodka and orange juice for breakfast. I don't care how stressed out he says he is.

Eric managed a bookstore and was also a part-time student at Cal State Long Beach. Unfortunately, he was one of those men who thought the world revolved around him. I'm usually good at spotting this particular male dysfunction right off. I don't know how I missed it with Eric during those first few dates, but it wasn't too long before I noticed how he'd go on and on about his day, go on and on about all the people he knew, all the books he'd read, yet rarely ask me a question about my life or my interests. The man could hold entire conversations with himself without noticing that I wasn't paying him any attention, that I was sitting there with my eyes glazed over, bored to death.

Calvin was too smart for his own good. We met at a bar on Pico Boulevard. I should've known he wasn't worth my time by the way he went on about his SAT scores. Bring up any subject and Calvin would undoubtedly have something to say about it. He enjoyed showing off his vocabulary and was fond of calling me "capricious." When I broke up with him he said things like "We had such an auspicious beginning. Why give up now?" "Are you so impervious to my point of view you that you won't even bother hearing me out?"

Looking back, I think I dated Tyler because he was the exact opposite of Calvin. I liked him because he had a limited vocabulary and had barely graduated from high school. We met at one of those ten-minute oil changer places where he worked. He gave me a free air filter and free transmission fluid then charmed me into writing my name and number on his arm with a marker. "Go on. Write it as big as you can. I don't wonna lose this." After a few dates with Tyler, I soon realized it was just as difficult to date someone who was on the slower side as it was to date someone who thought he knew everything. Tyler blew bubbles in his drinks, loved to tell knock-knock jokes, and knew nothing about the world outside of sports and action movies. I ended it with him one night after we had gone out to dinner with Deborah and her boyfriend at the time. We were headed back to the car when we suddenly couldn't find Tyler anywhere. It wasn't until Deborah mentioned something about maybe calling the police that we heard snickering from somewhere far off. "Hey, y'all, I'm up here. Look up here!" A sudden clump of leaves fell our heads. The fool had climbed a tree—was way up on the top branch swinging and swaying like Tarzan. I was so embarrassed. "Don't bother calling me again," I told him before closing the door on his goofy butt.

The problem is that men don't necessarily get on your nerves right away. Usually you think you've met a nice person and who knows? A certain amount of time has to pass before you discover that he thinks he's Malcolm X; or climbs trees for fun; or uses words like *lubricious* when he could just as well say smooth. All I'm trying to say is, I've never regretted being careful about saying the words *I love you* because I've learned that the same person you think you're so in love with those first few weeks will most likely become someone you'd just as soon forget.

I'm sure all my boyfriends had truly fallen in love with me. Go down their lists and my name would be written in blue felt-tip pen or black ballpoint directly under the heading "Love of My Life" or "Sexiest Woman I've Ever Been With." I know without a doubt that if I had said I love you to any of *them*, they would have said more than "That's so nice" and gone right back to sleep. I couldn't understand why the hell Darren hadn't taken me into his arms and told me that he loved me. I had finally found a man I'd never become bored with, or who'd never embarrass me, and what happened? He ruined the most romantic moment in my life.

But Darren was full of surprises, surprises that were too hard to fight against. While I was worrying about his love or lack of love for me, two days after I told him that I loved him, he had had three dozen irises delivered to the bank. *Three dozen.* And what are you supposed to think when a man sends three dozen irises to your job? That he could care less about you? That he thinks of you as a pal? I don't think so.

The deliveryman had sounded confused and frustrated

when he yelled out my name. "Is there a *Baby-sitter* here?" Deborah and Byron said in unison, "It's Baby*sister*," then pointed toward my station.

I almost passed out when I realized all those irises were for me. Even the woman I was helping at the time said, "Don't faint on me now. I need to make my deposit." After slipping me her money under the bulletproof glass, she added, "Your man must really love you. Or is he trying to make up for something he did wrong? Did he do something wrong?" I walked out to the open area of the bank and took the flowers from the deliveryman. "He loves me," I told her. "He does this kind of stuff all the time."

The card read:

> B—
>> *Thinking of you.*
>> —D

Marsha, who never says anything to anyone, came over during her break and buried her head in my flowers. She had on one of her typical spinster dresses, a polka-dotted thing that went past her knees and made her look too old for her age. "My husband did something like this for me once." "Oh really?" I said, ready to finally hear her talk about something personal. But all she said was "These are really beautiful," then glided away without another word.

Everyone asked who they were from. Was it my birthday? What's the special occasion? I wanted to say, Remember that fine brother who came in the bank about three months ago? The flowers are from *him*. He's an architect, graduated from UCLA. But I couldn't very well say that. Not with Deborah going on about how romantic "Rob" was for sending me flowers while giving me a hug, and if anything, making me feel more guilt than I wanted to deal with at the moment.

I called Darren from a pay phone outside of Ramiro's during my lunch break. I was having lunch with Tonya but thought that I might try to catch Darren in his office. While I waited for him to pick up his line, I imagined him standing in front of a huge desk with his sleeves rolled up, pointing at tiny models of important buildings or drawings of extravagant houses—a group of men standing behind him in expensive business suits, nodding their heads in unison. *Excuse me, gentlemen, this will have to wait, my girlfriend is on the other line.*

"So I take it you got the flowers."

"Thank you. They're beautiful. I was so surprised."

"I'm glad you liked them."

"I loved them."

I peeked inside Ramiro's to see if Tonya was okay. She was going through one of her funks and spent most of our lunch describing the various types of beans in the world. "Not just refried pinto beans mind you. There are all sorts of colorful varieties: black beans, white beans, pink beans, red beans."

Darren said, "So I was also going to surprise you with dinner, but I'm afraid I'm swamped. I'm going to be here pretty late so I doubt if I'll be able to see you tonight. I'll probably have to take some of the work home with me if I'm going to finish on time."

I wanted to see him but I could hear how tired he was so I didn't press the issue. "I'll miss you."

"I'll miss you, too," he whispered. "Let's talk later, okay?"

Once at home, I put the irises in the center of my coffee table and decided that since I couldn't see Darren, I'd simply enjoy a quiet night alone. No Rob, no friends, no talking on the phone, no TV. I'd take a long hot bath and afterward begin one of the novels Darren had loaned me, *Another Country* or maybe *Sula*.

I did get to take that bath, and got as far as the third chapter of *Sula* when I heard a knock at the door. No one could've been more surprised than me to see Malcolm and his girlfriend, Sharice, standing in the hallway. Malcolm and I rarely visited each other. He'd stop by once every so often when I was cooking for Daddy, and I might stop by his place if Daddy asked me to pick up something Malcolm had borrowed and hadn't returned, but that was it. I had yet to visit him since he had moved in with Sharice, in fact.

"Babysister! It's been so long!" Sharice gave me a long hug. As usual she smelled like incense and body oil. "Are you surprised to see us? You must be. We *walked*. Malcolm wanted to drive, but I said, Why drive? We could use the exercise. You surprised?" She paused a second, covered her mouth with her hands, then rushed over to my irises, practically pushing Malcolm out of her way. "Awww look! How beautiful! I think irises must be the most beautiful, delicate flower around. What a stunning bouquet! *Mmmm* heaven." She grabbed one and tried to tickle Malcolm's nose.

"I don't know if those were grown without pesticides," I said, "so you might want to be careful with that. Where's your little boy?"

"Oh, he's with his daddy for a week. That's partly why we're here. We're trying to get out as much as we can while he's away." She led Malcolm to the couch, and after sitting down, carefully straightened her skirt, the million bracelets she wore tinkling about her arms like chimes.

She tapped Malcolm's stomach. "How long did it take us to walk over here, baby?"

"One hour, seventeen minutes."

"See there. We're healthier now and the air is cleaner because we didn't drive. I'll tell you, cars will be the downfall of us all someday. We need more roses on the planet and less cars. Wouldn't the world be beautiful with more roses and trees and grass? It breaks my heart that we seem to care more about our transportation than we do the air we breathe."

Sharice could be annoyingly emotional about certain things. The girl was capable of getting worked up over a dead insect. I'm not kidding. She had walked in on me once as I was spraying a trail of ants that had made their way to my father's sugar bowl. She gave me a speech about everything being connected, lectured me like I was a lost soul, evil destroyer of ant communities. "Death of any kind is sad. We're connected to these ants, you know what I mean? They lead such amazing lives, too. They're more together than we'll ever be." She took the ant spray and tossed it in the trash. "And Babysister, don't use that poison. It's so dangerous, especially in the kitchen. Put some garlic out on the counter or wipe them down with a sponge." Not even five minutes later she started talking about a TV movie we had both watched. This was classic Sharice. One minute she was carrying on like a hippie girl who'd done one too many drugs, the next she was capable of having a normal conversation about TV or something.

Malcolm nodded toward the irises. "So who you messin' with now?"

"What do you mean by that?"

"You always trying to rope in one brother or another." He smirked like he was trying to be funny.

"Actually, I met a very nice man. An *architect*."

Sharice clasped her hands together. "Babysister's gone and found herself a prince."

Malcolm said, "He ain't white is he?"

"No," I said, rolling my eyes. "There are such things as black architects, you know. Just like there are black doctors and black lawyers and black businessmen."

"Okay, okay."

Normally he would have said something like, That smart mouth of yours is going to get you in big trouble one day, little girl. But the real Malcolm had a way of disappearing when his African queen was around.

Sharice wrapped her arm around Malcolm's and dropped her head on his shoulder. "I think there are still several good black men to be found. I don't care what women say."

Malcolm kissed her forehead. "Yeah, but in order to get a good man you have to be a good woman. A brother doesn't want to have to put up with power struggles."

"Yeah," I said, "but a good man isn't threatened by a woman who knows what she wants."

Sharice said, "I'll tell you, your father did such a good job raising his son. Malcolm has no problems with housework, unlike most of our fine young brothers."

My eyebrows shot up. "Since when does Malcolm do housework?"

"Last week I came home from work and Malcolm had the entire house cleaned and dinner on the table, didn't you, baby?"

"Yep."

"Tell her what you made, baby."

"A couscous-tofu stir-fry." He stretched his arms out like there was a crowd of applauding women in the room.

"See, a real man doesn't mind helping his woman out once in a while. But what man wants to help out a woman who thinks she knows everything? I'm not trying to say a man has to be in control twenty-four seven. I mean, I've learned a lot from Sharice. Things I wouldn't have learned if I hadn't taken the time to listen to her, and even more important, not try to get my way all the time."

"Your brother is one of the most supportive men I've ever known."

I looked around my apartment to see if there was anything I could puke in.

"I'm just trying to help you out a little, Sis." He motioned toward my irises with his chin. "Those white-collar brothers don't want to put up with a lot of attitude. That's why so many of 'em date white women." He chuckled like he had made a funny joke.

"Thanks for the advice. Considering how long your relationships last, I should probably do my best to pay attention."

"Oh, Babysister," Sharice said. "Those other relationships weren't his fault. He just needed to find the right queen."

She squeezed his hand and made goo-goo faces.

I give them another month, I thought. Two tops. The real Malcolm was bound to come out sooner or later, and when he did, Sharice would find out how often he complained. She'd also find out that if he didn't have to lift a finger to help out around the house, he wouldn't. And besides all that, he loved meat.

"Finding love takes time," Sharice said. "But it's out there. I'm thankful that all my life experiences and all my past mistakes have led me to your brother."

Sharice was two years younger than me. She was a

beautiful woman, there was no way around this fact. Five feet eleven with small almond-shaped eyes, full lips. She had the sort of beauty that made you think of other places. Made you want to ask her where she was from. Malcolm was more in love with her beauty than anything else, but I'm sure countless other men had fallen in love with her for the same reasons. There was no telling how many other men had given up meat and started talking like a hippie in order to be with her. Unlike my brother, who only had the occasional modeling job here and there, Sharice had actually made her living as a model for several years. When she got bored with modeling, she decided to study art. After she dropped out of art school, she went to Africa for two months, then came back to study massage and African dance. She had also had a son with a photographer who did a lot of work for *Essence* magazine. Her latest idea was to open an upscale vegetarian restaurant.

Malcolm went over to my CD collection, asked if he could borrow my Patti Labelle CD then complained about the fact that I didn't have any "world" music. Since it looked like they weren't leaving anytime soon, I offered to make coffee. They almost declined when they found out the coffee wasn't organic, but seemed to feel better about accepting it after lecturing me on the plight of coffee pickers around the world. They also mentioned that the walk had made them hungry but because my refrigerator was filled with meat and meat by-products, they had to settle on peanut butter and jelly sandwiches.

When Sharice came into the kitchen to help out, I told her it was a wonder she and Malcolm didn't starve. Don't ask me why I said this, I ended up getting a lecture on everything from how to find protein in vegetables, to the evolution and eating habits of humans. The only way I could get her to shut up was to ask about her son—not that I wasn't genuinely curious.

"So where does Prophet's father live?" I asked.

"Huntington Beach. His father has a house a few blocks away from the beach so it's great for Prophet. He's an Aquarian so you know he loves the water. Malcolm and I are having fun, but we miss him. We miss Prophet, don't we honey?" She had to raise her voice because Malcolm had turned on my TV and was watching a basketball game. "I was telling your sister how much we miss Prophet."

"Yeah, it's not the same without him."

"Awww," Sharice said. "You know things are good when your man likes your kid."

Sharice's son was seven years old. His full name was Prophet Hotep Shabazz. I met Prophet for the first time at Daddy's house. Sharice had him dressed in an African shirt that went down to his knees. After dinner, she had him recite a speech he had given to his second-grade class on an African warrior who had the powers of a hundred men. At the end of the speech he played his bongo and did a few dance steps. It all would have been cute if Malcolm and Sharice hadn't kept interrupting, prodding Prophet on like he was performing at the March on Washington instead of simply speaking in front of my family. "No baby, do that part again. That's right! Good! Say, A . . . sa . . . lam Ma . . . lakem, Prophet. Say, Aslam Malakem!"

Sharice placed the sandwiches she made for Malcolm on a plate. Before taking them into the other room, she said, "Malcolm is so good with Prophet. He's a good man in general, I'll tell you. He's very supportive."

"Yeah, I can see how supportive he is. Look who's carrying the food and who's watching the TV."

"Oh, Babysister," she said, then walked up close. "And he's so good-looking, too. He really turns me—"

"Sharice, please." I raised my hand. I really was going to puke if she didn't shut up.

"Sorry." She smiled. "I sometimes forget he's your brother."

"I wish I could."

As she gave the sandwiches to her African warrior, I noticed how he moved his head slightly so he could see the TV as she kissed him—not even his beloved African queen could divert his attention from basketball. She returned to the kitchen, hopped her tall lanky self onto the counter, and bit into her sandwich. "So tell me about this new man in your life. Is he cute?"

I can't tell you how good it felt to talk about Darren. I mean, since we'd started dating I hadn't said a thing about him to anyone. Sharice was full of questions. I described him for her from head to toe, emphasized certain key words: Baldwin Hills. Architect. UCLA. Six feet three. We ended up having such a nice talk, I wound up sitting on the kitchen counter as well. Sharice really wasn't so bad if you stayed clear of certain topics.

"He sounds great, Babysister."

"He is, Sharice. To tell the truth, I've never felt so strongly about a man before. I can't stop thinking about him! And that's not like me at all."

"Awww, Babysister, you're in love, aren't you?"

"I love him so much, Sharice. He's intelligent. He treats me well. He's beautiful." I pressed my lips together as though I was tasting something sweet and delicious. "This one I'd marry in a second. I really would." As soon as I realized what I had said, I covered my mouth and giggled nervously.

Malcolm interrupted us just then. He wanted another sandwich and had the nerve to call to Sharice from where he sat like he truly was a king.

She jumped from the counter as if she had felt a shock on her ass. "Sure, baby, I'll make you another sandwich."

"You better keep your eye on him," I told her. "You don't want to end up making all the sandwiches in the relationship. Malcolm can be lazy."

"I can hear you, Babysister!" Malcolm yelled. "You're the last person who can say anything about someone being lazy, as spoiled as you are. Tell Sharice how many cars Pops bought for you."

"What does that have to do with being lazy?"

"I worked far more than you ever had to when we were kids. I work hard now. I deserve to be treated well by my girlfriend every now and then." He was still facing the TV, but began raising fingers in the air and counting aloud. "One, two, three . . . four cars. Am I right?"

"It wasn't like they were all new."

"All I know is, you can't grow into a respectable adult if you get everything you want as a child." He turned around so he could face Sharice. "Babysister got everything she wanted. *Everything*. Daddy didn't know how to say no to her. Still doesn't."

"And so?"

"You've never learned the meaning of give-and-take because all you ever had to do in life was take."

"Like you're somebody to be talking about give-and-take."

"I give a lot. Don't I, Sharice?"

As soon as we started arguing Sharice began busying

herself with Malcolm's food, acting as if making a peanut butter and jelly sandwich was especially complicated. I watched as she gently sliced the sandwich into quarters. "You definitely give a lot to this relationship," she said finally. "But you and Babysister need to get along. Life is too short. One day all you'll have is each other."

"Lord help us," I said.

Sharice gave Malcolm his sandwich then joined him on the couch. They immediately started making goo-goo faces at each other.

"Have you ever told Sharice how mean you were when we were little?"

"I wasn't mean."

"All he cared about was torturing me," I said. "He was a psycho."

"*Malcolm?*"

"Yeah, Malcolm. He threw a rat on me once."

"A *rat?*"

Malcolm waved his hand as though I was being ridiculous. "We were just fooling around. I was a kid."

"Yeah, and I was a helpless six-year-old girl."

Sharice stuck out her lower lip. "Oh, Babysister, you poor thing."

Actually, I was eight years old when everything went down. Malcolm and his friend Louie had found the rat hiding behind a Dumpster. The rat had a broken leg and couldn't get away. Malcolm held it by its tail so he could get a better look at it, then for no reason at all, squashed it under a board. I saw the entire thing because I was playing at the other end of the alley. As soon as he and Louie realized I was watching, they ran after me. I didn't get very far before I tripped and fell. Next thing I knew Malcolm was swinging the rat above my face and when I threatened to tell, he dropped the rat on me and ran off. I couldn't stop screaming. Seems like the more I tried to brush the rat away, the more I felt it on different parts of my body. My neck, my stomach. It was terrifying. I had nightmares for a solid week after that. Daddy swore every time I cried about lost sleep because of a nightmare, he'd give Malcolm a spanking. And because I made sure to whine about nightmares long after the nightmares had stopped, Malcolm got a spanking almost every day that month.

I told Sharice the entire story in complete detail. Malcolm would try to interrupt me, but Sharice would say, "Hush, Malcolm, let Babysister finish." I made sure she understood how cruel Malcolm had been, not only to me, of course, but to that poor, helpless, handicapped rat who might have had babies somewhere for all we knew, and who was a creature of the earth who should not have been tormented. I had that girl practically in tears by the time I finished.

"How could you be so evil, Malcolm? I thought you said you were a good child. I thought you said you and Babysister were close."

"That was just one incident. I was a *kid*."

"Do you still have nightmares, Babysister?" Sharice asked.

"Yeah," I lied.

"Oh, give me a break, Babysister. You don't get nightmares. Besides, I've apologized a thousand times for what I did."

His lie was bigger than mine, but I didn't say anything. Let Sharice deal with him, I thought.

Malcolm put a hesitant arm around Sharice. "You wanna take a bus home, baby?"

"Whatever," she said and then without making a single goo-goo face, stood and said she was ready to go home.

The African prince is in some serious trouble, I thought as I walked them to the door. Served him right, too. I could already hear the lectures he was going to get on animal abuse, child abuse, the importance of family in African culture. And I won't even go into the satisfaction I felt watching Malcolm reach for Sharice's hand only to have her roll her almond eyes and push it away in a huff.

Nine

No MATTER THE SITUATION, I've always tried to be as direct as possible when breaking up with a man. I don't go for playing games like not returning phone calls and hoping that he gets the hint. I dated a man named Eddie once who turned out to be a strong macho type. Truth be told, I'd much rather have a weak man who can carry a conversation than a macho man who says nothing.

Eddie and I met while I was having lunch at the park near Ramiro's. I was sitting on the park bench and watching him do his push-ups in these loose shorts that floated in the air every time he lowered himself to the ground with a grunt. I went over to him after I had finished my enchilada and asked if he could do a one-handed push-up. He laughed and did ten with his left hand and ten with his right. Turns out he taught PE at a private high school out in Pasadena.

Eddie was the type of man who was fun for about a month because he looks good, but then you begin to miss having an actual conversation. I mean, you couldn't expect more than a ten-word response to any given question. So how was your day today? Fine. So what did you do? Nothing much. What do you feel like doing tonight? Whatever.

Breaking up with men like Eddie is easy because you don't have to deal with lengthy discussions. You don't have to analyze the hows or whys, you simply tell them it's over. I dropped a postcard in the mail when I broke up with Eddie. On the front of the card, there was a black-and-white picture of an oak tree with an empty swing hanging from a branch. On the back I wrote: *It's time we go our separate ways. I wish you the best. Sincerely, Babysister.*

At the opposite end of men who hardly say a word about anything, you have the type of man who'll argue with you to the death if you dare try to break up with him. A postcard won't work with men like this. They need to see the cold detachment in your eyes as you tell them it's over. They need to see how you fold your arms and pinch the sides of your mouth as they beg you not to break up.

Marcel worked as a bartender in West Hollywood. Things started off well, but because he worked most nights we didn't see each other as much as I wanted. I got bored after about three months because we could only go out once or twice a week. When I was ready to break up with him, I suggested we meet at a restaurant. I figured by going to a restaurant, I could limit the conversation to the time we spent eating and then we'd conveniently go our separate ways. I told him that I wanted to see other people as I was cutting into a slice of roast beef. "We're not making it as a couple, Marcel, but if you want, we can still be friends."

"How can it be over when I still love you? We can work

this out, Babysister. It takes two people to make a relationship succeed or fail. You're not holding up your end. I can change my hours so we can have more time together. I know we can work this out." I let him go on and on. The great thing about breaking up with someone at a restaurant is that you can concentrate on your food while the other person argues with himself. After finishing my dinner I looked him in the eye and said, "Face it, Marcel, it's over. I'll get the check, though. It's the least I can do."

Breaking up with someone like Rob is different, because while it's rare when it happens, sometimes you honestly do want to remain friends. But usually there's no point in dragging things out. The way I see it, if you're ready to get on with your life you should let the other person get on with his.

All I'm trying to say is, I had always expected that if and when a person I was dating ever wanted to break up with me, he would be man enough to tell me directly. So when the trouble began with Darren, I didn't see any of the warning signs. Not a one. As far as I saw it, we were headed down the road to wedded bliss. We were moving at a slow pace, but the end result would be the same so what did I care?

Things started to change the day after I saw Malcolm and Sharice. Darren and I were supposed to have dinner together so I called him as soon as I got home from work.

"I feel bad about this, baby, but I'm still working on this damn project. I'm sorry. Will you forgive me?"

A part of me wanted to throw a fit: You promised me dinner! Fuck all your lame-ass apologies. Fuck these damn flowers. I want to see you! But what I said was, "Of course I forgive you."

"I'll make it up to you tomorrow, okay?"

"Promise?"

"Promise."

It had been three weeks since I last saw Rob, but I called him anyway.

"I miss you, Rob. It's been too long. Want to order some Chinese food and watch a video?"

He showed up with a movie and more Chinese food than we could possibly eat. He even brought a bunch of daisies for me. Poor thing was pretty hurt when he saw my irises. He began walking away dejected and sad, practically dragging the daisies on the floor.

I stopped him at my door. "You got it all wrong, sweetie. Those are from . . . Well, to be honest, I bought them for myself. I've been depressed. I thought if I bought myself some flowers, they'd cheer me up. Beautiful, huh?"

"You expect me to believe that?"

I gave him a hurt face. "It's true."

"I could buy you flowers, you know. I would buy you all the flowers you could want."

"Aww, that's sweet. But I like these flowers just as much." I took the daisies in one hand and his hand in the other. "It's good to see you."

"You should call me when you get depressed. You said you wanted to be friends. You should call. I'm your friend."

"You are," I said, giving him a hug. "I'm sorry I didn't call. Forgive me?"

We fell right into our old, comfortable routine. We didn't have sex, but Rob did put his arm around me while we watched *All About Eve*. I was grateful for the company. I couldn't stop thinking about Darren the entire time Rob was there, but at least I wasn't alone.

Darren and I saw each other the next night. He made dinner for me at my place. A pasta dish with capers and sun-dried tomatoes. He said he wanted to cook something nice as a way of "paying penance." He was full of Oh baby's and kisses for most of the night. Everything was right back to normal, in fact, except for one thing: he didn't take his underwear off while we made love. Not at all. He had on designer underwear, boxer shorts with colorful fish swimming through the ocean. The scene looked as if it had been hand-painted onto his shorts. But did I care how fancy his underwear was? To me, you simply do not make love to your woman in your underwear. I don't care how pretty they look or how much you paid for them. Every time I went to caress his body, I swear I wanted to grab hold of the elastic and snap it against his skin. I couldn't stop thinking about passionless married couples who only have sex every two months. The woman lying there with limp arms, daydreaming into the ceiling. The guy still dressed in his T-shirt, giving her a kiss on the cheek for foreplay, his right hand sliding her gown up no further than the knee, his erection pushing through his boxer shorts. A peck on the cheek afterward and they fall asleep.

I didn't say anything at first because I didn't want to start an argument, but afterward I pointed to an orange fish and sort of laughed. "What's up with not taking your underwear off?"

"I wanted you so bad I couldn't wait."

Yeah, right, I thought. I didn't believe that line for a minute.

He didn't call the following night. I tried to keep myself busy so that I wouldn't call him first. I read for a while, then watched TV. When I still hadn't heard from him, I finally broke down and phoned.

"Hey, sweetie, how have you been?"

"Fine. I'm sorry I haven't called. I was going to, but I thought it might be too late."

I pressed the phone to my ear because I loved hearing his voice. "It's never too late for you to call, you know that."

There was a brief silence and then he said, "Listen, baby, I've been getting behind at work. I need to put some energy back into my job. How would you feel about cooling it for a couple weeks? Just a couple. I really have to get on top of things."

"Yeah, sure," I lied. "That would be fine. I could use the time to take care of a few things myself."

He told me he'd miss my beautiful body and we'd only be apart for a couple of weeks. "I occupy so much of your time. Think of all the things you'll get done."

It was only ten o'clock after we hung up, but I felt so miserable about not being able to see him for two weeks I went straight to bed.

The days without Darren reminded me of the record player I owned when I was a kid. My days were so slow they felt like the times I'd turn the knob from 45 to LP, slowing the singer's voice until it sounded as warped as a drugged demon's.

Most days I told myself that he needed to work and that it was good that he cared about his job. Other days I came close to driving to his office and begging him to at least have dinner with me. I tried to send him mental messages to call. When I wasn't at the bank I ate way too much food and watched way too much TV, that's it. I didn't contact Rob or anyone else. I didn't want to see anyone but Darren. I felt like the dog the woman across the street owned. She kept it tied up in the backyard so he had nothing to do but wait around for someone out front to walk by so as to have an excuse to bark, tug at his chain. He spent his days waiting until dark because that's when the woman finally came out to feed him and give him water, and if he was lucky, a pat on the head.

On the seventh day of our separation, I heard a knock at my door. Naturally I assumed it was Darren. I had a huge sundae in my lap, uncombed hair, and was watching a sitcom I knew he'd call brainless so my immediate reaction was to head for the window because I was about to get busted. Thing is, when I got up the nerve to ask who it was, I heard Deborah's voice. She literally waltzed into my apartment and grabbed my hand, forcing me to dance with her.

"You'll never guess what happened! Not in a million years. Not in a million, trillion years." She spun around on one foot, her hair trailing behind after her.

"I *know* you won't be able to guess." She sat down on the couch and took off her shoes. Her toes ran in place as if there were cockroaches under her feet. "I've been with Darren, girl! We kissed!"

I stumbled backward because the floor suddenly seemed to be made of ice.

"Don't just stand there with your mouth open. Say something!"

I had to balance myself against my chair. "You lie."

"I know I should have told you that we've been talking. I was going to, honest. I'm sorry. It's just that I know how you feel about Darren. I know you don't like him much because of the way he treated me. But you can be happy for me. I know he regrets how he acted. He won't stop apologizing."

"How long have you been talking?"

"About a week I guess. I didn't want you coming down on him. Anyway, he's been begging me to see him, so tonight I finally said okay. We had dinner together. He was acting so shy, Babysister. Telling me how much he missed me and wants to try again. I know he's sincere, too. I *know* he is. He told me the two months we had together were the happiest he's ever been."

"So he wants you back?"

"You look as surprised as I feel. I know it's crazy. But it's not crazy at the same time. I never stopped caring about him, and he admitted that he never stopped caring about me. It felt so good to be with him again. It felt right, you know?"

She noticed my melting sundae and asked if I had any more ice cream. They had eaten sushi and she was still hungry.

I told her to help herself then buried my face in my hands. Don't blow it Babysister, I told myself. She doesn't know anything. *Stay calm.*

"Are you okay?"

"Yeah, I ate too much is all." I looked up. "I have to wonder about this, Deborah. If he was so happy while you guys were together, why'd he stop seeing you? He wouldn't even return your calls."

"Well, the first time he called—"

"When was that?"

"What?"

"The first time he called."

"Last Friday."

The night he said he needed to cool things down because he needed to concentrate on his job.

"The first time he called I was cold. I mean, you're right. He had dogged me. And this was after we had grown so close. But that's the thing. He says he got afraid. He had never felt so close to another woman. It scared him. He says these past three months without me have helped him realize he never wants to be without me. That's how powerful his feelings for me are. Stop looking at me like that, Babysister, I know he's sincere. He started *crying* tonight he felt so bad. *Tears*, Babysister. I know he's sorry. I know we should be together."

She got up to make her sundae. I watched her closely as she walked around my kitchen. Scooping ice cream, melting the fudge, the strap from her dress falling every once in a while, her finger disappearing into her mouth then reappearing with a smack. "Mmmm, good fudge." I told myself, if I could simply concentrate on watching Deborah in my kitchen I wouldn't have to think about what was happening; otherwise, I was really going to lose it.

"He says he'd do anything to try again. He says he can't deny his true feelings for me anymore because they're too strong."

"Did he say anything about what he's been doing these past months?"

She ate a mouthful of her sundae, shoved in a big spoonful. "Naw, and to be honest, I don't really care. I'm no fool. I realize he was probably dating someone, fine as he is, but to tell you the truth I think that was probably good too. He's ready for the kind of commitment *I* want now. If only you could have seen him tonight . . ." She hugged herself and fell back into the couch. "I know he's through with all the others. I know we're going to work this out. Well, aren't you going to say something?"

I listened to music from the downstairs apartment seep up through my floor. I heard a steady beat and the singer crying out in Spanish. I told myself that after she left, I'd go to Darren's place and find out what was *really* going on then walked over to her and gave her a hug. I had the urge to yank out her silver earring when I felt it against my cheek. "Congratulations, Deborah," I said. "I'm so happy for you. . . ."

Ten

I MET MY first serious boyfriend, Henry Watkins, when I was fifteen years old. He had moved from Texas to California after his father got a job at LAX loading bags onto planes. You couldn't miss Henry when walking around our school. He was very dark-skinned and at sixteen was over six feet five inches tall. When I saw him in the halls, towering over a crowd of students, I often thought of the poster my history teacher had in her room of a tribe of African nomads dressed in deep red robes and walking with their cattle through the desert. Henry was set to play pro basketball. I had heard that he eventually played basketball in Europe somewhere. He also played college ball. I knew because years later I saw him on TV. I had dropped out of community college for the second or third time and was still living at home. It was a typical afternoon, Daddy and Malcolm were watching some game in the living room. The next thing I knew, they started yelling over the TV, "Babysister, get in here! Your old boyfriend is playing!" And there was Henry, still tall, still dark, only now it was five years later and he possessed a newfound sense of confidence and ease. He made everyone else on the court look stiff and unsure of themselves. Sweat poured off his face and down his arms and legs so that every muscle glistened. He looked delicious. I stood there eyeing the television until Malcolm said, "Damn, you sure blew that one." I didn't bother responding because at that moment I felt like Malcolm was absolutely right, I *had* blown it. I mean, if things had been different, instead of living at home I could have been married to Henry, waving at him from the stands, smiling into the camera each time it came in for a closeup of his adoring wife.

Henry sat behind me in Mrs. Cooper's English class. He had let it be known after one week into the semester that he was in love with me and wanted to take me back to Texas to raise pigs. I would look at him like he was crazy when he'd tell me these things. "There's no way in hell I'm raising anybody's pigs," I'd say while popping my gum. But he kept trying. When school clubs sold candygrams, he'd send two or three to all my classes: *Would you be mine? Signed a Secret Admirer. I like you, do you like me? Love, Henry.* It wasn't long before my rolling eyes turned into giggles, and one day I finally said yes to his umpteenth date proposal.

We went to a movie and afterward drove around in his father's 1977 lime-green Lincoln Continental. I found myself talking a lot more than I would have because unlike all the other boys I had gone out with who only seemed interested in making out, Henry didn't try to make a single pass and actually seemed to enjoy nothing more than talking. Before walking me to the door, he told me in his soft country voice that he had the best intentions and only wanted to make me happy. He would be honored if I would be his lady.

A week later while we were in his bedroom, I convinced

him to have sex with me. I had lost my virginity that summer with a boy named Keante. Keante was junior class president and very popular. We had dated for four months before I agreed to have sex with him. The sex was not nearly as eventful as I had hoped it would be, and after a few more tries I broke up with him. But after that summer, I couldn't stop thinking about what it would be like to sleep with someone who had more experience or who I had stronger feelings for. Seems like I walked around school with the tip of my finger in my mouth, checking out boys with a cool stare as though I were in a supermarket and had the choice of any item I wanted. Henry made me swear that I didn't mind he was still a virgin, and after promising I wouldn't laugh—no matter what—I slowly undid the top button of his beige corduroy pants, then pulled off his shirt. Two minutes later he was holding me next to him on his twin bed. When he asked me whether or not I thought he had truly lost his virginity—he had barely made it in before he came—I kissed him on the cheek and told him yes.

Maybe it was because he was from Texas, but Henry did treat me like I was special. During a basketball game, he'd point to me after every slam dunk, kiss me goodbye after walking me to each of my classes. And Henry and I could actually talk to each other too. We talked about everything, in fact. Our families, our dreams. Our favorite date was to go to the roof of King's Supermarket where he worked and simply hang out. We'd go through the storeroom, which had a stairway that led to the roof, and lie on the blanket I'd bring. I remember how our shoes would scrape against gravel and rocks whenever we started to kiss and how we'd search for the few stars and satellites bright enough to break through the smog.

Often Henry would tell me about the country, what it was like to live there. I'd listen quietly as his voice rose over the sounds of distant sirens or blaring horns. He told me once about how he had helped a cow give birth. "I actually had to put my hand right up in her," he said. "I had to turn the darn calf, 'cause its head wasn't where it was supposed to be. Daddy was standin' right there so I wasn't scared for her or nothin'. Turned out to be one beautiful calf." He gave me detailed instructions on how to milk a cow, his hands motioning in the air as if the cow was standing in front of him. He also explained how to barbecue a pig by burying its body under the ground, how to make rock candy and molasses. I wouldn't say much because I loved listening to him talk. I'd put my head on his chest and he'd say, "Babysister, it's so quiet there in the mornings, in the night, too, just crickets and things, but never any sirens or planes or cars. You feel like you're the only one around. You ever had that feeling? It's a nice feeling. You can't get that here, but see, you stay with me, and I'll take you somewhere where it's you and nature and quiet." I'd press my head in closer, hold on to his polyester shirt with *King's* sewed over the top pocket. "You don't even have stars here. After we're married, though, I'll take you someplace where you can see some stars." While Henry went on and on about life in the country, I'd find myself daydreaming about living there. I imagined myself standing on a large porch ringing a triangular bell, eating huge amounts of barbecue pig for dinner, saying country things like Aw shucks or Hot dang! I mean, let's face it, I was a city girl through and through, but I was also fifteen years old, an age when you can romanticize almost any situation.

I broke up with Henry when my closet girlfriends (all

four of them, except Deborah, who liked Henry and wanted us to stay together) kept telling me that I could do better. They wouldn't stop teasing me. "He's so *skinny*, Babysister. What's it like to be with such a *skinny* boy? I'd never date no boy skinnier than my own damn thigh."

"Why can't he learn to talk right? Shit, girl, this ain't *Green Acres,* this is the fucking city."

"He's so *black*, Babysister. He's too dark. Look like one of them blue-black niggahs from Africa or somethin'."

"What's it like being with a man so dark? Can you see him at night? Do you gotta tell him to smile so you know where his face is at?"

They talked about him so much I soon convinced myself that he *was* too skinny, too dark, too country. I convinced myself that everything I liked about Henry Watkins was exactly what was wrong with him.

I told Henry to come pick me up because I needed to talk to him. I didn't feel like going to the rooftop so we drove around the neighborhood in his father's lime-green Continental until we ended up in front of my old elementary school. He was telling me about the different ways to kill a chicken. "There's nothing in the world like fresh chicken. It tastes way better than the kind you buy in the store. You get that bird and slice at the neck real quick or you can shove a toothpick through the roof of his mouth right on up through the brain, stun him real good and then kill him."

The car was thick with the smell of his aftershave and all the hair grease on both of our heads. I blurted it out before I lost my nerve. "I want to break up, Henry." He went on about chickens for half a sentence then said, "What did you say?" He almost sounded angry, so I said it again, quietly. "I want to break up."

"Why? What's wrong?" He gripped the steering wheel so that his knuckles stuck out. "You don't love me anymore?"

"I never said I did." I was afraid to look him in the eye so I gazed at my old school, which looked spooky in the dark. I heard my girlfriends' voices: He's so country, Babysister. Do you have to tell him to smile so you can see him?

Tears were shining in his eyes and he tried to blink them away. He probably told himself, Don't cry in front of her, man. Don't do it. He wiped the tears away as though, if he could only wipe fast enough, maybe I wouldn't see. But I sat there staring at him. I had never seen a boy his age cry before. His shoulders hunched up and down. He used his right hand to cover his face, the same hand that could hold and maneuver a large basketball as easy as a tennis ball. He sniffled and snorted. There was no Kleenex so he used his jacket sleeve. "I hate it here," he said.

I felt ashamed that I had made him sad enough to cry, sad enough to regret moving to L.A. and meeting me, but I was too full of myself to say I take it back, I made a mistake, of course I want to be your girlfriend. Instead I acted cold, pretended I didn't care. I had already told him I wanted to break up, may as well follow through. I put on all my fifteen-year-old attitude and rolled my eyes as if seeing a boy crying was too disgusting to handle. "You need to grow the fuck up," I said. "Take me home. And you bet' not come begging to me to take your sorry ass back 'cause I won't."

I would find myself thinking about Henry Watkins after I drove to Darren's place. I mean, when Darren bowed his head and said, "This isn't working for me, Babysister. I never stopped thinking about her," my memory of Henry was so strong, I might as well have been sitting in the

Continental staring at his dark profile. Except this time I would have better understood how he must have felt, better understood how cruel I had been.

I went to Darren's condo right after Deborah left and tried to peep through his window without making myself obvious. The last thing I needed was someone calling the cops about the crazy black woman snooping around people's houses at eleven at night. I could see him through the slants of his blinds playing with the dials on his stereo. He disappeared into the kitchen then came back with a bag of chips and a beer. My view was so good I could see his jaws pressing as he ate. My plan had been to confront him, put him in his place for even saying two words to Deborah, let alone having dinner with her, but now that I was standing at his door, I didn't know if confronting him was what I should do. He probably had a perfectly logical explanation as to why he had seen Deborah. And who knows, Deborah probably had exaggerated about everything. Maybe he hadn't actually *kissed* her, maybe it was more like a peck on the cheek. He probably feels guilty as hell, I thought. I'll definitely make him suffer a little before I forgive him, but in the end I need to show him that he can rely on me when things get stressful. I took out my compact and used the light coming from the window to check my makeup. I put on a bit more lipstick, counted to three, knocked.

He opened the door and stared at me without the least bit of surprise. It took me a second, but in that instant, I realized that I knew the look on his face all too well, not a hint of guilt to be found, only a touch of fatigue.

I had it all wrong, I thought. He doesn't feel bad at all for having seen Deborah. He's bothered by the fact that he has to deal with the inconvenience of breaking up with me.

I won't lie, the look in his eyes made me feel completely worthless, but I somehow managed to act as if I had no idea what was going on. "You don't seem too surprised to see me," I said.

"I knew Deborah would be talking to you sooner or later. He gestured toward the living room. "Do you want to come in?"

I walked past him and sat down on the edge of the couch. You might as well get on with it, I thought.

He sat opposite from me on his big leather chair. The same chair we had made love in once after sharing a bowl of strawberries. "I know it was wrong for me not to tell you we had been talking. I apologize for not saying anything. I don't mean to hurt you, Babysister, but this isn't working for me. I never stopped thinking about her."

"Excuse me?"

He hit the table once with his finger. "It's like this. I do have feelings for you, you know that. We've had a nice time together. Very nice time. But I need something more. And you deserve something more yourself. You deserve a man who can give you more than I can. As much as I thought I was over her, I've never stopped loving her. You must have known there was a chance we might get back together."

He spoke to me as though we were in a business meeting. If you didn't know what was going on, you would have thought I was a client hearing plans for a new building.

"That first night we were together, you knew I still had feelings for her. And to be honest, I've always had doubts about us. I know you must have had your own doubts as well. Our interests are so different. Our backgrounds." He opened his hands as if he were carrying a box then closed them again. "Regardless, I think what scared me away from Deborah was fear of commitment and you offered a sense of fun, and I ended up rushing into something I shouldn't have. I mean, we had a bad start anyway. You guys were *friends*. We never should have been together in the first place. You must have known this was coming." He cleared his throat. "And I want you to know, Babysister, this wasn't an easy decision. I was afraid of even calling her. She must think I'm a fool dropping her the way I did."

He waited for me to say something, to agree with him or yell at him but I couldn't speak. I knew that as soon as I opened my mouth—even if it was to call him a bastard or lie and say that I didn't care that we were breaking up—I would surely start crying.

"Are you okay?"

I felt a tightening in the back of my throat and stared at my hands. Please don't cry, I thought. I crossed my legs and began bouncing my foot, but as soon as he came to sit next to me on the couch and took my hand—"Hey, you know I'll always care about you, right?"—I felt the tears begin to pour down my face fast and even. Darren tried to hand me a tissue, but I shrugged him away. I stood up without looking at him and walked toward the door as best as I could. Snappy comebacks came to mind, but I simply let them pass. I had been on Darren's end so many times, I knew that pleading or arguing does no good. When a person is set on breaking up with you, you have to let them go on and do it.

I took a week off from work. On Monday morning I called Mrs. Hodges and told her that my grandfather had died and I needed the time to be with my family and help my father with the funeral arrangements. She gave me one of her drawn-out sighs, but kept her lecture brief because while I might talk too much at work, I rarely miss a day. I went back to eating and watching television.

Tuesday morning I woke to find an envelope under my apartment door. It was a card from Deborah with a letter folded up inside. The card had a picture of two little black girls dressed in white dresses and white hats, holding hands in a field of daisies. I almost didn't open it. My life was depressing enough as it was without having to hear from Miss Perfect.

> Dear Friend,
>   I guess I haven't heard from you because you think I hate you, but you're wrong. I have always felt that you have been more to me than my friend —my best friend—I have always thought of you as a sister. We have known each other since pre-school. PRE-SCHOOL! Grew up near each other. Always told each other everything. Anyway I know about you and Darren. He told me everything. You might think I'm crazy, but I still want to remain friends. Don't get me wrong, I'm angry with you and have every right to be, but I also feel we've never let anyone come between us. We shouldn't let a man come between us now. I don't think it's completely your fault. I think your mother's death has a lot to do with some of the choices you make. But Babysister, you need help. From the time we were kids to now, you've always looked to men to make you happy, material things to make you happy. But I'm here to tell you, Babysister, only YOU can make you happy. You need some serious spiritual help. Therapy as well. If you get the help

*you need, you won't need men or money to make
you feel good, and you certainly won't have to go
stealing your best friend's man in order to find
some delusional sense of happiness.*

*Please don't take this the wrong way, but I feel I
have to ask. I've been going over why all this might
have happened and wondered if you had slept with
Darren out of jealousy. I know how Satan works.
He can use jealousy as a tool and the next thing
you know, people will kill because of their jealous
emotions. What exactly made you so jealous that
you simply couldn't be happy for me when I told
you about Darren and had to go and sleep with
him? What made you do it, Babysister? I still can't
believe you did it.* Why would you want to hurt
me like this??!!

*I don't want to judge you. This letter isn't about
me judging you. I'm judging the sin. As I've said, I
don't think it's entirely your fault. I think we were
put on this Earth to forgive each other as He
forgave us. That's why I forgive you. That's why I
forgive Darren. I'm angry, but I forgive you and I'm
willing to talk.*

WE CAN WORK THIS OUT!!!

Love always,
Deborah

P.S. *For God so loved the world, he gave his only
begotten son that whosoever believeth in him should
not perish, but have everlasting life.*

John 3:16

I started laughing after I got over the initial shock of that letter—I did! All her references to devils and sin made me shake my head. She and Darren were so different. Darren never talked about God or religion and that was all Deborah knew. They would never work out. Period. And while I couldn't understand why Darren couldn't get Deborah out of his system once and for all, I believed that once he did, he'd come back to me.

Deborah called on Thursday. I let her leave a message on my machine like everyone else who had phoned during the week.

"Are you there? Hello?" She waited. "So I was wondering if you got my letter." She waited again, but there was no way I was going to pick up the phone. "Anyway, you don't have to avoid going to work, Babysister. I mean, all your grandparents died years ago. Nothing is going to happen to you. I mean, I haven't told anyone." There was a very long silence then I heard her start to sniffle. "I don't understand why you did it, Babysister. You hurt me so much. You both did. I—" The answering machine beeped then began clicking itself off.

She called again five minutes later. "I'm not the bad guy here. You should be apologizing to *me*. Aren't you ashamed? Wait. That's not what I wanted to say. I just want to stress the fact that we can get through this. Maybe we can talk after you come back to work. I'm willing to talk if you want. Okay. Bye."

I stood over my answering machine wondering why on earth she could possibly think I'd want to be friends with her. What would we have to talk about? So how was your date with Darren? Did you two kids have a good time? And even if by some miracle we managed to make up, I'd have easily given up my friendship with her all over again if it meant I could have Darren back.

I called Rob.

"Can you come over?"

"Yeah, sure. Are you okay?"

"Not really."

"Give me twenty minutes."

He met me at the door with a single rose and hopeful smile. As soon as I saw him, I knew I shouldn't have called. I didn't want to see him. I didn't want to see anyone but Darren. But it was too late so I smiled and thanked him for the rose and told him to come inside.

"What happened?"

I tried to brush my hair down with my hands, but knew it was hopeless. "You want to get drunk with me?"

"What's wrong?"

"You want to get drunk with me or not?"

"Sure. I guess."

"Rum and Cokes?"

"That's fine."

It took me forever to find my wallet, but once I did, I handed him all the bills. "Would you mind going down to the liquor store, I don't have any rum."

He pushed my hand away. "You must think I'm a fool. You offer me drinks then tell me to go to the store and buy them?"

I moved in so that our chests touched. He seemed shorter than ever and I wondered again what I had ever seen in him. I tickled his nose with my nose like I had seen Sharice tickle Malcolm. "I don't think you're a fool, Rob. I think you're my very good friend. I'm going through a hard time right now."

"What happened?"

"Nothing really. Problems at work. I got chewed out because I messed up a transaction. You wouldn't understand. So anyway, I took a couple of days off." I rested my head against his chest.

"I bet you could use a drink then, huh?"

"Yeah, I could."

"Okay, I'll be right back."

"And would you get me a pack of cigarettes and some chips, please?"

"No problem," he said.

We drank and watched TV. Rob gave me a massage after I had had too much alcohol to refuse. I wasn't so drunk, though, that he could convince me to take off all my clothes. I let him take my T-shirt off but kept my bra and sweats on.

It wasn't long before he was kissing me on the back. "I know something else that might help you to feel better," he said.

Oh, please, I thought. There I was with my uncombed hair, nasty-smelling breath, red eyes, dirty sweats, dog tired and hardly able to move and he *still* had the nerve to want sex. Men are amazing.

I mumbled something about alcohol and regrets. Then I guess I fell asleep because the next morning when I woke, I was neatly tucked in the bed.

I found a note on my nightstand:

> *Babysister—*
>   *I don't know exactly what it is you're going through right now, but you know I got your back. Call me tonight.*
>
>   *Love, Rob*

Eleven

THE FOLLOWING MONDAY I went to work and acted like nothing had happened at all. The only difference on that particular Monday from all the other Mondays was that I didn't talk to Deborah. She rose from her seat clearly ready to speak as I walked past her desk, but quickly closed her mouth and sat back down once she realized I wasn't planning on stopping.

By the end of the week, the other tellers could tell we'd had a fight. "Did you see that? She walked right past her." "They must be fighting." "I hope neither of them is packing a gun." Everyone, except for Silent Marsha and Mrs. Hodges, kept a close eye on us. They watched as we said hello and goodbye to everyone but each other; watched us pass each other with tight lips as if we had something sour in our mouths; watched us go off on our breaks without offering to get the other a cup of coffee; watched as we ate lunch with other people or by ourselves. Danisha told me that Byron had the nerve to start a pool on whether or not we were fighting over a man. Just because he and Deborah were both loan officers he thought he understood her better than the others. "I told him he was crazy," Danisha said. "You and Deborah don't even have the same taste in men." We both started laughing. Everyone was dying to know what was going on. "How are you and Deborah doing, Babysister?" "Is Deborah okay, Babysister?" "Deborah sure has some nerve ignoring you, Babysister. You didn't do anything, did you?" I gave them all the same answer in the same no-nonsense voice: We're no longer on speaking terms. That's all there is to say.

The last time Deborah and I had gone without talking we were in ninth grade. It didn't last long because Deborah hated the silent treatment. Even if she was right about whatever the argument was, give her the silent treatment and she'd break down sooner or later. I don't remember what in the world I was upset about that last time. I think it had something to do with her not wanting to go to a party with me. Anyway, when she refused I didn't say a word to her for five days straight. As is the custom when you're a fourteen-year-old teenage girl, we divided our friends, set about rolling our eyes at each other, and pretended we were happy. But Deborah couldn't take it. One day she met me after my last-period class, crying away, begging me to talk to her again. "Okay, I give up. It would be better for you to cuss me out than ignore me like this!"

At any rate, I wasn't too surprised when the next Monday I found her standing in front of my car as I was about to leave for work.

She rushed up and said, "*You* should be apologizing to *me*. Don't you realize all the pain you've caused?"

I began fumbling around my purse even though I knew my car keys were in the front pocket. "I didn't think you'd find out," I said.

"Is that all you care about? That I would find out?"

"Yeah, it is. I knew you'd get hurt if you found out. It's not like I set out to hurt you." I went back to pretending to look for my keys. "I didn't mean to hurt you, Deborah."

"You don't get it do you?" She held my wrist so that I'd have to look at her. "What's happened to you, Babysister? What's going on?"

I was barely keeping it together is what was happening. I was actually grateful for the eight hours at the bank because otherwise all I did was sit at home eating and watching old movies.

I pulled my hand away. "Nothing has happened to me."

"*Nothing?* We were like sisters. How could you go and do what you did, then say it was nothing? You realize that if you can't admit your fault in all of this our friendship is over, don't you?"

I went directly for my keys this time. "I think it would be best if we didn't talk about it. What happened happened. It's over now."

"Babysister?"

She said my name as if she wasn't quite sure it was me, as if there was no way I could possibly be so cold. A wave of guilt rushed over me and I felt my lips begin to quiver. It wasn't as though I was proud of myself for going behind her back. I hadn't purposely set out to hurt her. I had set out to get Darren. Still, what was the point of trying to explain. What was the point of trying to hold on to a friendship that, in my opinion, had been dissolving anyway? I hastily made my way around her and got in my car. "Leave me alone, Deborah. I really don't care that our friendship is over."

"I don't believe you."

"Fine," I said before starting my car and driving off. "Don't believe me."

I had stopped to buy a cup of coffee on my way to work so Deborah had arrived at the bank a good ten minutes before me. She was bent over her desk with her head in her hands while Danisha gently patted her back. When Danisha glared at me like I had killed someone's mother, I knew right then that Deborah had told her everything. Danisha had the biggest mouth of us all so by telling her, Deborah might as well have told everyone we worked with one by one.

Danisha came over to my station with the money for my drawer but wouldn't hand it over. She wore a bright purple dress with bright purple stockings. She even had on bright purple lipstick that made her lips look bruised. I wondered if her herpes were acting up. "Deborah is too nice to say anything to you," she said. "But I'll say it. I'll say it to your face. You're a two-faced liar. I hope you get what you deserve for what you did." Her voice was quiet, but Vicky and Carol were already looking over from their stations.

"Mind your own business, Danisha. Who are you to tell me what to do? You're not involved in this situation so keep the hell out of it."

She put her hand on her hip and started to say something but Mrs. Hodges walked over. "And how are you two ladies this morning? Ready for a full day of work?"

We nodded yes without taking our eyes off each other.

"Good, good. Glad to hear it."

By lunchtime everyone knew what had happened. I heard Darren's name floating around, as well as the word *irises*. Byron won two hundred dollars from his Babysister vs. Deborah pool. No one spoke to me the next day. I was completely shut out. As days passed I felt their stares, but no one said a word.

And what was worse, Deborah told Lisette, who showed up at my apartment Wednesday night, wearing loose jeans, green sandals, and a polka-dotted shirt that I knew she had found in a thrift store because I was there when she bought it. Except for the fact that she was tapping her foot, she seemed pretty calm. But once inside my apartment, she let loose all of her Afro–Puerto Rican biracial, womanist self, so fast, so furious, I could hardly get a word in.

"How could you, Babysister, huh? Tell me that one thing. How could you do that to Deborah? How could you as a woman do that to another woman? How could you as a *woman*, okay?"

She walked around my apartment, hands on hips, voice close to shouting. "I don't understand it. I thought I knew you. I thought I *knew* you. I thought we were friends. You call yourself a proud black woman? You call yourself a *woman*? Women shouldn't do things like what you did."

"I—"

"Real women don't go around stealing their best friend's boyfriends. Let me tell you, a real woman doesn't need a man twenty-four and fucking seven to make her happy. I can't believe you were so desperate for a fucking man, to do this." She hit her fists on the top of her head. "I am so angry with you, Babysister. Deborah was crying her eyes out when I saw her last night. Let me tell you something else. You need to apologize, okay? A-pol-o-gize. You want me to spell it? A-p-o-l-o-g-i-z-e. You must have no love or self-respect for yourself." Then she started going off in Spanish. *Respectar*, Babysister. Do you know what that means? It means RESPECT. *Amistad*, Babysister. That means *friendship*, Babysister." And then she paused suddenly and said, "Can I have some water?"

"Can I say something in my defense?"

"What could you possibly say, huh? Tell me that one thing, please. How can you defend yourself? On what grounds? Was he Deborah's boyfriend? Did you sleep with him? Did you tell Deborah what you did? I don't want to hear nothing, Babysister. Nothing. *Nada*." She went into the kitchen and poured herself a glass of water. "The only reason I'm here is because Deborah is crazy too. Not nearly as crazy as you. Not a teeny bit as crazy, but for her to forgive that dog is some serious fucked-up shit. I try to tell her. He slept with your *best friend*. Let him go! But she won't listen to me either. No one wants to listen to me. All of you can live without a man. You can LIVE WITHOUT A MAN, okay?" She held up her glass of water but set it down. "I'm the only one with brains." She tapped her forehead. "I'm the only one with the fucking *huevos* to tell the truth around here. All of you are messed up. And you know something? I feel very very hurt by all of this. I feel hurt by everybody, especially you." She downed her water. "Especially you."

"I didn't think they'd work out."

She slammed the glass down. "Of course they're not going to work out. He's a dog, okay? But whether they work out or not is not for you to decide. Who can I talk to now and tell that I'm pissed? Gotta go to my group and light a candle about all this crazy mess." She gave me the same incredulous look Deborah had when we were standing out in the driveway. "And all that time you were telling Deborah to be strong."

I won't deny I felt small about this. "I didn't mean to hurt her, Lisette. I swear."

She put the glass in my sink. "Bullshit, Babysister."

And then she was gone, walked out of my apartment without saying another word.

I told myself that I didn't care. But in all honesty, I didn't know how I was going to last if everyone continued to shut me out. I hadn't meant to lose my friends.

I called in sick on Thursday and Friday. On Thursday, I drove to a cafe somewhere out in West Hollywood and tried to write Darren a letter. I wanted to tell him that I'd wait until he figured things out. That I loved him. That Deborah was all wrong for him. I got as far as a page, but the letter made me sound too whiny, so I tossed it in the trash. I eventually decided that Darren needed to realize he'd made a mistake on his own. I wanted him to come back to me without a single message or phone call. I wanted him to convince himself so that there would be no more doubts.

I drove to my father's house Friday evening. I whispered a thank-you to God when Malcolm wasn't there. I needed to be around someone who wouldn't judge me, who understood me, and who better but my father. Daddy sat in front of the TV, eating his dinner: a huge plate of smothered chicken, black-eyed peas, mashed potatoes, and a roll. One thing about my father: He knows how to cook and he knows how to eat.

"Hey, baby. Grab a plate. I was just sitting in here thinking about you. I made all this food and thought you might enjoy it. I was going to call you and tell you you better get over before your brother shows up and eats it all. Not that he'd eat the chicken. You know how he doesn't eat meat anymore."

I kissed his cheek, went into the kitchen, and returned with a full plate.

"How's that car of yours running?"

"Fine," I said.

"That's good. How's work? You still like messing with other people's money?" He chuckled.

"Work's not going all that well, Daddy. I'm thinking about changing jobs. I need something that I can grow in."

He turned from the show he was watching. "Like what?"

"I don't know. Something different."

"You have to be careful about giving up a steady paycheck, baby girl. Before you move on, if you move on, make sure you find something you're gonna stick with. Nothing wrong with new goals, though. Long as you got some goals, know what I'm sayin'?"

I looked at the pictures he had of Momma on the wall. He had put her high school graduation picture in between my picture and Malcolm's. What made my mother's picture stand out from millions of other high school graduation pictures is her serious expression. Her lips are parted but there's not a smile to be found. Thing is, my mother had the most beautiful smile. A mouth full of wide, white teeth and dark brown gums. I like to think that my mother hadn't smiled for her picture because while the guy was telling her to "Say cheese!" she was envisioning herself as a famous designer. High school was the last thing on her mind. She had been named most likely to succeed. She had made prom dresses for herself as well as two of her girlfriends. I don't have too many memories of her, but I do remember the feeling of sitting on her lap and playing paddy cake. I remember how she'd hold my hands by the wrists and make them clap together and move in a circle. I remember how she'd let me fall backward on her lap then pull me up close to her face. I remember looking into her big smile and watching her mouth the words paddy cake paddy cake.

I got a long lecture from Mrs. Hodges when I returned to work on Monday. She sat at her desk, perfectly still, holding a pencil over her memo pad and smiling at me as if I had been naughty. Her office was pretty standard except for the huge oil painting she kept on the wall behind her desk. The painting was a family portrait of Mrs. Hodges, her husband, Spencer, and their two dogs, Biscuit and Muffin. The painting looked like something you'd find above a fireplace, even had a gaudy gold frame. Mrs. Hodges's husband was a light-skinned man, cream-colored with a dark red Afro and tiny red freckles under his eyes. Mrs. Hodges colored her hair so that it matched her husband's even though she was a few shades darker and the color looked anything but natural. The funny thing about the portrait was that the two dogs they owned also had the same reddish-brown color. They were the kind of dogs whose fur stood straight out as though their paws had been put into a light socket.

While Mrs. Hodges lectured me on work ethics and team spirit, I kept my eye on the pin she had pierced through her brown tweed suit. Mrs. Hodges always wore a suit with some kind of pin: butterflies, cats, cars, you never knew what to expect. Today, the pin was a huge gold dragonfly that looked like it might attack her face any second.

"You've been with us for a long time now. You're an asset to our team . . ."

Why do managers say things like "asset to our team"?

". . . but I can't have you missing so much work. I've noticed there has been tension around here lately, but I've also noticed it has had no effect on your performance or general attitude toward our customers. However, as I've said, you cannot continue missing work. Ultimately, *you* make the decision to keep your job by not falling into habits which can only lead to termination."

I told her almost every line of bullshit that I could come up with. My grandfather's death had been hard on me. My job was extremely important. I enjoyed working with people and coming to work made me feel good about myself. I ended all the bullshit by commenting on her beautiful dragonfly pin. She gave me the exact same smile as in her portrait. Suddenly it was as if there were *two* Mrs. Hodges in the room—which let me tell you wasn't the most pleasant feeling in the world.

Mrs. Hodges was right about one thing, though: I needed to decide if I was going to stay at the bank or not. In the end, I wanted to prove that I was stronger than all of the stares and whispers, even stronger than Deborah's gleeful face as she walked in every morning—Hi everybody! It was more important to fight it out than to let them believe they were right about me in any way or to let them think they could get to me. I told myself that I didn't need them or their approval. I'd go to work, do my job, and if I needed to have a conversation, I'd talk to a customer.

Enough time passed so that I got so good at ignoring all the stares and whispers, a few people began to act a bit more cordial. Byron met me for lunch a couple of times. Tonya soon began to ask how my day was going. Danisha refused to say anything, but it wasn't like she was my favorite person in the world anyway. From time to time, Deborah would look over at me from her desk, but she'd quickly look away as soon as I caught her staring.

To keep myself busy and to lose the weight I had put on from sitting around so much, I joined a gym. I started reading more, too. I didn't have anyone to really talk to at work so I took a book with me, ended up reading during all my breaks and even after I got home. I bought titles I had seen on Darren's bookshelf. *Their Eyes Were Watching God, The House of the Spirits.* My goal was to have read all his favorites by the time we were together again.

One Friday night—four months, two weeks, and four days after Darren had broken up with me—I found a large manila envelope under my door. PLEASE READ! was underlined three times. I recognized Deborah's handwriting.

Inside the manila envelope was a letter and a small off-white envelope.

> *Dear Babysister,*
>   *I'm not going to beg you to talk to me. Everyone says you deserve to be ignored, so I guess if that's what you want—fine. Do whatever you need to do. I personally think it has been far too long for you to hold a grudge for something you did wrong.*
>   *I'm tired of this, Babysister!! I've prayed and*

*prayed about this situation and think I should just
tell you how I feel. To be perfectly honest, my
prayer is that we start over. That's what this letter
is about. I have news that I want you to hear from
me before people start talking about it at work.
Darren and I are getting married. Yes, I mean it.
Married.*

*We know marriage is what we want. We've
known it for some time now, actually. After Darren
proposed, we started seeing a counselor from my
church. I wanted him to be absolutely certain that
marriage was what he wanted. We've been
planning the wedding for a while now, my family
knows about it, but I haven't told anyone from
work because I was hoping things between us could
be resolved first. Hopefully, now that I'm telling
you about our marriage, you'll realize that Darren
and I are together forever and this realization will
help you get over your grudge or whatever it is
you're experiencing. I miss you. It has been very
difficult working with you and not being able to
speak to you. We don't even say hello! Now is the
best time for us to go on with our friendship.*

*We have always been there for each other. Have
you somehow forgotten all we've been through? I
was with you at your mother's funeral. You helped
me survive my parents' divorce. We've been
together through most of the major events in our
lives. Anyway, I want you to come to my wedding.
It will be the happiest day of my life. I want you to
be there. Major events aren't the same without you!*

*Darren also wants you to come, by the way. He
says he wants to continue being friends with you.*

*We have discussed it all and believe things can
work out!!!*

Your Friend,
Deborah

My first impulse was to rush out and find Darren. I
wanted to somehow help him come to his senses. What
are you doing, Darren? What are you trying to prove? But
just as quickly I was overcome by the feeling that everything was over and curled up on my couch and had a long
hard cry. An hour had probably passed before I got up
from the couch. I was washing my face when I remembered the small white envelope. Inside was the wedding
invitation of course. Two gold doves with rings in their
beaks floated above their names. Blah blah blah . . .
Miss Deborah Michelle Moore to Mr. Darren Forrest Wilson . . . blah blah blah . . . First Missionary Baptist
Church. When we were teenagers, Deborah and I would
tease each other about having our weddings at First Missionary Baptist. Who would have her wedding first, who
would have the most guests. And now her wedding was
only two months away. *Two months.*

I felt somewhat better as I burned the invitation over
my kitchen sink. I found my lighter and calmly watched
as the fire ate away at the raised gold letters and the Bible
verse Deborah had written at the bottom in matching gold
ink. I hadn't bothered reading the entire thing, but it had
something to do with friendship.

I called Rob.
"What's wrong?"
"Everything."
"What's going on with you, Babysister?"

"Everything."

"You want me to come over?"

"No, not really. Actually, I was wondering if you think I'm a nice person."

"I think you're great. Why do you think I put up with all the grief you keep giving me? Why do you think we're friends? I'm not with you anymore, but I still get a kick out of hanging out with you."

I was quiet.

"Do you want to get back together, Babysister? Is this what this is about? Do you miss being with me?"

"No." I still hadn't figured out why I'd called him. "Listen, I'm going to go. Thank you for talking with me."

I hung up before he had a chance to say anything else.

On Monday, as I was getting ready to take my morning break, Deborah walked up behind me and whispered over my shoulder.

"Did you get the letter?"

I nodded my head and without looking at her locked my drawer and turned off my computer.

She continued to follow me as I headed for the break room. "I wouldn't have given you the invitation if I didn't believe with all my heart in the power of prayer and forgiveness."

Silent Marsha sat in the back corner of the break room eating her lunch and reading a book. She let out a long sigh before turning a page.

"If you would just stop being so stubborn," Deborah said, "I think we could get through this."

"I guess I don't have as much faith as you, Deborah, because I don't see how we can ever be friends again."

"You know what's funny? I should be saying those

same words to you. Instead I'm the one going around begging for your friendship when you're the one who tried to destroy everything!" Her voice was high and shaky, but she stopped suddenly and waved her hand through the air. "Fine," she said. "You want to be alone and miserable and bitter for the rest of your life because you couldn't have *my* man? Fine. You deserve it." She whirled around and walked out of the room just as Carol and Vicky rushed in. Vicky's hand was over her chest as though she was trying to be ladylike. Carol simply looked bewildered.

"Too late," I said. "You've already missed it. I'm sure Deborah will supply you with all the details."

On Wednesday morning while we were preparing to open, Deborah went around the bank passing out the wedding invitations as though it was Valentine's Day and we were in elementary school. I could have hid out in the break room, but I wanted to prove that I could care less about her silly invitations and stayed at my station where I could see and hear everything that went down. Danisha began screaming and jumping up and down like she had won the lottery. Byron gave Deborah a hug and told her that even though he and his wife were having troubles, he still thought marriage was a great institution. Tonya started asking her questions about what she was going to wear and so on. When everyone had their invitation, Deborah stood in front of her desk as though she was about to give a speech. "The ceremony is going to be fabulous. My wedding day will be the happiest day of my life, and it would mean so much to me if each of you could attend. I want all of my friends to be there." With that, she cleared through the crowd of her adoring fans. She walked right past me without saying a word and made her way to Silent

Marsha's work area. "This is for you, Marsha. I hope you can come." She turned before Marsha could say thank you, and as she made her way back to her desk, glanced over at me. "Had your chance," she whispered. But I managed to keep my mouth shut. Something my father was known for saying when he watched a game came to mind: "It ain't over till it's over, so you best not start cheerin' yet."

Twelve

I FELT AS IF I were going to my own wedding as I stepped out of my car and walked toward First Missionary Baptist Church. I was wearing as much white as Deborah would be after all: a short white dress, white pumps, white chiffon scarf, white pearl necklace. I had taken over two hours getting ready that morning. I had pressed my nappy edges, set my hair in curlers, and after it dried, pinned it up into a swirl. I brushed on powders, drew in lines, painted, plucked, shaved, and tweezed. The final touch: a fingered curl perfectly placed so that it had the look of perpetually falling over my eye.

First Missionary Baptist was one of the nicest-looking churches in the area. No bars on the front windows, a large green lawn, three jacaranda trees, and a border lined with African daisies, rosebushes, violets, and Easter lilies. The building had a contemporary design: three small angular buildings connected to the main building, a wide bottom that grew smaller at the peak. The shape forced your eyes upward so that you couldn't help but look at the cross on top.

It had been raining for two days straight, but on that

morning the sky was a clean, clear blue, not the smoggish green-blue I was used to. I could even see the San Gabriel Mountains in the distance. The mountains reminded me of when Darren promised to take me camping. He had said there was nothing like being out in nature with someone you care about.

I pulled my car in next to Darren's BMW. His car was one of maybe five other cars in the parking lot and was covered with paper flowers. I was checking my makeup in my compact when a man walked up to my car. He introduced himself as Darren's cousin, but I didn't see any resemblance to Darren except for his height and skin color. He teased me about being so early then asked, "So are you a friend of the bride or the groom?"

"I'm a friend of Darren's," I said, then added that I hadn't seen him since we were at UCLA together. "We were such good friends back then. Staying up late. Studying together. Partying together. Those were the days." Ha, ha. "Is he around?" Big smile.

"Yeah, he's in the preacher's office. Through that door there, down the hall and to the right."

"Thanks."

"Nice day for a wedding, huh?" He lifted his hands toward the sky.

"It sure is. Couldn't ask for better."

I watched him walk to the front of the parking lot and light a cigarette.

It had been a little over six months since I last saw Darren. I had sworn that I wouldn't go to the wedding, but when I woke up that morning I knew I had to see him. I simply had to.

I checked my makeup for the thousandth time then made my way toward the church, my white slip brushing against my butt, my heels crunching in the gravel, my knees feeling like any second they might give out. As soon as I opened the side door I heard his voice and my stomach jumbled up into a small nervous ball. He was saying something about ties, then I heard him laugh. I followed that laugh all the way down the hall and found him in the preacher's office, standing under a picture of Jesus—the one where he's holding a peace sign except his fingers are closed. There were two other men in the room as well. They would have made perfect dates for Danisha and Vicky. One guy was short and round with fat cheeks and the other was tall and skinny with glasses that made his eyes look too big for his face. Like Darren, they wore black tuxedos, only Darren was wearing a pink rose and baby's breath in his lapel. He looked as unbelievably fine as always. All my fantasizing over the past months hadn't made him look any better or worse. Some things in life never change.

When he saw me he shook his head a bit, but didn't appear any more angry than a parent shaking his head at a child who is too cute to actually punish.

His short friend said, "Sorry, sister, no women allowed."

"He's right," Darren said. "You shouldn't be back here."

"I know," I said with a slight smile.

The taller man extended his hand. "Richard. Best man."

"Babysister," I said. "Ex-girlfriend."

"The infamous Babysister, huh?"

The short one rolled his eyes. "See, sisters like you give other sisters a bad rep as a whole. We heard all about you, girl."

I slid my hands up and down my chiffon scarf. I had to giggle. I was at least seven inches taller than him and had a clear view of the thinning black hair on the top of his head. He didn't seem like he'd be a friend of Darren's at all. I mean, he looked like one of the black Oompa Loompas from *Willy Wonka and the Chocolate Factory*. All he needed was a pair of white overalls and those tiny white shoes.

"The family knows about you," he said. "It's a shame that you could betray another sister the way you did. The family is standing behind Deborah by the way. You should know that."

"Listen, I just wanted to speak to Darren."

"He's getting married today."

"Oh *really*? So that explains the tuxedos and the church. I get it now."

Richard whispered something to Darren and he nodded his head like an official taking advice from an aide. I wanted to say, Jesus Christ, could everybody just relax, please?

Darren turned to the Oompa Loompa. "It's okay, Thorton. Wait outside. This won't take long."

Thorton?

"Yeah," I said. "We won't be long, and would you close the door on the way out."

Thorton said, "It's none of my business, man, but don't mess up."

Richard looked at Darren as if to say, you want me to leave or stay?

"It's okay. Wait outside. We won't be longer than a minute."

Darren actually grinned after Richard closed the door. "You really are something."

"I did receive an invitation. It's not like I wasn't invited."

"True."

His grin eased into a full smile. I pointed to his new pair of black boots.

"I couldn't resist," he said, lifting his pant leg so I could get a better look.

"Is she pregnant?"

He turned away as if my question was too pathetic to answer.

"Sorry. I was curious about the sudden need to get married. I mean, are you sure about this?"

"I wouldn't be here if I wasn't sure."

"Sorry." I moved in closer and rested my hip against the preacher's desk, then tried my best to look as if I might burst into tears. "I just never thought the next time I saw you, I'd be at your wedding." I dropped my shoulders into a slump, held my head down low, stared into my clasped hands. "I'm sorry. It's been hard for me."

"Hey, I shouldn't jump all over you. I'm glad you came." He bent down so he could see my face. "Really. It's good to see you."

I looked up and grinned sheepishly. He stretched out his arms and we hugged. When he stepped back, I brushed at his tux and straightened his collar. I let my hands pause for a moment on his chest. I could feel it rise with his breath. Up. Down. I realized I had nothing to lose. Nothing. "I want you back, baby," I said, as if announcing he had won a prize.

He took my hand and began stroking my thumb. In that instant, I knew that he was struggling between kissing me or kicking me out. "Listen, I don't have time for this. I'm getting *married* today. *Married.*"

"I know."

"It's over, Babysister. It's been over. I don't understand why you can't figure that out."

I kissed him on the cheek and he moved his head away as if embarrassed for me.

"I think you better leave."

I put my mouth against his neck, and when I felt him swallow, turned in and kissed his Adam's apple. I felt his body stiffen and heard a faint whistle come out through his nose, but the surprise was, he didn't move. So I kissed him again, put my arms over his shoulder to pull him closer, began kissing his face and lips. "I've missed you so much baby." My leg slowly climbed up and wrapped itself around his ass. I heard the deep low notes of the organ from outside then someone began singing. When I heard him sing, "God is a rock," I slid my tongue in between Darren's lips. I guess it was fitting that we were in a church with a hymn floating around our heads, because Lord knows my entire body was saying a prayer at that moment. I pried his teeth open and felt the tiny tastebuds on the top of his tongue and all the smoothness underneath. I felt his hand on my breast, his thumb brush over my nipple. He pushed me further against the preacher's desk. My hand slid against a stack of papers and they rustled to the floor like leaves. I began trying to undo his cummerbund and when that didn't work, I went for the buttons on his shirt. I was down to three and sliding my hand under the white cotton and reaching for skin when I felt him push me so hard I fell off my corner of the desk and stumbled backward.

He grabbed my arms and shook me. "Listen to me," he whispered, "*leave*. Get out of here! I love *Deborah*. I'm marrying Deborah. Leave us alone. Are you crazy or something?"

"But . . ."

Darren pushed me again, this time so hard I went flying against the wall. My foot twisted out of my shoe and down I went. He knelt over me while I was slumped on the floor then dug his fingers into my arms and started shaking me. Richard and Thorton rushed in and tried to pull him off, but the harder they pulled, the tighter he held on. They tried to convince him to let go of me, but it wasn't until Thorton said, "Calm down, man, she ain't even worth it," that he let go. I tried to stand up gracefully, but my shoe was missing so I looked lopsided. My arms hurt. I was surprised that I didn't see any bruises.

The preacher's office was a mess. Papers were everywhere; his name plaque turned over; his desk clock in his chair; the picture of Jesus on the floor. I picked up my purse. Richard handed me my shoe. I began straightening my dress when Thorton had the nerve to reach for my arm. "You little fucker, you better not touch me," I said, then I flung my chiffon scarf across my neck and lifted my chin like I had everything under control. I even had the nerve to try and switch my ass as I walked out the door.

Outside, there were several more cars in the parking lot. I had just opened the door of my Mustang when I noticed Danisha, Carol, and Vicky making their way toward the front of the church. They were too busy talking amongst themselves in their tribal circle to notice me. Danisha had on an orange suit that was so snug around the middle it looked as if she were wearing a corset. She also wore an orange hat with a feather sticking out on the side. The hat looked like something an elf would wear. Carol had on a loose skirt that gave her butt a watermelon-like shape. Martin the security guard stood next to her with his arms around her shoulder, so I assumed they were no longer a secret. Vicky towered above the little group. She had burgundy extensions in her hair that clashed horribly with her pink dress. Considering what I had been through in the preacher's office, the evil stepsisters were the last people I wanted to deal with. I started my car without much thought as to where I was going. All I knew was that I had to get out of there.

I ended up driving to the nearest coffee shop, a small place with six red booths along the window and a long counter with forest-green stools. There was an old register with those large buttons you have to push down in the front. On the wall there was a picture of the Virgin Mary and a framed one-dollar bill with a note that said WE'RE STILL HERE! taped underneath.

I sat at the counter, and after handing me a menu, my waitress said with a big smile: "You look like a beautiful bride in all that white. You look like you should be getting married today. Very pretty." I said thank you and immediately started crying into my paper napkin. "Oh, honey," she said, "let me get you a glass of milk," and then she rushed off as if something to drink would magically solve all my problems. She was back in a minute with the milk and a handful of extra napkins. I had cried some until I felt her cold hand on my wrist. "Ya, ya, ya," she said. "Everything will be okay." I looked up over my tissue. Her name tag read Guadelupe, but from all the blond hair and fifties-style makeup, it might as well have read Cindy Sue or Mary Beth. My guess was that when she was young she probably got it in her head that she wanted to look like Marilyn Monroe and was still trying twenty years later even though she was now old and fat. Her hair was dyed a bright yellow, cut short with a flip, and she had a small

light-brown mole over her lip, a beauty mark that probably turned all the boys on when they tried to tongue her
in the backseat of those huge cars people drove back then.

Guadalupe made me feel comfortable though, and it
felt good to have someone finally acknowledge that I was
hurting. When she asked me to tell her what was wrong, I
took a sip of milk and explained that it was my ex-
boyfriend's wedding day. He had broken up with me, but
I still loved him. I also told her that I had gone to the
church before the ceremony so we could talk. "I just saw
him," I said. "He was getting dressed. I think he's still
attracted to me. We kissed, but then he got scared."

Guadalupe hit her hand against the counter. "I bet he
still has feelings for you and now he's going to go and
marry the wrong woman."

"I know."

A couple walked in and she excused herself. When she
returned, she poured coffee into my cup. She gave me a
serious look as if while taking the couple's order she had
figured out exactly what advice to give. She poured herself
a glass of milk and leaned over the counter. "I myself
never had a wedding because I was married in a court-
house. I was married for thirty-eight years to my husband,
Maurice, and thirty-eight years is no joke, huh?" She went
on to tell me that Maurice was a good provider and great
musician, and that he was also a black man. Her parents
made her pray the rosary for two hours every night when
they got word that instead of visiting her cousin Rosaura
down the street, she had gone out with her trashy friend
from work to a nightclub where she had danced with a
black man. "We danced until four a.m.," she said. She fell
in love with the man that very night, but she was twenty
and still living with her parents. Her oldest brother beat

her up when he found out she had danced with a black man. Her father began to drive her to and from work, making the sign of the cross whenever she got in or out of the car. But she didn't care, she found ways to see him. One month later she climbed out the window while everyone was sleeping and ran to his car. "I didn't look back," she said. "My Maurice died three years ago. A good man. I knew it too. The day he came by my work and told me he was going to Los Angeles and asked me to go with him, I knew in my heart he was for me. Felt it here." She held her hands together and pressed hard over her breast. "I felt it in my heart. I wore my best dress. Left my family a long letter on top of the box of cereal they ate every morning. Froot Loops. Isn't that perfect?" She took out a towel and began wiping the counter. "Sometimes love will make you do courageous things or just plain silly things, too. You love your boyfriend very much. You should go to the wedding. See what happens. Might be like the soaps. Maybe he'll run away with you after all."

I looked at my watch. Twenty after one. Deborah was probably standing in the entryway on her father's arm waiting to walk down the aisle.

The drive from the coffee shop to the church took about fifteen minutes so the ceremony was well under way when I arrived. No one I knew saw me because I sat in one of the pews in the back. The inside of the church was large and airy and could easily seat up to four hundred people. There were six stained-glass windows that reached up to the ceiling so that colored sunlight spilled over on all the guests. There was a huge gold cross on the back wall. A man sat at the organ. There was also a piano and drum-set up front. A banner on one wall was decorated with two arrows: one pointed up, the other down. Next to the arrows was a question in bold green letters: *Where will you go when all is said and done?* Lisette was one of the bridesmaids. The lavender dress Deborah had her wear did nothing for her color. She wouldn't stop fidgeting with the gloves she had on either. Deborah's older sister Erica was the maid of honor. Richard and Thorton stood next to Darren, who looked together as ever. You never would've known the incident in the preacher's office had ever happened. He held his head high and seemed to be very proud, like someone standing next to his new car, jiggling the keys in his pocket, about to drive it off the lot for the first time.

Deborah, I had to admit, made a stunning bride. Her hair was pulled up high over her head with a few soft strands falling over her cheeks, outlining her huge brown eyes. The bodice of her dress looked as if it was made from antique lace and seemed to blend into her skin. The bottom half looked like shiny cream-colored silk which hung gracefully then flared slightly at the hem. Her bouquet was a mixture of pale pink, soft yellow, and cream-colored roses. Roses were everywhere, in fact. A large bouquet of white roses draped over the piano and over the organ, a stand with roses of every color in front of the pulpit. Roses had always been Deborah's favorite flower.

I started sniffling and began digging in my purse for a tissue. The woman next to me saw that I was tearing up and handed me one of her own. "Here, child," she whispered. She wore a yellow hat with white feathers floating around the brim. Grandmother type. "A wedding is a beautiful thing, ain't it? A blessing from God, 'specially these days."

I nodded.

"I'm Mrs. Lawson. I used to live near the Wilsons when that one there was a baby." She pointed toward Darren, who was gazing into Deborah's eyes.

The bald preacher nodded his head and a woman I couldn't recognize started ruining one of my favorite songs, "Always and Forever," by trying to sing like some opera diva. I wanted to tell her, Lower your voice, girl, you're singing R&B not opera. She was a frail-looking thing with a head of curls balancing on top of her birdlike head. I guessed that she was Thorton's girlfriend or something because she wasn't much taller and he stood beaming at her as though he couldn't be prouder. I noticed Darren's mother then. She sat in the front row, resting her head on her husband's shoulder, occasionally dabbing her upper lip with a handkerchief. She was about the one thing I didn't envy Deborah for, definitely the last woman you'd want for a mother-in-law. Darren's father was a beautiful man, of course, and every time he turned to look at his wife, I'd try to get a glimpse of his profile. Same color skin. Same jawline and mouth.

Everyone from work was there except for Silent Marsha. Martin the security guard and the evil stepsisters sat near the front row with bright smiles on their faces. I knew they were trying to remember every detail of the wedding so that when they were finally alone they could have a good gossip session. Byron and Tonya sat next to Mr. and Mrs. Hodges. I noticed Darren's ex-girlfriend, Angela, had shown up with her white husband. She still had her short Afro, while her husband's hair went past his shoulders and was a thick and shiny brown. They kept smiling at each other and giving each other goo-goo looks. At one point Angela started burying her fingers in her husband's hair, pulling at strands, lifting it and letting it fall. I had to wonder how she had the nerve to flirt with a white man in a church full of black people, even if he was her husband. I would have been worried that everyone there would be glaring at me and thinking about slavery and white slave-owners raping black women. I looked to see if anyone else was staring at them, but it seemed like all eyes were on the happy couple.

After the woman finished destroying my song, the preacher asked Darren and Deborah to turn and face each other. He said a few words about the sanctity of marriage then announced that Darren and Deborah wanted to share poems they had written to each other. Why Deborah thought rhyming words like love and dove and Darren and swearin' was a good idea was beyond me. Darren's poem, though, sent me slumping into the pew. The poem was all about the simple power of love. "Maybe we'll have a simple life," the last line said, "but as long as we share our simple life together, the power of our union, the power of our love, will affect our children and our children's children." After reading their poems, they walked to the large arrangement of roses in front of the pulpit and each picked a flower then walked back to the preacher. Darren gave Deborah a white rose then accepted a red rose from Deborah.

The entire ceremony was becoming much too much for me: the poems, the music, the smell of all those roses. That perfumey, too sweet, roses-are-red-violets-are-blue, happy-fucking-Valentine's-Day, just-after-a-shit-air-freshener-smell started working like a poison in my nostrils and I wanted to throw every single rose to the floor and crush those smelly petals beneath my white shoes. I prayed for enough courage to stop the wedding. Stop! Stop! This is a mistake! Prayed that I could be as bold as

Angela, who had enough guts to play with her white husband's hair and massage the base of his white neck at a black wedding. Or as bold as my waitress, Guadelupe, who left her family and friends to start a life with the person she loved.

I rested my elbows on the pew in front of me. Mrs. Lawson patted my back. All the white feathers on her hat floated up and fell as she leaned toward me. "You okay, child?" I blinked and everything went blurry. She pulled me to her and my head fell against her chest. She rocked me long enough so that I managed to smear a glob of mascara on her yellow suit. "You better try to smile, child. This is a wedding, not a funeral. Everyone should be happy for them."

Just then the preacher said the old line about kissing the bride and Deborah puckered her lips. She didn't know what the hell she was doing. She kissed him like a shy schoolgirl, lips pressed together tightly, giggle giggle. Anyone would tell you, a man like Darren should be kissed with parted lips, and after you feel his body give some, you slip your tongue into his mouth, shyly at first then with everything you have.

Open your mouth, girl, I thought. Put your hand around his neck and bring him in. Give him your tongue and take in as much of his sweet breath as possible.

"I should show her how to kiss him," I said. "She should at least know how to kiss him."

Mrs. Lawson said, "She should at least know *what*?"

"How to kiss him."

She looked at me suspiciously and narrowed her eyes. "Child, they're married now so you best forget about whatever it is you're talking about. You trying to put a curse on them?"

"I don't need to put a curse on them. Their marriage will never last."

She glared at me like I was some sort of voodoo priestess. "What God has joined together let no man put asunder!"

I rolled my eyes. "Whatever."

Her voice rose slightly. "Were you invited to this wedding? Does Mrs. Wilson know you're here? I know that boy's mother wouldn't allow someone with your attitude in this here church."

"Darren's mother can kiss my black ass," I said.

Her eyes went big and she grabbed her purse. "You ought to be ashamed of yourself," she said, and then waddled off to the pew in front of us without looking back.

Everyone applauded as Darren lifted Deborah's hand to his mouth and kissed it.

He had lifted my hand like that once, I thought. The time we saw the French movie he had lifted my hand all the way up to his mouth and given it a long soft kiss. We were walking out of the theater. He had kissed my hand and said, *"What are you doing to me, girl?"* Then he kissed me directly on the mouth, right there in front of all those people waiting in line for tickets.

Thirteen

THAT NIGHT I DREAMT that I stood at my bedroom window wearing a long white slip, watching Darren float in a starry sky like a leaf taking its own sweet time reaching the pavement. He reminded me of Peter Pan but instead of tights he had on boots and jeans and a short-sleeved shirt. I yelled at him to come inside, but he simply laughed. "I want you to see how handsome I am!" he yelled. "But I already know how handsome you are!" I yelled back. He floated toward me then and took my hand. All at once I was floating as well. We flew high over the city, light as balloons. Down below us there wasn't a person in sight and the city was still and quiet. We flew past the bank first. *Investment Services!* was painted across one window, but when Darren snapped his finger the words suddenly changed to *I love Babysister!* Next we went over to the church where he and Deborah were married. We kissed in front of the stained-glass window of the black Jesus then sat on the roof of the church and talked about what our own wedding would be like.

The dream shifted then and we found ourselves in Darren's bedroom. He was bare-chested now, rocking me back and forth in a slow sensual dance. "May I ask you a question?"

"Anything."

"Would you polish my boots?"

A rag magically appeared in his hand. "This means so much to me," he said.

I took the rag and carefully wiped down each boot. I made small circles near the heels and long wipes down the sides. The more I polished, the more aroused we both became. "Oh yeah," Darren moaned. "That feels so good, baby." I wiped faster and harder. "Yes, that's it!" Darren cried. "I love you, Babysister! I love you!" But then something strange happened. A satin shoe appeared out of nowhere, right next to the boot, and when I looked up, there was Deborah standing in her wedding dress fondling his chest and kissing his neck. When I screamed for her to stop, she kicked me on the shoulder and I went flying backward. "You'll never have him," she cackled. I began yelling Darren's name, but he was too busy kissing Deborah to notice. And that's how the dream ended, with me calling out Darren's name and being ignored.

I woke up in the late afternoon. The dream had left me feeling both sad and horny. I tried to go back to sleep, but my neighbor downstairs started blasting his music and from the wailing tones of the violins and the weepy voice of the Spanish singer, I guessed he was listening to some sad love song. Sad love songs are always the same, Spanish or English. I buried my head under my pillow, but as soon as I closed my eyes, it seemed like every detail from the church sprang to mind at once: the crack in Darren's voice at the beginning of his poem; the gentle way he helped Deborah straighten her dress; how perfect they looked standing together in the church, like a plastic couple on top of a wedding cake.

I gave up on sleep and went to the bathroom. I had to blink a few times when I saw myself in the mirror: my skin was ashen and gray, the bags under my eyes thick and heavy. The last time I looked that bad, I'd had food poisoning after eating at Eve's Rib, a barbecue place on Lincoln Boulevard. Deborah and I had just left a club and Eve's Rib was the only place open. I was sick for days.

I washed up and turned on the TV, hoping to find something, *anything,* that would help keep my mind off Darren, but every program seemed to remind me of him. I began watching an old musical, but when the hero started singing I got teary-eyed and had to change the channel. Darren had sung to me once. We were eating croissants at a bakery near his condo, sitting in the booth side by side and reading the paper. Ella Fitzgerald and Louis Armstrong came on the radio and Darren started singing "Isn't This a Lovely Day" close to my ear, right along with the music. I couldn't watch the western with Clint Eastwood because of the boots, of course. I tried to watch a rerun of *The Cosby Show* but instead of seeing a TV family, I saw an older Darren and Deborah with their three kids: two boys, one girl. Darren Jr. was sitting at the grand piano practicing his Tchaikovsky, Deborah was brushing her daughter Rebecca's hair, and Darren was helping little Antony with his homework. (Deborah had always liked the names Rebecca and Antony.) Darren's mother is there for a visit. She's wearing her sailor outfit and sitting at the dining room table to make sure the new maid polishes the silverware correctly and doesn't steal anything. I ended up watching a shopping network and buying an ugly blue sweater and some gadget that was supposed to help structure my butt.

That next morning I woke up on the couch, one foot on the floor, a painful ache in my right arm. The TV was still on and a cheerful anchorwoman with big teeth and bouffant hair was chatting away with a cheerful weatherman with big teeth and bouffant hair about the possibility of rain. It had been two days since the wedding, but I felt like I had been inside for two weeks. If the anchorwoman hadn't said something about the Monday morning commute, I probably would have forgotten that I had to go to work. The sun wasn't up yet so I knew I had plenty of time to get dressed, but I decided to stay put. I didn't feel at all like listening to the gossip hounds at the bank go on and on about what a good time they all had at the wedding: Did you see what so-and-so was wearing? Did you see how so-and-so was hitting on so-and-so? Did you see how much food so-and-so ate? And all the rest of their crap. I called Mrs. Hodges, grateful that it was too early for her to be in her office, and left a message on her voice mail that my brother was in a minor car accident and I needed to get to the hospital. Then I went back to the couch intending to spend the entire day with the tissue box by my side.

Mrs. Hodges called at ten after nine while I was watching a cooking show.

"This is Mrs. Hodges. I wanted to let you know that I did receive your message. I hope your brother is okay and we look forward to seeing you tomorrow."

Rob called twice. "Hey, Babysister. Yeah. I tried calling you at work, but they said you didn't go in. I hope you're okay and you're not sick or anything. Anyway, I'm calling because I was wondering if you'd like to go out for dinner tonight. My treat. Give me a call as soon as you get home so we can get together."

And later: "Yeah, it's me again. This is your last chance for a free meal. I'll have to go out with someone else if I don't hear from you. You know you're my first choice so call okay? I haven't seen you in a while, girl. Okay, bye."

Every time the phone rang I couldn't stop myself from hoping that it was Darren. (Babysister, I've made a huge mistake! Take me back! I love you!)

That afternoon I sat at my living room window and watched the four little sisters from downstairs play double Dutch. Each girl had her hair done in tiny twists with what looked like hundreds of barrettes in every color imaginable. The barrettes would fly up and down as they jumped rope, so that the colors seemed to swish around in the air. They were so close in age they looked more like a set of quadruplets, and if it weren't for the different outfits they had on I wouldn't have been able to tell them apart. I had been sitting at my upstairs window for a good hour before LaKeisha noticed me watching and called up from the sidewalk. "Why you watching us play? You ain't got no job?"

"Yeah, but I didn't go in today."

"Why didn't you go to work?" LaVita said. "You got fired?"

"No, I'm depressed."

LaNeisha said, "Why you depressed, you ain't got no friends?"

I rested both my arms on the windowsill. "My boyfriend broke up with me and married another woman."

LaQuita shook her head. "Dang, you ain't never gonna get married if your boyfriend don't marry you."

I watched them play until they heard their mother calling. "LaKeishaLaNeisha LaQuitaLaVita get in this house! I thought I told you about going outside before you finished your homework. Jumping rope is not going to get you to college and I have more to do with my time than to yell out this here window!" The girls started running all at once, their barrettes bouncing every which way.

The phone rang as I was making dinner—microwave pizza and a bag of chips. Again I hoped it might be Darren and waited with thumbnail in my mouth for the answering machine to pick up.

"Babysister? You there? It's Danisha."

Herpes woman.

"I heard your brother was in an accident. I hope he's okay. So I didn't want anything really. I saw you at the wedding. I was wondering what you thought about it. The church they chose sure was nice, but could you believe all those roses?"

I stared at my machine as she rambled on. I hated thinking about Darren and Deborah, but at the same time, I wanted to know about everything I'd missed at the reception. How was Darren acting? What song did he and Deborah dance to? Did he feed her a slice of the wedding cake nicely or did he get it all over her face? I know I was obsessing, but I couldn't stop myself. Before she had time to hang up, I picked up the phone. "I'm surprised to hear from you of all people."

"Well, word got out about your brother being in a car accident and we all wanted to know how he was doing."

"He's fine."

"People drive so crazy these days. Are you sure he's okay?"

"He had to get a few stitches, that's all, but thanks for asking."

"Well, you know, like I told Vicky and Carol today. The way I see it, we should all let bygones be bygones. Work is stressful enough without co-workers not getting along, don't you think? Besides, Deborah's married now. And it would take a fool not to see how happy they are. We all need to move on."

I believed her about as much as I believed Darren would actually call from his honeymoon suite.

I asked how things went at work then as casually as possible asked about the wedding reception—seeing as that I couldn't make it because of the birthday party I was throwing for my father and all.

"Too bad you had to miss it, girl. Vicky got so drunk! You should have seen her. Falling all over people and shit, acting a fool. The food was incredible, by the way. The cake must have been two feet high and was this fancy, chocolate-cream thing that tasted as light as a cloud! I ate two pieces myself. You think that's rude? I think there was some rum or something in the icing. Full-course meal, too. They had fish and chicken and all sorts of appetizers. Oh, and did I mention all the champagne? I'm talking about the good expensive stuff, honey. And they had one of those things set up where the champagne just poured and poured down all these champagne glasses. Everything was perfect. Everything. You should have seen them on the dance floor. That man is *fine*. That man's entire family is fine. I introduced myself to all of 'em. I danced with two of his cousins *and* his father. Did you know his father is some big-shot lawyer? Good-looking man. Looks as good as his son. And you know they went to Paris for the honeymoon, right? On top of everything else they went to Paris for their honeymoon."

I almost dropped the phone. *Paris.*

"Can you imagine? And here we are chucking twenties at Bank of the 'Hood. That brother must have some serious money to be flying off to Paris. I'll be honest, girl, I can understand why you were tempted. That man is something." She chuckled then and paused to catch a much-needed breath. "I've been wondering exactly how you ended up going to the wedding. Are you and Deborah friends again? Did you and Deborah finally have a talk? It's funny because that's exactly what I told Carol and Vicky, I told them that all you and Deborah needed to do was to sit down and have a serious talk."

I could picture the saliva falling from her mouth as she cupped the phone against her ear.

"You and Deborah must have had a talk and she ended up forgiving you. Is that why you went to the wedding?"

"Why are you so concerned about me and Deborah? Last I talked to you, you were calling me a two-faced liar."

"Aw, girl, it's not like that. Like I said, all is forgotten now. You can understand why I was angry, can't you? Like I said, we all need to move on. Besides, now that I've seen who you lost, my guess is that you must be in a lot of pain. You need your friends."

I bit down on my lower lip. Yeah, I felt like shit. A part of me believed that I would never be myself again—never laugh or flirt or feel romantic, but there was no way in hell I was going to have someone like Danisha thinking that I needed her pity.

I sweetened my voice. "So listen, Danisha, I'll tell you what. I'll confide in you, if you confide in me. How would you feel about that?"

"What do you want to know, girl? I don't have too many secrets—nothing I'm too ashamed of anyway."

"Well, I've always wondered if the rumor going around is true. Everyone says you have herpes and you passed on the disease to the last security guard. That's what they say anyway."

"I don't know who started that rumor. I don't even know why something like that needs to be discussed. I was calling, *like I said,* to help you out, but I can see you just want to be ugly."

"Danisha, *please*. You honestly expect me to believe that you called because you wanted to help me? All of you have nothing more to do with your lives but meddle and gossip."

"Who are you to talk about meddling?"

"All I know is, what I do with my life is my business. You stay out of my business; I'll stay out of yours."

"You really need to do something about that attitude."

"First of all, there's nothing wrong with my attitude; and second, if you have a problem with my attitude, you shouldn't be calling."

"You should be grateful that someone is thinking about you considering what you did."

"Yeah, Danisha, thanks. I appreciate it." And then I hung up the phone before she could say another word.

After my talk with Danisha that night, I realized that I had no desire whatsoever to return to the bank. I had proven to myself and everyone else that I could be scrutinized and ignored on a day-to-day basis and didn't see the point in trying to prove that I could work in the same place as the new Mrs. Darren Forrest Wilson. I didn't want to be around when she returned from Paris, and I didn't want to be around when Darren strolled in to meet her for lunch, or God help me, when she announced she was pregnant. Working at the bank had taught me the importance of saving my money, so it wasn't like I'd have to find a new job right away. I had time to look for something new. Besides, anything would be better than having to work with my ex-boyfriend's new wife.

I woke up Tuesday morning feeling depressed as ever, but because I knew I was going to the bank for the last time I somehow managed to get out of bed and get dressed. I felt calm as I drove into the parking lot. I told myself I'd go in, talk to Mrs. Hodges, and leave. I hadn't thought much beyond that. One decision at a time was all I could handle. The weather that day was typical, bright sun and lots of smog. Martin, the security guard, was out front leaning against his tree as I drove into the parking lot. He had his headphones on and his eyes were half open.

Once inside the bank, I saw that new posters must have been put up the day before. A poster of a black man standing in front of his new car dangled above the area where people stand in line. On the wall behind Deborah's and Byron's desks was a poster of a light-skinned Latino couple with their two light-skinned Latino children celebrating a birthday in front of their new house. On the wall behind the tellers there was a poster of an old black couple walking on the beach. The posters made it seem like getting a loan was as easy as walking in and asking. I was grateful not to be a part of that lie anymore.

I walked back to Mrs. Hodges's office, but she wasn't there so I went to look for her in the break room. Tonya was slumped over her chair when I walked in. She might've been trying to sleep, but you never knew what exactly was going on with that girl. Silent Marsha was creeping around the coffeemaker. She wore her hair in a bun and had on a blue dress with a white collar. Since I was quitting, I almost had the urge to go over and tell her that she was doing herself no good hiding behind all those spinster dresses, but once she caught me staring, I looked away. Carol and Vicky walked in then with their heads pressed together like Siamese twins. They were whispering and giggling about something, but as soon as Vicky saw me, she turned to Carol and said loudly, "I swear I have never seen such a beautiful wedding in all my life."

Carol nodded her head and smiled my way. She had on tiny black shoes that were begging to be stepped on. "I'll never forget Deborah's wedding as long as I live."

Vicky spoke directly to me. She sounded phony as hell. "Good morning, how's your brother?" She had in blue contacts that day, the kind of blue that would have looked fine on a car, but not a black woman's eyes.

"Fine. He'll be fine."

"I saw you at the wedding," she said. "It was nice, wasn't it?"

"Deborah sure is lucky," Carol added. "I'd be jealous if I wasn't seeing Martin."

"Yeah," I said. "He's a good man. I saw him out front against the tree a minute ago. He has a tough job." Vicky raised her eyebrow, but Carol was too slow to know that I was putting down her lazy boyfriend. "So all those rumors about you and Martin were true, huh? I saw you together at the wedding."

"Yeah, we thought we should go on and stop trying to keep our relationship a secret."

"Well, that's nice. Martin is one of the best security guards we've ever had. I've never felt safer."

Carol stared up at me like she wasn't quite sure if she should smile or not.

Vicky knew what I was up to, though. "As long as the relationship is honest and decent any woman has the right to be proud. It's when there's been some *deceitfulness* or *foul play* that people should be ashamed. But, hey, everyone makes mistakes. As long as there's a happy ending, right?"

Only a few months ago Vicky had been crying on my shoulder because of her husband's gambling debts. I had tried to comfort her by telling her about Gamblers Anonymous. People will turn high-and-mighty on you in a second. "Excuse me, *Victoria*," I said, knowing good and well she hated being called Victoria. "You don't know what went down between me and Deborah, so you should probably keep your comments to yourself."

I made my way around them, but heard Carol whisper, "I feel safer since Martin started working here. Don't you feel safer, Vicky?"

Mrs. Hodges was looking at her pocket mirror when I walked in. She was fussing over her hair and humming a little to herself. She carefully returned the mirror to her desk when she saw me in the doorway and pressed at her latest pin, a gold coffee mug complete with saucer and steam made from silver wires. "How's your brother?"

"Fine, fine. Turns out he only needed a few stitches."

She examined my face as though she had special managerial power to detect lies. But after looking me over, she probably assumed a person would never lie about her brother's getting hurt. "Glad he's okay," she said. "Have a seat."

She evened out a perfectly straight stack of papers,

wiped her hand over the edge of her spotless desk, then tilted her head to the side so that she was in the exact position as her portrait. "What can I do for you?"

"Well, I'm afraid that I can't work here anymore, Mrs. Hodges."

She leaned back into her chair and crossed her legs. "Can't or won't?"

"I guess you can take your pick. I don't see a difference."

She stared at me as though she was trying to decide which don't-quit-your-job speech she should use, then pressed at the silver coffee mug pin like it might've somehow fallen out of place. "I won't say that I haven't heard any of the rumors floating around here because I have. This is a tough place to work. But it's tough because we all care about each other. We're like any other family. Tensions rise, we have our squabbles now and then, but when it comes down to it, we support each other."

Managers are some of the most clueless people you'll ever meet.

Her eyes lit up. "As a matter of fact, I was planning on talking about strengthening morale in our next meeting."

"Well, I think it's a little too late for that—in my case anyway."

She looked me over again as if seeing me in a new light, a light that told her she might try to butter me up. "I'm impressed with how you've turned your performance around. Excluding yesterday's absence, you haven't missed a day in a long while and you've been on time."

I wondered what any of that had to do with me quitting.

"And you know, I don't see you as a teller for the rest of your employment here. You're very sharp and I can't say I haven't noticed how quick your math skills are. You rarely use your calculator, am I right?"

"I'm pretty good with doing everything in my head I guess."

"See there, you have a gift. And I say why leave a job where your chances of moving up are pretty much a given. Listen, if anyone else came through that door saying she wanted to quit I'd say, okay, sign out, but you've been a good employee and I don't want to see you getting out there and finding out how tough it is."

I decided to lie. "I don't think you understand. I was offered a position in customer service with another bank."

Her eyebrows shot up. "Really, now. Well, if that's the case then I guess I should say congratulations. May I ask which bank?"

Shit.

"Bank of America? Wells Fargo? Citibank? Glenn National?"

I found myself mumbling yes, just to get her to stop guessing.

"Glenn National? Oh, really? Which branch?"

"I'd rather not go into it, if you don't mind. But I think I'll be happier if I move on. They've given me more responsibilities. To be honest I was growing bored as a teller."

She tapped her desk with her copper-colored nails and let out a sigh. "Well, we all do what have to, don't we. You're giving me my two weeks before you move on I hope."

"Actually, I told them I'd start right away."

"You realize you're putting everyone in a tough position until I find someone to replace you?"

I could care less about putting the people I worked

with in a tough position. I glanced up at her portrait then, but for some reason instead of being annoyed, I realized that she and her husband looked truly happy. I mean, their smiles didn't seem so phony for some reason. There was something very sweet about the way Mr. Hodges tilted his head toward his wife's.

I looked from Mrs. Hodges to the portrait. "How long have you been married, Mrs. Hodges?"

She blinked a few times. An employee had probably never asked her a question that wasn't in her manager's handbook. "Me? Oh, it's been thirty-one years now."

"What do you think makes a successful marriage?"

She picked up her pen and tapped it against her desk then set it down. "Love, of course. Friendship. Attraction. You have to have things in common. Spencer and I both bowl, you know. God." She flipped both her hands up. "And money. Love can't pay the bills and I think it would be hard to keep a marriage going if you had to struggle all the time." She nodded toward her portrait and smiled warmly. "Marriage can be difficult, but there's nothing like a loving family."

"Yeah, I'm sure you're right."

She looked at me for a moment. It was the first time she'd probably *really* looked at me since I was hired. "Well, don't worry. I have a feeling no matter what you put your mind to, things will work out for you. You're a very determined young lady and your determination will get you whatever you want. I can tell. You were a very good employee, Babysister."

It felt like years since anyone had paid me a compliment. I could feel myself blushing. "Thanks, Mrs. Hodges," I said.

"You're welcome, Babysister. Good luck to you, sweet-heart."

I went to the break room to collect my things from my locker: the book I had been reading, my sweater, a small stack of magazines. The evil stepsisters were standing around the coffeepot with their backs turned. I heard Danisha's voice, but couldn't see her because Vicky—tall as a redwood—was directly in front of her. Carol was at Vicky's side nodding attentively. They had no idea I could hear them talking.

Danisha's voice grew louder and louder. "I was merely trying to help the woman out," she said. "I believe we all gotta work here, may as well try to get along, right? But I'm not putting up with her anymore. Not after the way she treated me on the phone last night. I'm through with that girl *and* her stuck-up attitude. I wish you could've heard her. That girl has got problems. I don't need—"

I walked over to my locker. Carol saw me first and cleared her throat. Vicky stepped aside. That's when Danisha finally saw me as well. She was dressed entirely in yellow and looked like a bruised banana. For a split second, there was a look of embarrassment in her eyes, but since she was surrounded by her groupies, she knew she'd better back up all that crap she had been dishing out. She rolled her shoulder back and slid out her foot, which had been stuffed in a yellow pump, but just as she opened her mouth, Byron walked in. "We've got twenty-two minutes before doors open, ladies. And that gives me just enough time for my breakfast sandwich. I'm hungry, too." He went over to the beeping microwave. "My new master-piece. Ham, bell peppers, and a scrambled egg all sitting pretty on a poppy seed bagel." He was about to take a bite when he noticed me taking my things from my locker. "Hey, Babysister, why are you getting your stuff?" He checked his watch and stared at us all curiously. "What's going on? Why y'all chattermouths so quiet?"

Danisha picked up the coffeepot and found her mug. "Who's quiet? I was making myself a cup of coffee. Anyone else want coffee?"

Byron said, "Why you getting your stuff, Babysister?"

"I'm quitting."

"*Quitting?* When did this happen?"

"Today."

"Thank God," Danisha mumbled.

Carol giggled softly.

Byron walked over to my locker, but the room was so small, we might as well have been onstage. "What happened?"

I shoved my sweater into my bag. "I told you. I'm quitting."

Danisha set her coffee down and folded her arms. "Oh, Byron, quit trying to act like you don't know what's been going on."

Tonya finally looked up from her chair. She started kneading the bridge of her nose. "You're making me nervous, Danisha. Why are you acting so hostile?"

Danisha stepped in front of me. "I didn't appreciate the way you talked to me on the phone last night. And none of us appreciated what you did to Deborah."

"Like I said, Danisha, to both you and Victoria here: you don't know what went on between me and Deborah so keep the hell out of it."

Byron came over and patted us on the back. "Ladies, ladies, are you PMS-ing or what?"

Danisha kept her gaze steady. She was so close I could

see where her fake eyelashes met her real ones. Not a pretty sight. "Quitting is not going to make your life any easier, Babysister."

"I didn't say it would, Danisha."

I put my book in my bag. I decided not to bother with the magazines. I just wanted to get out of there. The situation was getting too tacky for my taste.

Danisha tightened her lips and started moving her finger back and forth. "Sleep with your best friend's man. Now that's some pathetic shit."

"No more pathetic than giving people venereal diseases."

Everyone in the room inhaled at once. Danisha's nose quivered like she was going to sneeze. "I didn't give anyone a disease. That's a filthy rumor."

"Whatever," I said, and turned to leave.

I took two—maybe three—steps and then heard Byron yell, "Danisha!" Next thing I knew, it sounded like someone was peeing somewhere in the room . . . and then the smell of coffee . . . something warm on my shoulder. *No she didn't,* I thought, but when I looked down, I saw a puddle of coffee at my feet, and when I turned, I saw Danisha holding her empty mug.

I dropped my things and was on her in a second. I had been in enough fights with my brother to know you don't wait for the other person to make a move, you move in as quickly as possible and cause pain wherever you see an opening. I hit her hard on the side of the face with my purse and before she could think straight, slapped her with my left hand near her eye. I was about to use my purse again when Byron wrapped himself around me. Danisha lunged when she saw I couldn't get away, but Vicky caught her by the wrist.

"Calm down," Byron said softly. "I know everyone has been driving you crazy, but don't go down to their level." He leaned in close enough so that I could smell the ham on his breath. "You're better than this, Babysister." I stopped trying to pull away and he loosened his hold. "Get your things, okay. *Be cool*."

Danisha began patting her hair down and straightening her clothes while Vicky and Carol fussed all over her. Tonya was crying near the water cooler.

Silent Marsha seemed to appear out of nowhere and surprised us all by reaching for my magazines. "I'll walk you to your car," she said, then slowly took in the room. "You all should be ashamed of yourselves. My children know how to behave better than this. Come on here, Babysister."

After we walked to my car Silent Marsha pulled out a handkerchief from her Amish ensemble and started wiping the back of my suit. I told her not to bother, but she wiped anyway, naming all sorts of concoctions I could use to remove the coffee stain. "Good thing your jacket is nice and thick, or you probably would have been burned." She helped me take the jacket off then started twisting her handkerchief. "You're lucky you can leave this place."

"You can leave," I said. "It doesn't take much to quit a job."

"I've got three kids and a husband who doesn't make much more than I do. I'm not going anywhere anytime soon. I figure I'll come here and ignore all this madness till my kids go to college or I get as crazy as Tonya—whichever comes first."

I had never thought about Marsha's life outside the bank. I mean, who would have thought she had three kids?

"Thanks for helping me with my stuff. I appreciate it."

"No problem. Thank *you* for slapping Danisha. You don't know how many times I wanted to do that. I can't wait to get home so I can tell Teddy all about how you kicked Danisha's butt. That was the best thing that has happened around here in a long, long time."

"Well, girl, you should try going off on her yourself sometime. It felt pretty good."

"Maybe I will," she said, and we both started laughing.

I felt my eyes tear up as I watched her walk away. I thought for a moment that I was upset because of the fight, but as I got into my car, I realized that I simply missed Deborah. At least at that particular moment I missed her. I thought about how she had helped me get the job at the bank and how we had always been allies there. We could usually laugh about all the crap we had to deal with. It would've been nice to share a cigarette and talk about what had happened. At some point she would tell me that I was a mess, but that she loved me. She always told me this when I had let my mouth get me into trouble. But those days were over.

I started my car and began backing out of the parking lot. I told myself that there was no sense thinking about the past and that I had everything to look forward to. I was starting from scratch, that's all. I would come out stronger in the end. And as I drove out of the parking lot, the bank growing smaller and smaller in my rearview mirror, I almost believed myself.

Fourteen

WHEN MY FATHER CALLED to invite me to dinner that night, I went ahead and told him I quit my job. I made up some story about how I'd been planning to quit because it was clear that the manager didn't see my full potential and was never going to advance me. He said he didn't understand why anyone would quit a steady job, but that he was sure I could find something else. "I made that coconut cake you like so much and it's sitting in the kitchen waiting to cheer your spirits up," he said. "Why don't you come on over?" After what I'd been through at the bank that morning, the idea of pigging out on my father's coconut cake sounded good to me. I mean, Darren was in Paris with his new wife so I certainly didn't care about gaining weight.

Unfortunately, even my own father had the damn wedding on his mind. As soon as we sat down to eat, he asked how it went.

"I'm surprised you haven't said a single word about the wedding yet."

"She's probably jealous," Malcolm said.

"Shut up, Malcolm."

Daddy and Malcolm had received invitations to the wedding but both had declined: my father had already made plans to visit Vegas with a group of friends and Malcolm had plans to go with Sharice to visit her family in Arizona.

Daddy cut into his chicken with a look of concern on his face. "You did go to the wedding, didn't you?"

"Of course I did. I was one of the bridesmaids, remember? It was nice."

Malcolm said, "I bet Deborah made a pretty bride, huh?"

"Yeah, real pretty."

"So where's the honeymoon?" Daddy asked.

"Paris."

"Paris, huh? Well, I sure do wish them the best."

Malcolm dropped his fork down as if he'd suddenly lost his appetite. "Couples need more than best wishes."

"What's wrong with you?" I asked.

"Him and that girl broke up," Daddy said dryly.

"*Sharice?*"

Malcolm was quiet.

"When did you guys break up? Didn't you go to Arizona with her?"

"That trip got canceled."

"Canceled?"

Daddy shrugged his shoulders and started scooping up his food with his fork. "Hmmph. He's been staying here going on ten days now. You haven't noticed his stuff all over the place? He brought five bags' worth of clothes. Go on in there and you'll see 'em. Five big bags."

"I like clothes, Pops. Babysister has more clothes than me, but you don't say nothing about that."

I let his comment slide because not only was it true, I

was curious about what had happened with Sharice. Normally I wasn't surprised when he and one of his many girlfriends broke up, but I honestly thought he had Sharice fooled. "So what happened?"

"What do you mean what happened? We broke up. You never heard of people breaking up?"

"You don't need to get smart with me. I was just asking a question. If you want to know the truth, I'm surprised your relationship lasted as long as it did considering that temper of yours."

Daddy said, "Well, you break up with one and meet another. You never had trouble in that department, Malcolm."

"Yeah, Daddy, but this isn't high school. Sharice and Malcolm had been living together for almost a year."

Did I just say that?

Malcolm glanced over at me like I must be up to something, but I shrugged and kept eating.

"He's lived with women before, too," Daddy said.

Malcolm lifted his fork. "Yeah, but I've never been kicked out."

I said, "So the African queen kicked your butt off the throne, huh?" Daddy and I laughed some.

"At least I made something last for a while."

"At least I've never been kicked out of a man's house. You won't see me moving back to Daddy's. How many times have you moved back here anyway? Nine? Ten?"

He stroked the stubble growing in on his neck, then picked at his salad. "Anyhow, I'm thinking that she might take me back. She'll come around. We had a beautiful thing."

Daddy said, "Just because it's beautiful, don't mean it's right for you."

"See there, Pops. I could tell you never liked her."

"Now I might've said that I don't like tofu, but you know good and well I never said nothing about not liking that girl."

"It's the way you act."

"Why you so concerned about what I think about her? If you ask me, it don't matter now, anyhow."

"He's got a point there," I said.

"You stay out of it," Malcolm said, pointing his knife.

"I know you're not pointing that knife in this direction."

"Awright you two," Daddy said.

The grandfather clock chimed and I made the mistake of wondering aloud about what time it was in Paris.

"What's it matter to you?" Malcolm said. "Told you you were jealous."

"Malcolm, leave Babysister alone please."

"Oh, but it's okay for her to say whatever she wants to me, is that it? I swear this family will never change."

"Don't start actin' up now, you hear?"

"Why you always gotta be so hard on *me*, Pops? What about *her*? You act like she never does anything wrong."

"Leave me out of it, Malcolm. And don't you think you're a little too old to be whining?"

"I'm not whining. I'm trying to make a point. He doesn't get on you nearly as much as he does me."

"Babysister's doing fine, Malcolm. You both are. Now, why don't you calm down and finish your food."

"You don't get it at all, do you?"

"Didn't I ask you not to raise your voice?"

"Forget it." He pushed his chair back and stood. "No sense talking when no one is listening to you."

He walked out and I heard the bathroom door shut. He

was definitely acting like a brat, but once again, oh horror, I found myself feeling sorry for him. "It's hard when someone breaks up with you, Daddy. Malcolm is upset."

"But you've never gone through any of that sort of mess."

When I didn't respond he said, "Am I right?"

"Well, I'm just saying if someone I loved happened to break up with me it would be very painful."

"Well, I wish that boy could learn from your example, I honestly do."

He wouldn't want Malcolm to learn from my example if he knew what had happened between Deborah and me. But I certainly wasn't going to bring that up.

"You know Malcolm means no harm, Daddy. And you know you like Sharice, too."

"Never said I didn't, now did I?"

Malcolm returned just then and started clearing off the table without saying anything. Helping out was his way of saying, Sorry I lost my temper, Pops. And when Daddy passed him his glass and said something about a game that was on that night, what he was really saying was, I'm sorry, too. This was communication at its best for those two. Sometimes I had to wonder how I turned out as well as I had.

It was close to seven after I left my father's house. I thought about going to see a movie, but decided to pay a visit to Sharice's place instead. She lived near the Forum in one of those neighborhoods that probably hadn't changed any since it was first built. Small houses with spotless lawns sat in neat rows, a palm tree in front of every house. I told myself that I'd put in a nice word on Malcolm's behalf and leave, but as I stood on her porch I couldn't think of a single nice thing to say. Besides, hadn't I helped enough? Malcolm and I had no special bond. We'd been forced to grow up in the same house simply because my parents had sex one night three years before I was born.

I was turning to leave when Sharice opened the door. She had puffy eyes and a crumpled tissue in her hand. I knew the look well. "What are you . . . ? Oh, God, is something wrong with Malcolm?"

"No, no. I was in the neighborhood. I wasn't sure if I had the right house."

She stood blocking her door, staring blankly like she had no idea who I was.

"Well?"

"I'm sorry. Come on in. We were finishing dinner."

She had on jeans and a halter top. I'd never seen her in anything other than a long skirt or dress. I knew the girl was skinny, but man, except for the layer of flesh on her bones she was a walking skeleton. Prophet was at the table eating what looked like a hot dog. Sharice caught me eyeing it. "It's a *tofu* dog, Babysister. Hundred percent vegetarian. They're made with absolutely no meat or meat by-products."

"You like that, Prophet?" I asked.

He nodded. His cheeks were full of the stuff.

"What do you say to Babysister, Prophet?"

"Greetings my African sister." I couldn't help but get a glimpse of chewed up tofu dog swishing around in his mouth. "Asalam Malakem!"

Sharice told Prophet to put his plate in the sink when he was finished, then led me to the living room which was decorated with all sorts of floor pillows, plants and two ceiling fans. It reminded me of *Casablanca*. You half

expected Sam to walk out and start playing the piano
Sharice kept near the windows. I knew Darren would
have liked her place. He liked old houses with dark wood
and hardwood floors. He would have liked the glass door-
knobs and the built-in bookshelves. He had drawn a
sketch of his dream house for me while we were in bed
once. It reminded me of the houses you see in San Francisco. He said that even though he was an architect, he'd
rather fix up an old house than design his own. I hugged
myself and walked over to the photo Sharice had on the
wall. I didn't want her to see that I was getting teary-eyed.
The picture was a large black-and-white photo of a
woman who was partially hiding herself from the camera.
She was biting into an apple and wore an African skirt, no
top, a few beaded necklaces.

"That's me," Sharice said. "I was eighteen. Can you
believe it? I look older, huh? I still get assignments, but
modeling bores me. I guess I shouldn't complain too
much. All that modeling paid for this house." She stared
up at the picture then and smooshed her bony fist up
against her nose. Her greenish-brownish eyes, usually
bright and clear, were completely red.

"So what did Malcolm do, Sharice?"

"What didn't he do? It's just hard, you know? I couldn't
take it."

"Couldn't take what?"

"I want to grow. He says he wants me to fly, but he's
this weight holding me down at the same time." She bit
the thick part of her palm. "The problem is that I miss
him. That's the problem."

"That is a problem," I said.

She put two large pillows on the floor and we sat down

together like hippies. "I know it probably looked like paradise from the outside, but me and your brother have always had our share of problems. I tend to get into relationships that oppose my energy instead of nurture it. When the yin and the yang thing works, it's beautiful, but when the separate halves don't form a whole, what do you have? Two separate entities in constant struggle."

"What did he do, Sharice?"

"He won't let me breathe. He has to be around me constantly. If I have an assignment, he has to be there with me; or if he can't, he's calling to check up. He constantly shows up at the restaurant while I'm trying to work. He says he's just getting a drink, but that's bull. He's jealous. I won't be smothered. Either trust me or forget it, know what I mean?"

I had attracted enough overly dependent men in my lifetime to know exactly what she meant. Men who couldn't go anywhere unless I went along. Men who called me at work every twenty minutes like I had nothing to do with my time but chitchat. Who would've thought that my very own brother, Mr. I-don't-give-a-shit-about-nothin'-but-myself, would have turned out to be jealous and smothering.

"So two weeks ago he sees me leaving my massage class over in Culver City. I was leaving with my friend Kevin. Kevin and I are holding hands. You know why we're holding hands?"

I shook my head.

"Kevin's *boyfriend's* father died. I was trying to *console* him. And here comes your brother. He starts shoving Kevin and acting crazy. I was so embarrassed. And what was Malcolm doing out in Culver City if not to follow me around?"

Sounded to me like Sharice had every reason to kick his ass out.

"But the problem is, I still love him. I do." She started sobbing again. "I love him with all my heart."

She was a total wreck. I couldn't help but think about how much we had in common at that moment. I put my hand on her shoulder. Things were over with Darren and me, but I should at least try to help her out.

"My brother is an ass, Sharice, there is no getting around that fact, but I can tell that he loves you." There, I said it.

"I just saw him at my father's and he's pretty upset over all of this. He said something about how hard the breakup is because he wanted to spend his life with you."

"He did?"

"And he even took the time to pick out the salt pork Daddy had put in the green beans."

"Really?"

I nodded.

"I'm so confused, Babysister. I don't know what to do."

You're going to owe me big time for this, Malcolm, I thought before giving her a nudge.

"Listen, Sharice, when you meet a man, you have to ask yourself three questions. The first is, is he trained? It's a rare man who doesn't need any training at all. The ones who don't had a decent childhood or some ex-girlfriend who put in all the work for you, but they are few and far between. The second question is, can he be trained? And the third is, do I have the patience to train him? Most men need to be trained. If you have the patience, you can train a man on how to make you happy. Believe it or not, I think Malcolm is trainable. I think it would take a special woman like yourself to train him, but it can be done. I mean, he *loved* meat before he met you. Now look at him."

She stared at the ceiling. "I hate the feeling of being smothered, you know?"

"Who doesn't. But you know what's worse, don't you?"

"What?"

"Men who are still in love with their mothers."

We laughed some and I said, "I dated this man once who went to visit his mother every day. And I'm not talking about a woman who was sick or dying or anything. The woman was healthy—and mean, too. She couldn't stand me. And she had him under her thumb. I got tired of it. And so I told him: Listen, baby, you've got to choose. Do you want to suck my titty or do you want to suck your momma's titty 'cause this going back and forth mess ain't gonna work."

"What happened?"

"He chose his momma, probably over there sucking right now."

She laughed again and wiped the corners of her eyes. "Men are more needy than we are, but nobody ever says it."

"Ain't it the truth."

She got up to check on Prophet and returned with two glasses of red wine. "How's that architect of yours doing?"

I'd almost forgotten that I had told her about Darren. I felt like it had been years since we'd been sitting in my kitchen, since he'd given me that bouquet of irises. My voice was barely audible. "We broke up," I said, feeling like an alcoholic in her first AA meeting. "Darren broke up with me."

"Oh, poor thing, and here I am going on about Malcolm." She clasped my hand. "You poor, poor thing. You were so happy!" Deborah was the only woman I had ever truly confided in and while I liked Sharice and knew she meant well, I can't say that I felt like pouring out my soul to her. I didn't want her feeling sorry for me either. "I'm fine, Sharice. It's not like we were in love. Men come and go. My real problem is that I'm out of work. That's why I'm down. I dread having to look through the classifieds."

"What happened?"

I decided to keep lying. Lying was much easier than dealing with the truth.

"I couldn't get along with the new manager to save my life. Our personalities clashed."

"What was her sign?"

"I have no idea. I just know that I hated going into work. I couldn't take it."

Without saying anything, Sharice lit a stick of incense and two candles on the coffee table. She closed her eyes and started fanning the sweet smoke from the incense toward her face, mumbling something about needing strength.

"Things will be all right," she said, still fanning herself with closed eyes. "You've got to rely on the strength of our royal ancestors." She stopped then and opened her eyes. "You are an African queen, don't you ever forget that."

"I don't know about all that king and queen stuff, girl. Wherever there's a king and queen there are usually some servants. Everybody couldn't be royalty."

"Oh, Babysister," she said, jumping up suddenly and clapping her hands. "Babysister!"

"What?"

"This is perfect."

"What is?"

"They're hiring at Medina's. I would have called you if I had known you were out of work. You can work there!"

"Well, I don't—"

"It's perfect! You wouldn't believe how much I make in tips. There's a good crowd, too. Many of our fine African kings go there for dinner. I wouldn't be surprised if you met someone."

Meeting another man was the last thing I felt like doing. No, no, I wasn't looking for a job based on the availability of men. But the idea of working somewhere that was completely different from the bank did sound good.

Sharice had invited Deborah and me to stop by Medina's for dinner not long after she and Malcolm started dating. I immediately fell in love with the place. From the outside, the restaurant looked like an abandoned industrial building. Inside, there was a full bar, wood-burning rotisserie, and a huge fireplace. I had ordered chicken from the rotisserie; it was about the prettiest meal I'd ever seen. The chicken leg was placed just so on the plate with whipped garlic potatoes swirling around near the thigh and the carrots were cut to look like flowers. I have to admit that I enjoyed watching Sharice move around the room, opening bottles of wine, laughing and talking with the customers. So did I want to work at Medina's? Hell, yeah.

"But I've never waited tables before," I said.

"You'll get the hang of it. Ever use a cappuccino machine?"

"No."

"Do you know anything about wines?"

"No."

"Don't worry. I can teach you everything you need to

know. We have to get started right away, though. I mean, I still have to talk to the manager, but I know he'll like you. This is going to be so much fun! What do you think?"

I imagined myself balancing delicate portions of over-priced food high above my head, making fancy coffees with the exact amount of foam. "Well, I guess it can't hurt to try. My luck has been so bad lately things can only get better, right?"

Fifteen

I MADE A HORRIBLE WAITRESS. Horrible. On my first day, I tripped and sent a plate of ravioli stuffed with wild mushrooms and spinach flying across the dining room. On my second night I knocked a glass of water into a woman's lap. I had no idea working as a waitress would be so difficult. At the bank I stood in place all day and dealt with people one at a time, but at Medina's I was expected not only to serve the food, but to know the ingredients, to say words like *chateaubriand, frittata,* and *prosciutto* as effortlessly as fried chicken. Plus there were the odd requests and questions I had to deal with: "May I have the salad dressing warmed and on the side please?" "Could you make that a nonfat decaf latte with extra foam?" "Was the chicken organically fed?"

My biggest problem was confusing orders. I'd never been around so many white people before and couldn't tell one from the other. I mean, have you ever served food to a group of white businessmen in suits or a group of blondes all wearing the same trendy outfits and makeup? So when a bunch of white people sat at one of my tables, I'd hear things like "No, *he* had the fish; *I* had the chicken." I tried my best, but I swear, all I saw were different shades of pink.

To make matters worse, I was still struggling with memories of Darren. Sometimes I would think that I saw him out of the corner of my eye, only to discover that no, it wasn't Darren at all but another man who was almost as tall, almost his color, and then my heart would sink and I'd be left wondering whose order I had in my hand or which table wanted the coffee. I went home at night feeling like a complete failure. Not only had I lost my chance at happiness, but every night at Medina's I made a fool of myself in one way or another.

My ass would have been out of there quick if not for my mouth. For all my clumsiness, for all the times I gave the wrong dish to the wrong person, no one could deny that I had a way with the customers. Darius, the manager, would come up to me just as perplexed as can be. "Don't think that I don't see all the mistakes, Babysister, but I want you to know your tables only have good things to say about you. I don't know what you're doing to win these people over but keep it up." I wasn't doing much more than talking and joking with everyone. Black, white, ugly, attractive, made no difference. I could have a table cracking up before their appetizers were served. Don't get me wrong, I wouldn't pull any of that let-me-kiss-your-ass-Mammy shit, but I did enjoy being able to converse with people about something besides money and accounts. I enjoyed being around people who seemed to be doing interesting things with their lives. People who would come in and discuss politics, music, or the play they had just seen. I'd put my nosy self into their conversations if I felt they were open to talking. It also helped that I got along with the people who usually worked the same shift as I did. Most of them were nice enough to cover for my mistakes during those first few weeks. Diane and Jessica were white and in their mid- to late twenties. Diane had a way of keeping to herself until the perfect opportunity then she'd say something sarcastic. Jessica wasn't afraid to talk about anything, especially sex, and knew all kinds of dirty jokes. The girl had a mouth. But you'd never know what Jessica and Diane were like if they were serving your meal. Like everyone who worked at Medina's, once they were walking out to a table it was all professionalism and class.

Another person who turned out to be helpful was Darius, the manager. He was brown-skinned and had big eyes, hair cut so short it always looked like it was barely coming in, big cheeks, and a toothy smile. Darius was one of those people who simply had a good heart—sort of like Deborah—and was the person who actually kept Medina's together. His uncle had initially bought the restaurant, named it after his daughter, and then let Darius handle everything else. His uncle came in once in a while with a group of friends, smelling of cigar smoke and playing the fat boss, but that was it.

Before my first staff meeting, Darius took me aside and gave my hand a few pats. "I wanted you to come in early so I could show you around. I don't want this place to overwhelm you." Seeing the restaurant empty made it look twice as big as when I had eaten there. Darius didn't seem to notice I was nervous, though, and started telling me all about the decor of the place. "The bar is made of mahogany. The stones for the fireplace were flown in from Ireland. The plants are from . . . let's see, Arizona, Hawaii, Mexico, the tall one over there is Brazilian. Amazing, huh?" The paintings had changed since the time I'd been there. When Darius saw me staring at them he said, "The paintings are by an artist named Maru. They're incredible, don't you think?" On the wall behind the bar there was a painting of a black man washing a white man's car window. "The title of that piece is *Whatever It Takes,* but I say a painting like *that* in a place like *this* is called *Irony.*" He took my hand. "Come on. I'll show you the kitchen."

The kitchen was bigger than my apartment. There was a large stainless steel counter, three refrigerators, a walk-in freezer, and two stoves. The chef was a tall white man with curly gray hair and watery green eyes. He looked like he was about eight months pregnant. When Darius introduced us, he stopped chopping the celery on the counter long enough to nod his head and blink a few times then went right back to work. "He's from Russia," Darius whispered. "Don't be afraid of telling him what you need. He's grumpy, but he's your friend." Then he waved to this gorgeous man who was standing at the end of the counter writing something down on a notepad. He was slightly taller than Darius, with skin almost as dark as mine and jet-black hair long enough to wear in a ponytail that went past his shoulder. "This is Jorge Martinez." Darius couldn't stop squeezing the top of Jorge's shoulder. "He's our head-waiter and my righthand man. What I know, Jorge knows. Jorge will also help you out, right, Jorge?" Darius squeezed his shoulder again. Jorge shook my hand, smiled at Darius, then walked through the swinging doors that led to the office in the back. "He's fine," I said. "Yeah," Darius said. "I'm a lucky man." And that was as far as any discussion of their relationship went. When I asked Sharice about them later, she rolled her eyes. "They've been together forever and they still act like they just started dating. Aquarians and Geminis always get along. Everyone should be as lucky as those two."

It was Darius who, twelve nights after I started, took me by the arm when he saw I was having a particularly bad time. I was serving a table with two bearded white men who looked like identical professors. I couldn't tell them apart to save my life and kept confusing their orders. I was about to serve them dinner but stood at their table with pasta in one hand and lamb in the other, biting my lip and trying to remember who had what. My eyes started welling up because I felt so frustrated and depressed. Not two minutes before, I had knocked over a bowl of carrots in the kitchen. The chef started yelling something that sounded like *Nyet! Nyet!* while pointing his finger in the air and turning a bright pink. Jorge rushed over and told me not to worry about the carrots and go serve my table, but I still felt like a fool. I was standing frozen by the identical professors when Darius walked over and touched my arm. I thought I might drop their plates and burst into tears, but he took the dinners and said, "Babysister, let me help you with these. You poor thing, you haven't had your break yet, have you?" I stared at him blankly. I'd had my break about thirty minutes before and he knew it. "You must be dead on your feet." He asked Jessica to take over my table and told me to make myself a cup of tea and meet him in his office.

I knew my ass was fired. This is it, Babysister, I thought as I took a seat in his office. Back to square one: no man, no job. I sipped my tea. At least he offered me a final drink.

Darius walked in right as I was telling myself I should go on and leave. "Listen, Babysis', you need to relax. You're too nervous. But I know you can do this job! You have a gift with those people. They all love you even when you make mistakes—terrible mistakes."

I sat up in my chair. Maybe I wasn't going to get fired after all.

"But love is not enough. We expect perfection at Medina's. I've never been wrong about an employee yet, good or bad. I have a feeling if you would concentrate you'd be fine." He paused and folded his hands. "Look at your shoulders. Now push them down. That's it. Now inhale with me. Come on. Now slowly exhale. Good. One more time. Inhale. That's good. Exhale. Ahhh."

I had to force down the impulse to roll my eyes. I mean, what made him think I went for the hippy-dippy stuff? My name wasn't Sharice.

"Okay. Now I want you to go home and take a long hot bath or something. But tomorrow I want you to breathe before you go out to the tables. Hold your chin up and *breathe*."

"So you're not firing me?" I said.

"Hell no. I'm not going to let you make me out to be a fool for hiring you. You need to believe that you can do this job, though. Otherwise you're wasting both our time. *Kappish*?"

I figured I had absolutely nothing to lose and tried the breathing exercises the next night. I felt foolish at first and couldn't stop picturing myself as a woman about to deliver her first child, inhaling and exhaling frantically, her eyes big with fear. But ridiculous as it seemed, I kept it up. Sharice caught me taking a deep breath one night and when I told her about the breathing exercises, she got all excited. "Yes! Darius is right. I think that's excellent advice. And remember: As you breathe you should focus on exorcising the demons within. Inhale positive energy;

exhale fear." She started inhaling and exhaling, repeating something about being one with the light. As soon as she closed her eyes and asked me to join in, though, I said something about a table and rushed off.

I breathed my way through my second week at Medina's with minimal mistakes and by the fourth week I felt as if I could do no wrong. I knew which wines and after-dinner drinks to suggest; said things like "This merlot has an oak flavor, but isn't too strong"; could convince everyone at the table to order dessert so my tip would be higher. I even taught myself how to tell the white people apart by concentrating on something other than skin color. (Okay, the *bald* one gets the beef; the one with the big nose gets the fish; the one without the jacket gets the pasta.)

I'd been working at Medina's for almost four months when I realized I wasn't turning my head every time a brother over six feet tall walked in, wasn't thinking about Darren between tables or fantasizing about the day he might come in and swoop me off my feet. Darius called me in two months after I'd started. "See, what did I tell you, Babysis? I knew I was right about you. You're doing a wonderful job, girl. Hundreds of people would love to work at this place. Gorgeous wannabe actors with top skills in waiting tables would do almost anything to work during the dinner shift at Medina's, but I gave the position to you. And you know why? When I saw you I knew I had a dynamite waitress on my hands. And was I right?"

"You were right."

"Okay. I got my eye on you, girl. Keep up the good work. Keep smiling."

I was beaming as I left Darius's office. I felt so proud of myself I started daydreaming about one day running

Medina's, owning it. Starting another restaurant and calling it Babysister's Place, a fancy soul food restaurant where my father would be head chef and Malcolm the janitor.

I worked from four in the afternoon until eleven or twelve at night. Once I was home, I'd watch a late movie and eat dinner. I went to bed after two or three o' clock every night just so I'd sleep through most of the following day, that way by the time I woke up, I had nothing to do but get dressed and grab a bite to eat, maybe find a cafe near the restaurant and read. I'd still dream about Darren, and I'd still get weepy when I let myself remember our time together—how good things had been—but as time passed I found myself feeling better—at least while I was at the restaurant. I was making more money than I ever had earned as a teller—usually as much as a hundred and fifty a night in tips, but it wasn't just the money that was rewarding. For the first time in a long while, I actually looked forward to going to work. Sometimes I'd have a drink with Jorge or Diane after closing—I never would have thought to hang out with Danisha or Vicky or most of the other idiots at the bank in a million years. If Sharice and I shared a break, we would make a cup of tea or coffee and sit out back. Once in a while I'd bum a cigarette from someone, and after making sure I understood the cancerous effects of smoking, Sharice would take a few hits and tell me about Malcolm's progress. He had moved back in the house and they were seeing a counselor and lighting candles together in the Yoruba tradition—whatever the hell that meant.

I also decided that just because I couldn't imagine loving anyone but Darren, it didn't mean I couldn't show myself off some. I looked as good if not better than most of the women who came in to Medina's and unlike many of them, all of my body parts were real. I went to a salon and the beautician colored my hair a rich velvety black then styled it into soft layers that fell lightly to my shoulders. All the waiters had to wear a white top with either black pants or a black skirt; I started wearing a short black mini with an extra-tight white blouse and push-up bra.

I ventured out to Fox Hills Mall about a month after my talk with Darius. I was feeling good and woke up wanting to buy myself a treat. Any treat. A new coat, new boots, something expensive. I had been shopping for nearly an hour and was coming out of a bookstore (I was still reading the books Darren liked) when God help me, I spotted the evil stepsisters walking out of a card shop. Unfortunately, they saw me before I could escape. They walked up dressed in their complete shopping attire, hands on hips, faces sour. Carol had on a red jumpsuit with tiny red pumps and thin gold belt. Danisha wore a low-cut mini-dress and awful silver-white lipstick that made it look as though she'd kissed a powdered doughnut. Vicky towered above them in a green and lavender dress with matching green contacts and a weave that was so thick and long, you had to wonder how many women had given up their hair just so she could look like a wet Afghan hound.

Danisha got to me first. She started right in too. "That was some tacky mess you pulled at the bank. I was trying to be nice and you had to make everything ugly."

"Don't even start with me, Danisha."

"I'm not trying to start anything. You're the one who was hitting people."

"You threw your coffee at me."

She tossed her head and started scratching at the back

of her neck. "Well . . . *anyway* . . . Deborah seems happier than ever, in case you're wondering."

"And her husband stops in all the time," Vicky said.

"Ooh," Carol squealed, "I think her husband is one big chocolate hunk. He is so cute. If I didn't have my Martin I just might be jealous."

I rolled my eyes. As if they could compare.

Danisha said, "So I heard you're working at Glenn National."

"Actually, I got bored with working at banks. I'm working at a place called Medina's now."

Carol's eyes widened. "I heard that that place is expensive. I had a friend who said she saw Denzel Washington there once. You ever see Denzel Washington, Babysister?"

I lied, of course. "Oh, yeah. He's been in a few times. Now there's a beautiful man."

Vicky and Carol nodded their heads.

Danisha squinted at her two evil stepsisters. "So Deborah says she and her husband are working on starting a family. That's exciting news, don't you think?"

"Can you imagine what beautiful kids they're going to make?" Vicky said, flipping at her extensions.

Danisha smiled sweetly. "Deborah says if their first child is a boy she's going to name him Antony, and if it's a girl, Rebecca."

I pictured Deborah at eight or nine months pregnant and Darren resting his head against her belly. *They were planning to start a family?* I did not need to hear that. I'd been feeling better. I'd been feeling good.

Danisha jutted her head forward as if to say, Well what do you think about that? Vicky bit down on the inside of her cheek so that her lips pressed together at the corner. Their news had thrown me, but I certainly wasn't going to let them see I was upset. "Well, that's great news," I said cheerfully. "Good for them." I adjusted the bags in my hand and checked my watch. "Anyway, I've got a date tonight and I still haven't found a dress. I should get going."

I made my way to the escalator as fast as I could. I was just about to go down when I heard Carol shout, "What time does Denzel usually show up at Medina's, Baby-sister?"

"Dinnertime," I shouted back. "And if they ever start paying you all more at the bank, maybe you can afford to come by."

I couldn't concentrate at work that night. I kept picturing Deborah as this glowing pregnant woman and Darren as the perfect husband who runs out late to get her peanut butter and pickles to eat. And I kept picturing myself as a mean old spinster, the kind who used to come into the bank without ever having anything good to say. Why you got all these windows open if you ain't got enough tellers to stand in front of them? Why y'all got the air conditioner on? You tryin' to freeze me to death?

I had to do something. I needed to get on with my life once and for all—and this is where Grant comes in.

Grant wasn't as tall as Darren, not as handsome, not as stylish, certainly not as interesting, but for whatever reason he was the man the women wanted at Medina's. Any time he'd come in, all weaved and unweaved heads would turn and stare. Who is that fine brother? Mm, mm, mm, take a look at that man. Grant drove a Jaguar. Grant wore Italian suits. Grant drank expensive Scotch and after-dinner drinks. Grant worked for an advertising company in Sherman Oaks. Grant had been to Japan and Europe.

Grant started asking to be seated at my station whenever he and his goofy-looking co-worker came in for dinner. He'd tell me about his job or about some trip he'd taken as I served his dinner and then he'd leave some outrageous tip. Seems like the more I ignored him, the more he'd ask me to go out. I hardly thought about him until the day I'd heard that Darren and Deborah were trying to get pregnant.

He showed up at Medina's two nights after my run-in with the evil stepsisters. After telling him and his goofy-looking friend about the specials, I said, "So if you still would like to go out with me, I'm off on Monday."

"Well, now," he said to his friend, "this must be my lucky day." He smiled up at me. "I want nothing more than to spoil you. Have you ever been to Chez Veronique's in the Valley? It's the best French food I've had since . . . well, since my last trip to France."

"How about coming to my apartment. Eight o'clock?"

"Oh, you are something, aren't you?" He looked at his friend again. "Well, I must admit I have a thing for women who know what they want. Eight o'clock it is."

When he smiled, it occurred to me that he really wasn't all *that* bad-looking. He had nice light-brown eyes and a nice mustache. Maybe Monday wouldn't be so bad.

Grant arrived with a bottle of wine and a box of chocolates, excuse me, truffles. "Imported truffles," he had told me after I opened the box. "Hand-rolled and made with the finest liqueurs. I found them in a quaint shop in Beverly Hills."

He looked around my apartment after sitting on the couch. "So this your place, huh?"

I opened the wine and listened to him go on about himself until I couldn't stand it anymore. "Listen," I said, "would you mind massaging my back? I've had a hard week."

A look of surprise came over his face, but he regained his composure. "Why certainly. You know, I had one of the best massages of my life during one of my visits to Japan. The Japanese have so much to teach us about the art of living."

I sat in front of him on the couch so that he could massage my back. For all his talk, Grant did know how to give a good massage. I had on a light blue lace top, thin enough for me to feel the warmth of his hand. Between the wine and the massage I felt myself relax. I started thinking about sex and the fact that it had been close to a year since I had made love to Darren. *One year!* Sex with someone else was exactly what I needed.

"The West," Grant said, "hasn't caught on to the ancient medicine of acupuncture, but it's a perfect treatment for back pain. I have my own acupuncturist and a masseuse. You might think that's overdoing it, but my job is so stressful that all of that is necessary."

I turned so that I could massage his crotch. I heard him swallow and then felt his breath on my neck. "You are really something," he said. "I like a wom—"

"Be quiet, Grant," I said.

We hadn't been kissing for a good minute before I felt his hand reach under my top and latch on to my breast. "Slow down, Grant."

"Yes, you're right. The French have a saying about taking time to enjoy a meal as well as other pleasures." He kissed me again, slowly and soft. I pressed my body against his. He smelled light and clean like a very expensive perfume, the kind that you sniff at the cosmetic counter but can't afford to buy. I took his hand and led him to the bedroom. After we climbed into bed he said, "I must be dreaming. You're so beautiful." I rolled on top of him and kissed him lightly on the nose. It felt so good to be appreciated. We started kissing again and when he reached for my breast I didn't stop him.

Grant, unfortunately, started talking after we began to make love. "How do you like that, huh? Do you like me, Babysister? Do you like how this feels?" I pulled him down and kissed him so that he'd shut up. He began moving faster and I raised my hips to meet his. For one long moment I didn't have a single thing on my mind, nothing at all except the pleasure I was feeling and the nagging question of why the hell I'd gone so long without sex. But unfortunately Grant started talking again immediately afterward. "That was nice, huh? Did you enjoy yourself? I pride myself on holding out until the woman reaches her climax."

I sat up and started rubbing my forehead. "You know, all of a sudden, I'm just not feeling all that well. I'm so sorry about this. Would you mind letting yourself out? I don't mean to be rude, but I should probably get some rest."

"Leave now? But the night's still young."

I clutched at my stomach and moaned a little.

He patted my back, then reached for his watch. "Wore you out, huh? Yeah, I knew you had a good time. I aim to please."

Oh my Lord, I thought. I could definitely do better than his conceited ass. I fell back on my bed. "You better get going," I said. "I'm feeling a little nauseous."

Sixteen

Babysister,

I miss you. You said you wanted to be friends, but I don't know how we can be friends if we never see each other. I know when a woman says she wants to be friends that that usually means stop calling, but you and me had a good thing (i.e., friendship). I thought we had a good thing. I believe you thought we had a good thing, too. I know you probably have a new man in your life by now (as fine as you are), and it is not my intention to get in the way of that. I am also seeing someone (nothing serious), but would still like to spend time with you. I know you don't like to be pressured, but I don't want to disappear from your life. So this is me, Rob, trying to get you, Babysister, to start seeing me again. Maybe we can watch a movie together sometime.

I miss you, girl.

Sincerely,
Robert C. Woods

ALONG WITH THE letter, Rob had given me two movies he knew I always wanted on video. *She's Gotta Have It* and *Notorious*. He'd left the package with the little girls from downstairs who'd been outside playing hopscotch.

"That football player left this bag for you," LaNeisha said after I got out of my car. It was my day off and I had gone to get my hair done.

"He gave us a dollar to tell you that he said that you should call 'cause you are pretty and he loves you." The girls started giggling.

LaQuita said, "LaKeisha, stop lying. He didn't say that. Tell the truth."

"He said to tell you to call."

I told them thanks and took the bag. LaQuita put her hand on her hip and popped her gum. "You gon' marry him so you won't have to be looking out the window all depressed?"

"I don't think so, but if anything happens, I'll let you all know."

LaNeisha said, "You gonna let us come to the wedding?"

"Yeah," I said. "If I ever get married, all four of you can come."

They started jumping up and down, barrettes flying every which way.

After my night with Grant, seems like I couldn't stop myself from thinking about sex. That's why I was so happy to hear from Rob. At least I wouldn't have to worry about him interviewing me as we made love. I mean, after reading his letter I knew that we would end up in bed and even found myself feeling a little gushy toward him. I held the letter close to my face and thought that it would be nice to wrap my arms around my old friend Rob.

Let's-stay-home-and-relax Rob. Rob of the I'm-fine-with-a-movie-and-some-Chinese-food. The type of man who's as comfortable as your favorite pair of gray sweats. It had been close to four months since I had seen him. I called him right away and explained that I had been busy because of my new job. "I missed you too," I said. "Please come over!"

Three hours later, he was standing in my doorway with a big grin on his face.

"I'm so happy to see you!" I gave him a warm hug then stood back to get a good look at him. "You look great."

"So you like the beard, huh?"

That's what was different. He had grown a nice soft beard. Made you want to rub up against his cheek or stick a pipe in his mouth. Best of all, the beard gave his face some much-needed shape. He had on a black leather jacket that was big enough to cover all those muscles. A black leather hat. Black pants. His clothes were a nice improvement over the usual beige khakis and your basic shirt or sweater.

"And you got a new jacket I see."

"Yeah, I guess I discovered why you like to shop so much. I went in for a new pair of pants one day and came out with four shopping bags' worth of new clothes." He lifted his arms out and turned back and forth.

"So you want something to drink?" I asked.

"Actually, I was wondering if you'd like to go out dancing."

"That sounds like fun." I kept my eyes on him while touching his chest with the tip of my finger. "Since when do you like to go out dancing?"

"I've been up to a lot of things since you last saw me. And if you would have returned my damn calls we could have gone out sooner." He started wagging his finger at me. "Four months is a long time, Babysister."

"Yeah, it's been too long. Thanks for the videos, though."

I felt a growing sense of warmth as I watched him shift on his feet. I felt like I had been away on a very long trip and had just walked into my home and was grateful to be back, grateful to find that nothing had changed. I definitely wanted to make love with him. Sometimes a woman simply wants some nice old-fashioned, I-know-your-every-move sex.

We went to a small bar in Long Beach. The place had a dance floor and a few tables in the back, jukebox and pinball machine. A pool table was near one wall. It was blues night and Rob and I were so into the music we never bothered to sit down. We simply held our drinks in our hands and moved our bodies closer and closer together as the night went on.

After his fourth drink, Rob started asking me where I'd been for the past months as though I'd left the country. "I miiiissed you sooo much, Babysister. Don't ever disappear like that again, okay?" I'd had too much to drink myself and would burst out into a fit of giggles every time he'd beg me not to leave him again. "Babysister . . . Babysister . . . Don't leave me, okay? I can't keep up with you, girl."

We had been dancing for a good three hours when he brushed his new beard against my cheek. "I miiiissed you, girl." He rocked his hip to the left, which forced me to move with him. The horny part of me started screaming, Why we gotta dance so much? When are we gonna make love? I want to make love! I held Rob's face between my hands. Ruth Brown was blasting from the speakers, but I didn't have to raise my voice for him to hear what I had to say. "So you want to go someplace where we can be more comfortable?" He stood straight up, instantly sober, then grabbed my hand, placed our drinks down at the bar, led me through the crowd of people and out through the swinging doors.

We drove north on the 405. It was after two, but you wouldn't have known it by the amount of cars on the freeway. I made Rob stay in the slow lane because I didn't know exactly how drunk he was. He had a calm, satisfied look about him as he drove, like he was feeling all was right in his particular world. He had a good-looking woman in his car, nice clothes, job promotion. Yeah, bro', you are one bad dude. You got your shit together, man. He asked why I was staring when he noticed me checking him out. "No reason," I said with a smile. "So are you seeing anybody?"

"Not really. I've gone out a few times with a woman I met at the mall, but you know me, I'm not into the dating thing all that much."

"Is the woman you met at the mall behind your new look?"

"She works at the store where I usually do my shopping. She talked me into buying the leather jacket and trying out some new colors. I asked her out."

"What's her name?" I was curious as hell.

"Why do you want to know her name?"

"I just want to know."

"You sound jealous."

"I'm not jealous. There's a difference between curiosity and jealousy, you know."

"It's Katie."

"*Katie?* What kind of name is that?"

"What kind of name is Babysister?" He kissed the back of my hand and held it in his lap. "We've been on a few dates. It's nothing serious. Honestly. She's on the mousy side."

"With a name like Katie it's no wonder."

"She's nice. She's into birds. She has two cockatiels: Maximilian and Butter Bird."

"Okay, okay, enough about Bird Woman already." I folded my arms.

"Aw, girl, don't be jealous. It's over. I like an independent woman. A woman who can speak her mind." He tried to lean over to give me a kiss.

"Keep your eyes on the road," I said.

"You know you're the only woman for me." He put his hand on my knee and I stroked it quietly. Next thing you know, the tip of my tongue was running from the bottom of his index finger all the way to the top. I covered his finger with my lips, sucked some then licked his finger again as if it were covered with chocolate icing. "I can't stand this anymore," he said, and started driving faster and faster. I prayed for our lives, but couldn't stop laughing. I unfastened my seat belt when he turned off the freeway and began licking his ear and playing with his soft beard. I didn't stop until we reached my apartment and Rob got out of my car like a military man with a purpose. He opened the door and pulled me out and up, drew me to him and kissed me forcefully. Rob does nothing forcefully so I found myself getting very excited. He picked me up like a bride and walked me up the stairs. "Rob!" I laughed. "Hush," he said, and kissed me on the lips. Once inside, we fell to the couch. As we kissed I unbuckled his belt, unbuttoned and unzipped his pants and found his penis all with one hand. Rob, though, had no success whatsoever, couldn't even unhook my bra. I let out an exasperated "I'll do it," then unfastened the hooks myself. He started kissing me everywhere all at once, my face, my chin, my arms. I wrapped my hand around his erection, guided him as carefully as you can when you're making love on a couch. I was glad he was so familiar. With all the changes I had been through, making love to Rob felt like falling into a bubble bath after a long day at work. He spent the night and we held each other and talked about the past months in soft, quiet voices.

I felt good.

Seventeen

TWO MONTHS AFTER ROB carried me up to my apartment like a military man, Sharice invited us to dinner. She had also invited my father and Darius and Jorge. Malcolm was there, too, of course, acting like Mr. Family Man and welcoming us to his home as though his name was on the mortgage right next to hers.

Daddy had driven along with Rob and me. When we went to pick him up, Rob earned ten bonus points on the spot by giving Daddy's hand a firm shake and saying, "It's nice to meet you, sir." And I'm sure Daddy was almost ready to welcome Rob into the family when Rob commented on how good his beloved Fairmont looked sitting out in the driveway. This would be the same Fairmont Daddy and Momma attempted to drive to their honeymoon. After Momma and Daddy left the reception, all set to drive the Fairmont to San Francisco, the car wouldn't start. Daddy told Rob the story about the Fairmont on the way to Sharice's. "I had to borrow my friend Tate's car, but he could only loan it to us for the weekend, you know, so we drove to Vegas instead. And you know that darn car hasn't given me any trouble since?"

Sharice met us at the door, looking like a vision. She wore a dress she had bought in Africa, one of those big, roomy dresses, dark blue with blue embroidery around the neckline and in the front. I have to admit that while I didn't think that every black person had royal ancestry, from the way she stood at the doorway with her arms stretched out, I thought that her great-great-great-somebody probably had sat on a throne made of gold and had beautiful African warriors at her every command. It wasn't that Rob, Daddy, and me were looking all that shabby. Rob had on his leather jacket. I wore a nice lavender suit. Daddy had on a pair of slacks and the burgundy sweater I'd given him one Christmas.

Malcolm and Prophet met us in the entryway in matching yellow and green dashikis. They stood there with their heads raised looking like they belonged in the sixties and might start raising their fists and shouting about fighting The Man. Malcolm nudged Prophet and Prophet exclaimed, "Greetings my African brothers and my African sister. Welcome to our home! *Habari gani!*"

"That's Swahili," Malcolm said proudly. "We're teaching him the language of the motherland."

Malcolm was pleasant enough when I introduced him to Rob, but as Sharice led Rob and Daddy into the living room, he leaned over and said, "Sharice told me that white-collar brother—that architect—broke up with you. I tried to tell you brothers like that don't like attitude, now didn't I?" He touched the cleft in his chin before pointing at Rob. "So what's wrong with this one here?"

"Nothing's wrong with him. Mind your damn business."

" 'Scuse me for showing some concern."

Sharice poured everyone a drink, put on a CD, lit

incense, and rushed off to the kitchen to finish preparing the food while Malcolm sat on his pampered ass. Darius showed up right before we were about to head to the dining room. He shook everyone's hand and gave Sharice and me kisses on the cheek. He'd brought wine and flowers and was full of energy just like at the restaurant. "I'm so sorry I'm late. You got my message, right? Jorge is so sorry he couldn't make it. It's just too difficult for both of us to get away from Medina's at the same time. I swear, I could stay at that place twenty-four seven and still have things to do. If these flowers look familiar it's because they're from the table in the waiting area. I had to stop by because Vlady had the nerve to threaten to quit again. He's a genius in the kitchen but can be so temperamental." He paused and looked around the living room. "So this is your place, huh? It's lovely."

Sharice took Darius's coat and offered to take Rob, Darius, and my father on a quick tour before we sat down to eat.

Malcolm tapped me on the back after they left. "I know all about that Darius, and that Jorge dude," he whispered. "I didn't want them over, but Sharice had a *fit*. He better not try to come on to me is all I got to say about the subject or I'm going to kick him out."

"Why in the world would you think Darius would want your sorry, lazy ass. Besides, he's in a committed relationship just like you are."

"I don't care what you say, Babysister. That shit ain't natural."

"And what do you think about two women sleeping together, Malcolm?"

"That's different. That's erotic."

"Jesus you can be stupid."

"Hey watch your mouth. Your problem is that you've never learned how to act like a lady."

"Your problem is that you've never learned to act like a human."

Sharice came out then. "Dinner's on, you two. And no arguing tonight. Could you just do that one favor for me, *please?*"

The dining room had been lit with candles. A vase filled with white roses stood in the center of the table along with three tall candles—one red, one green, one black. There were also platters and bowls of food. "It's all vegetarian, but I didn't get too exotic or anything. Spinach salad. Hummus and pita bread. Dolmas. The main course tonight is tofu ravioli. It's one of Malcolm's favorite pasta dishes." Sharice beamed. Malcolm beamed. He hugged her tightly at the waist then pulled Prophet over. It would've been a perfect photo opportunity if any of us had been interested.

The meal was actually pretty good, everyone cleaned their plates and even asked for seconds. Darius, who sat across from Sharice, carried on about her cooking and they fell into a discussion about Sharice's idea to start an upscale vegetarian restaurant.

"You can focus on ethnic foods," Darius said. "Ethnic food is very in. Oh and you'd have to have a killer atmosphere. The restaurant business is thirty percent food, thirty percent atmosphere, twenty percent service, and twenty percent crowd. At least in my humble opinion."

Malcolm, who sat at the head of the table, of course, hadn't been too happy about being shut out of Darius and Sharice's conversation. He would try to put his two cents in about how he had helped Sharice prepare the meal, but they pretty much ignored him and he soon started rolling his eyes and shaking his head at them like they were wasting time over a pipe dream. When she and Darius started talking about what the interior of her restaurant could look like, Malcolm interrupted Darius mid-sentence. "Hey, man, your kind knows all about interior decoration and stuff like that, huh?"

Daddy had been concentrating on his meal, but paused and said, "Your mother knew a lot about interior decorating. Tell Darius about all the things she used to sew."

Darius stared at Malcolm as if he couldn't decide if my brother had purposely been offensive or if he was just plain stupid. "What do you mean by 'your kind'?" Darius didn't take shit. We'd seen him kick out men twice his size whenever they harassed any of the staff.

Sharice poured Darius more water. "He means people in the restaurant business. *Right, Malcolm*?" She glared at him and Malcolm nodded quietly. He then turned to Prophet, who was playing with his fork at the end of the table.

"Hey, Prophet, why don't you recite that poem your mother and I taught you."

"Do I have to?"

"If you want dessert you do."

"What if I don't want dessert?"

We all chuckled.

Rob leaned over and whispered, "He sure is a cute little boy."

"Yeah and I hope living with Malcolm doesn't destroy him."

Malcolm's voice rose. "Recite the poem, Prophet."

Prophet slowly stood. "The sun . . . the sun . . ."

He stared up at the ceiling as if the words of the poem

might be hiding up there somewhere in easy-to-read block letters.

Sharice said, "What about the sun, honey?"

Prophet stood frozen. He had Sharice's brown-green eyes and high forehead, and like Sharice he was usually all smiles and happiness. It was sad to see him standing there like he was nothing more than my brother's showpiece.

"He's not a puppet, Malcolm," I said.

Darius shrugged. "He's probably just nervous. Let's not pressure the boy."

Malcolm picked up his fork and pointed at Darius. "Excuse me, but this is between me and Prophet."

Darius folded his hands together. "In other words, I should probably stick to interior decorating and other subjects familiar to 'my type.'"

Sharice went over to Prophet. "Honey, why don't you go on in your room. You can have some cake later, okay?"

As soon as Prophet was gone I said, "You are such a jerk, Malcolm. You don't treat kids that way."

"What do you know about raising children? You can't even keep a man past a week."

"What does that have to do with anything? Not that what I do is any of your business."

Just then Sharice came back to her seat looking tired and defeated.

"Let me pour you some more wine, honey," Darius said.

"*I'll* pour her some wine." Malcolm grabbed the bottle before Darius could touch it.

We all grew quiet. Sharice muttered something about getting the cake and walked into the kitchen. Malcolm grinned over at me and Rob then and stroked his chin.

"So, Rob, what exactly are your intentions toward my sister?"

Rob held his wineglass to his lips as though it were stuck. He swallowed and looked around the table.

"Leave 'em alone," Daddy said lightly.

"I'm curious. It's not often my little sister brings a real live man around for dinner and everything. Are you two serious?"

Talk about embarrassed. Beneath my brown skin I was as red as the candle on the table. "God, you're nosy. You need to mind your own business."

"It's okay," Rob said, taking my hand. "I have nothing to hide. I love your sister. I feel like we were made for each other. Nothing much more than that."

Sharice came in with the cake and started slicing. "Awww, that's so sweet."

Malcolm started laughing. "You two ain't sleeping together are you? 'Cause I'll have to beat you up if you're not respectful."

Sharice hit Malcolm with a towel she was holding. "Malcolm! Stop teasing them. You know he's just teasing you right, Rob?"

"I don't mind, like I said, I've got nothing to hide."

I smiled as I pulled my hand away. "Can we change the subject please?"

"You two should let me do a reading," Sharice said, slicing into the cake. "What's your sign, Rob?"

"Aquarius."

"Aw, just like Prophet. Aquarians are such good men."

Malcolm looked over at Darius. "So I guess you wouldn't know much about love between a man and a woman."

"I know more about it than I care to," Darius said dryly.

"So you're saying you've been with a woman? 'Cause I always thought you all just never tried it. That's the only thing that makes sense, if you ask me."

"Nobody asked you, Malcolm," Daddy said. "Why don't you help Sharice with the cake."

But it was too late. Darius stood up, tugged at the sleeves of his suit. "Well, Sharice. Thank you for dinner."

"You're leaving?"

He frowned at Malcolm. "I think I'd better."

Sharice shot Malcolm a look that said he had gone too far. "Well at least take some cake with you." She rushed off to the kitchen.

After he said goodbye to Daddy and Rob, I followed Darius out to the door.

"Is he always like that?" he whispered.

"Unfortunately, yes. And I blame myself that Sharice is still with him."

He shook his head. "Your guilt must be enormous."

"It would be except that Sharice is happy with him. And for the life of me I don't know why."

"Well, maybe you should bring him by the restaurant sometime and we'll have Vlady fix him up a nice scampi laced with cyanide. Sorry, I shouldn't talk like that. He is your brother."

"Yeah, well, it's not like I chose him."

Sharice walked up with a slice of cake wrapped in cellophane.

"Are you sure about him?" Darius asked.

"He means well, Darius. He's not at his best in groups. He's really a very nice person."

I let out an odd-sounding cough.

"Well, it's your life, Sharice," he sighed.

When he was gone Sharice said, "I can't believe some of the things that come out of your brother's mouth sometimes."

"Who you telling? Believe it or not. I think your influence has rubbed off. Things could've been a lot worse, trust me."

Later that night, as we lay in bed, Rob held me close to his chest and told me how much he had enjoyed the dinner and how much he liked my family.

I started cracking up.

"What's so funny?" he asked. "I'm serious. Malcolm is an instigator, but I don't think he means any harm. It's nice what he and Sharice have, don't you think? It felt good to be there with you. And Prophet is a great kid." He ran his hand over my hair and was quiet. "Do you want kids Babysister?"

I was silent.

"I was thinking, too, that we should take our relationship a step further. We should deepen our commitment."

"What does that mean?"

"I don't know. Move in together. Get married. Think about our future. A home, kids, family dinners."

I was silent.

"I guess I'm wasting my time if you don't feel the same way." He sat up in bed for a moment then looked down at me. "You do care about me don't you?"

I immediately felt horrible. "Of course I care about you!" I took him in my arms and went on and on about what a kind man he was and how close I felt to him. I even said that I would think about moving in together. I mean, I would have said anything to make him feel better, and I did care about him, after all.

Eighteen

ROB STARTED LEAVING a few of his things around my apartment, proof that he was serious about "furthering our commitment." First there were the white briefs and the red-and-black-flannel pajamas he put in my dresser. He also started coming over four, five nights a week. I never got around to making him a key, but that didn't stop him from treating my place as if it was his second home. I didn't say anything. Part of me liked having him around so I figured I should wait and see. If I waited long enough, who knows? Maybe I'd one day look over at Rob and feel something more than mild attraction and close friendship.

And then this happened.

It was a Tuesday night, my night off, nearly six weeks after Rob and I had the commitment talk in my bedroom. I'd just come back from shopping and was putting groceries away when the phone rang.

"Hello?"

"Babysister?"

"Yeah."

"It's Darren."

Holy fucking shit.

I dropped the can of soup I was holding and watched it roll across the kitchen floor until it hit the refrigerator with a thud. I stared at the phone like I had no idea what a phone was or who the hell was on the other line. And then, as if the phone had given off a shock, I slammed the receiver back in the cradle.

A few seconds passed before it rang again. Soft laughter rippled into my ear. "Don't hang up, okay? I come in peace! Honest."

"Where are you calling from?"

Don't ask me why, after fourteen long months, this was all I could think to say.

"I'm calling from my condo. I'm still here. We both are."

I let the words *we both are* settle in my ear. "I'm going to hang up," I said softly.

"Please, don't. Please. It was hard for me to get up the courage to call. Could you at least give me a minute?"

"What do you want?"

"I wanted to know what you've been up to, that's all. I've been thinking about you. How have you been?"

"Fine."

"I understand you left the bank."

"Yeah."

"So are you at another bank?"

"I'm working at a restaurant called Medina's."

"Medina's, huh? That's a nice place. You like it? You happy?"

"What do you want, Darren?"

"You'll never change, will you? And I hope you never do. Right to the point. That's one of your best qualities, you know. So what do I want? I want to see you, that's what I want."

"Last time I saw you, you wanted nothing to do with me. You were getting *married* remember?"

"Yeah, I know. But we had no business doing what we were doing either." He chuckled some but stopped when I didn't join in. "I'm sorry about all that. But I *would* like to get together. We were good friends. I'd like to hear how things are going for you." He paused briefly. "I'd like to see you, Babysister. What do you say? We could meet for lunch."

What do you say, Babysister? You could meet him for lunch. You could fall in love all over again and then he could screw you over. It'll be fun.

"I don't think so."

"You sure?"

"Yeah," I said. And this time when I hung up the phone, he didn't call back.

I walked straight to the liquor store and bought a pack of cigarettes. When I got home, I poured a glass of wine from a bottle of pinot noir Darius told me I could take after a table sent it back. I sat on my couch with my drink and a cigarette and went over our conversation sentence by sentence. What exactly had he meant when he said we were good friends? Was that supposed to mean I had been nothing more than a good friend while we were together and that's why he'd broken up with me? What had he meant exactly when he said it was hard for him to get up the courage to call? And why does he want to get together all of a sudden?

I was still on the couch when Rob arrived an hour later. I got up to let him in and went back to the couch without saying anything. He looked around at the bags of groceries that still needed to be put away then he lifted the wine bottle from the counter. "A little early don't you think?"

"You haven't moved in yet, Rob."

"What's wrong?"

"Believe me you don't want to know."

"Come on, what is it?"

I made up something about a urinary tract infection, told him I was feeling depressed because I'd been sick on my day off. My lie worked. He kissed me on the forehead and told me he'd put away the groceries and fix dinner.

I reached for the wine.

"Are you sure you should be drinking alcohol if you're sick?"

"Oh, yeah," I said, "fluids are important." And then I leaned back and started thinking about my conversation with Darren again. I started from the beginning with the way he had said, "It's me. Darren." I mean, by the casual tone in his voice, you never would've guessed he had broken my heart.

The next day before work I drove out to Darren's condo. I told myself that if I saw his house I might be able to get a better feel for what his life with Deborah was like. I drove by on a weekday, close to one o'clock, so I was pretty sure he and Deborah would be at work. I parked across the street, two houses away. Both their cars were gone and the blinds closed. Except for the new wind chimes over the porch, you'd never know Deborah had moved in. There were no crosses or fish symbols or signs that said Jesus Saves. The place hadn't really changed at all. I thought about our first date as I stared at the condo and the first time we'd made love and how afterward he buried his nose in my hair. "I could see myself getting addicted to you," he said, and then he wrapped his arms around me and rubbed his cheek against mine.

I lit a cigarette and let my head drop against the steering wheel. Just like that, I started crying as though he had broken up with me only hours before. I don't know how long I sat in my car hunched over my steering wheel, but I sobbed and sobbed until something Lisette told me a few years before came to mind. We were out shopping. She had just tried on a dress and came out of the dressing room unzipped and with the price tag dangling from her wrist. "I was thinking of something while I was putting on this dress," she said. "You have to take care of your self-esteem like it's a baby, you know? Like it's this small six-month-old baby." She studied herself in the mirror, held her stomach in. "Let me tell you something else, Baby-sister. I don't care what a man might say or how he might act, if you're crying more than you're laughing, you need to get your ass as far away from the dog as possible. You know what I'm saying? All you have to do is remember these two things, okay? Crying is bad. Laughing is good. 'Cause the rest of it is all bullshit." At the time I laughed at what she had said, but she was right. When all is said and done, a man should make you feel good.

I wiped my face with the back of my hand, then started my car and turned on the radio. I took a last hit of my cigarette and tossed it toward his condo. "Goodbye, Darren," I said softly, then drove off without looking back.

Two days later when I was preparing coffee for a table, Sharice came up to me with wide eyes and a funny grin on her face. "What's wrong with you?"

"There is one *fine* African warrior sitting at the bar."

"I thought you only had eyes for my crazy brother."

"I do, but this one is gorgeous." She led me out by the elbow.

I stopped dead in my tracks when I saw him. One black boot on the floor, the other propped up against the barstool on his right. A bouquet of pink and yellow daisies in his hand.

I grabbed Sharice's arm.

"Ow!"

"I *know* him," I said.

"You do? Wow!"

"Remember that architect I told you about?"

"*That's* the architect?"

I ducked back into the kitchen. "I gotta get out of here."

"You can't leave!"

She was right. "Do me a favor, Sharice?"

She nodded her head slowly like I might be delirious. "Serve table nine their coffee then go tell him I don't want to see him so he might as well leave."

"Why can't you tell him? Looks to me like he's come back with his tail between his legs."

"Please, Sharice, just do it, okay?"

She came back with the empty coffee tray in one hand and the bouquet of daisies in the other.

"What did he say?"

"He said to give you these flowers and then he got up and left."

"He didn't say anything else?"

"No."

"How did he act?"

"I don't know. He sort of smiled and then got up to leave. What's going on?"

"Nothing. Feel free to keep those flowers, though. I don't want them."

I was jumpy for the rest of the night. Maybe he'd come

back and catch me off guard and then I'd drop whatever I was carrying and make a fool of myself. I didn't understand what was going on at all. What the hell did he want with me? He had dumped me and married Deborah; now it's "We could meet for lunch"? I mean really.

I was unlocking my car in the lot after work when I heard the crunch of gravel behind me.

"Babysister?"

I turned around and there was Darren.

"Why are you following me?"

"I'm sorry," he said. "I can understand why you wouldn't want to talk to me inside. So I thought I'd try to talk to you out here."

He was more handsome than ever, but I wasn't going to let myself be distracted by how good he looked. I tossed my things in my car and stared at him coldly.

"Listen, Babysister. I'm sorry about how things turned out. I'm more sorry than you can imagine. That's why I'm here—why I've been wanting to talk to you. I wanted to apologize."

I thought of one of his favorite books, *Their Eyes Were Watching God*. I had read it twice since I last saw him and wanted to tell him, You know how much Janie loved Tea Cake and how wonderful they made each other feel? That's how it was for me. I loved you like that and you took what we had and threw it away. You made me feel like shit.

I stared at him coolly. "Where's your wife?"

"If it makes you feel any better, I've experienced my share of pain since we last saw each other. It's hard to admit when you've made a mistake, especially when there are other people involved, but I've learned a few things, you know. If you give me a chance, I sure would like to talk to you about everything." He paused and held up his finger. "One time. That's all. After that, it'll be up to you as far as what happens next."

I tried to search his face to see if he was sincere or not and was about to tell him no when he said, "The thing is, I could always talk to you, Babysister. Remember how we used to talk? I miss that. We were good friends. Very good friends."

It felt good to hear him admit that we could talk to each other and were friends—so good I felt myself finally relax.

"Okay. I'm off Tuesday. What time?"

"Six o'clock?"

"Where?"

"How about that Thai place you liked so much, the one off of Wilshire, remember?"

"Yeah, I remember."

"You'll show up, won't you?"

I nodded and got into my car.

"It's nice seeing you again," he said.

"Yeah," I said, my expression strained. "I'm sure it is."

I drove straight home. Rob was sitting in front of my apartment door. "You're late, Babysister. And when are you going to get that key made?" I jumped into his arms so that he had to catch me or fall over. "So what the hell happened at work tonight?" he laughed. "You eat some aphrodisiac on your break?"

We made love up against the living room wall. I thought about Darren the entire time. While Rob kissed me, I imagined myself in the parking lot with Darren. I imagined that instead of driving away, I grabbed his tie and pulled him down into my car so that he fell on top of me with all of his weight. I imagined him kissing my neck and feeling along my inner thighs, lifting my leg so that it reached around his back, slowly pulling off my underwear and touching me one finger at a time.

Darren was talking to a waitress when I walked into the restaurant. He pulled out a chair for me, then asked if it was okay that he had ordered for both of us because he was starving. We didn't talk about much through dinner —his job, my job, the weather. While we went through each boring topic, all I could think was: So what the hell do you want? Why am I here? When he started talking about his new computer I had to interrupt him.

"What do you want, Darren? You could've told me about your new computer over the phone."

"Like I said, it's always right to the point with you."

"We've been sitting here for a while. Besides, you're the one who showed up at my job and begged me to talk to you. I assumed you wanted to talk about more than the weather. Does Deborah know that you're seeing me tonight?"

I felt strange saying her name with Darren sitting right across from me. I hadn't talked about Deborah except when lying to Rob or my family about how we had grown apart since she'd gotten married. Saying *Deborah* in front of Darren made it feel as though her name had become a code word that could unravel the deepest of secrets between Darren and me.

"No, she doesn't. I'm at a meeting."

"You couldn't come up with anything more original?"

"Deborah misses you, you know. She hasn't said it directly, but I can tell. You were like a sister to her."

"This is what you wanted to talk about?"

"No. I wanted to talk about forgiveness. I wanted to

talk about the fact that I was an asshole. I thought I was doing the right thing, but everything happened way too fast."

"I've always had my doubts about the two of you."

"Yeah, I know."

The waitress came with our food then. I told him about Medina's as we ate, how working at the restaurant was a hell of a lot better than working at the bank. For one thing, I liked the people I worked with. I also liked the people who came in to eat. They were interesting and I actually liked talking to most of them. I even told him about everyone who worked there. I can't say that I was surprised that I was talking so much. Darren had always been a good listener and there was no denying the fact that I'd missed talking to him. We also talked about a couple of movies we'd both seen. After we finished, Darren paid and helped me with my coat. When he asked if I'd like to take a walk, I said sure.

We made our way through the area in Westwood with all the shops and movie theaters, then turned onto Wilshire Boulevard. That's when Darren took my hand. "Deborah's the kindest person I've ever met, but that didn't mean I had to marry her."

"I could have told you that."

"Yeah, you tried. Do you miss her?"

"Sometimes. How is she?"

"Not happy. I try to talk to her, but then she starts crying and then I start to feel bad. We go in circles. She's ready for children and I don't even know if I want to be married. I guess I thought I was marrying someone else and she probably thought the same about me. From the outside looking in we're a perfect couple, but neither of us is happy. We're very, very different people. I thought our differences were an asset, but I don't know if you can sustain a marriage on differences. You and me, for instance, could hang out and have fun. With Deborah, everything turns into an argument."

"So what are you going to do?"

"I'm seeing a therapist for starters. I told her about you, as a matter of fact. I told her all about your feisty spirit." He let go of my hand and put his hands in his pockets. "I was happy when I was with you, Babysister. I've *missed* you."

"I've missed you, too," I said, feeling my entire body blush.

And then without any warning, he bent down and kissed me—just like that, as if he couldn't help himself. Afterward we stood grinning at each other, not knowing exactly what to do next. I said something about feeling cold and he gave me a hug. "You *are* cold. Here." He put his coat over my shoulders. "You want to walk some more? Or do you have to go home?"

I began rubbing my hands together. The last thing I wanted to do was say good night. Who knew when I'd see him again. "You want to come over for a drink?"

His mouth dropped, and then that smile, those perfect white teeth. "I'd love to."

"Don't be getting all happy, now. One drink and your ass is going home."

"One drink," he said. "I promise."

I was pouring our wine when Darren noticed a pair of Rob's shoes in front of my stereo.

"Whose are those?"

"My boyfriend's."

"Boyfriend, huh? You guys serious?"

"Not as serious as he thinks."

Darren laughed, then lifted the glass of wine to his lips. I watched as he drank. Actually, I kept my eye on his Adam's apple. Next to his mouth it was always what I went for when we kissed. He turned to say something, but a helicopter flew overhead. We both rolled our eyes, but I found myself feeling embarrassed that I lived in an area where there were police helicopters instead of little cafes and palm trees.

When it was quiet again, he lifted his glass. "Here's to you."

"Yes, indeed."

The phone rang, but I let the machine pick it up.

"Was that him?"

"Probably."

"He's a lucky man."

"Yeah," I said, "so were you." I put my head on his shoulder and began touching his hand as though I were blind: tracing it with my fingers, cradling it. "We can't do anything, you know."

"I know, but that doesn't mean I don't want to. I haven't stopped thinking about you since we broke up. I've tried, but I can't help myself."

I let go of his hand and took my wine over to the window. There was a strong wind and I watched the two trees in front of the apartment building sway. I had wanted to collect my thoughts, but before I knew it, I could feel his breath on the tip of my ear.

"I wanted you that day in the preacher's office, but I was scared."

I kept my eyes on the trees. "What about Deborah?"

"I'll tell her I want out. I wanted to know how you felt."

"I don't know how I feel. I haven't seen you in fourteen

months, Darren. Now here you are talking about getting back together."

"Do you ever think about me?"

"Sometimes."

He began massaging my shoulders. "Relax, okay? Things will work out."

The excuses I came up with had probably been used by every other woman about to sleep with a married man: Deborah wouldn't have to know anything. And I won't see Darren again until he is out of the marriage. Period.

I turned around and smiled. "You're messed up, you know that? It's good you're getting some help."

I felt his finger follow my shoulder to the base of my neck, all the way around my jawline to my lips. "Shhh." We kissed in front of my window until I couldn't stand it any longer and led him to my bedroom. Once there, he went down to his knees and began hugging me at the waist like a man who had just found out his wife was having his baby. "Stand up," I giggled. "No," he said, lifting my blouse, kissing my stomach. "Let me worship you." I dug my fingers into his thick hair, buried my nose in it; ran my hands again and again over his face. His breath felt warm and sweet on my belly. "I missed you so much," he said. I lifted his chin with my finger so he could watch me unbutton my blouse. He reached up and touched my breast with his hand; I felt the other hand under my skirt, his finger moving my panties aside, his finger on my clitoris. My knees went weak and I had to balance myself against his shoulder. He held me by the arms so I wouldn't move and then I felt his mouth, his tongue. I heard myself moaning loudly, but couldn't stop. It wasn't until I came that he moved me to the bed. He'd enter me only to pause for a kiss or hold his face against mine, whisper something in my ear. "I've been thinking about this moment for so long." I'd never been made love to with such care. He didn't move faster until I wrapped my legs tightly around his back and buried my head in that safe, dark space between his neck and shoulders.

Nineteen

THE NEXT AFTERNOON I found Darren in my doorway, twirling his keys with one hand and holding a plastic grocery bag with the other. "I thought I'd make us lunch," he said. "I brought along everything I need to whip up a couple of my famous omelets." It was a little after twelve but I still hadn't dressed. I'd spent most of the morning in bed, in fact, trying to make sense of Darren's surprise return. He was married now, after all, and if Deborah found out we'd slept together—*again*—surely she'd be devastated. Worse, what if the night before had merely been a one-shot deal? How did I know if he'd break my heart—*again*?

He waved a green pepper in front of me. "All natural ingredients. I know how much you love my omelets."

I tightened the belt of my robe and leaned against the door. "What are you doing here on a Wednesday afternoon? Quit your job?"

"I'm on a lunch break," he grinned. "I couldn't stop thinking about you and thought we could hang out. I have an hour before I have to get back. What time do you have to be at Medina's?"

"Five."

"See there, my timing is perfect."

I watched him prepare our omelets on the small counter that separated the kitchen from the living room. He liked to cook as much as my father and moved around the kitchen with the same sense of contentment— whistling, humming to himself, doing four or five things at once. Growing up, I liked sitting in the kitchen to do my homework while Daddy cooked. He and I didn't talk much, but something about sitting at the table surrounded by the smell of red beans boiling in a pot or skillet corn bread baking in the oven made me feel relaxed and safe. I felt the same way watching Darren. At that moment, it didn't matter that he had dumped me or was a married man. How many men come along who make you feel like a girl again, safe in her father's kitchen?

I was quiet as we ate. We both were. We would make small talk only to let the conversation fade, the tension about the future hanging between us like a sign reading CAUTION or DANGER AHEAD. Darren finally broke the silence. "Listen," he said, "I know this situation is awkward, more than awkward, but I'd like to know if you're willing to be with me again, Babysister. I was a fool for breaking up with you, but I've learned from everything that's happened. I've learned that I want you and I'm willing to do anything to prove myself so you'll trust me again. I'm sorry I hurt you."

"You are?" I said, not sure I believed what I was hearing.

"Yeah, baby, of course I am. Breaking up with you was one of the biggest mistakes of my life." He bit his lip then and stared down at the last bit of omelette left on his plate. "I know I don't have any right to ask this, but I need to know if you'll be there for me. Things are going to get difficult. We're going to have to lay low until Deborah and I can reach some kind of agreement. But I'll tell you this: If you take me back I promise to do all I can to get out of the marriage quickly. I don't want you thinking I'm into secret meetings or sneaking around or anything because I'm not into that sort of crap anymore. That's not what I'm about now, but divorces can get ugly and I don't know if it would be worth the hassle if you weren't waiting for me after everything was said and done. I'll need your support in all of this."

I felt as if my body had been tense for months—years —and only now could I let my shoulders drop, let my legs and arms stretch out. He'd finally explain everything to Deborah. He'd tell her our love was too strong to fight, that we didn't want to hurt her, but we were meant to be together. We'd get married. We'd have a real life together.

"What are you smiling about?" he asked.

I moved over so I could sit in his lap. "I'm smiling because of what you just said. I'm smiling because we're together again and we're going to stay together this time. It's me and you from here on out, okay?"

"Okay," he said. "I feel good about this, baby."

"Me, too."

Later, after we said goodbye, I watched him walk to his car from my upstairs window. The four little sisters were downstairs playing double Dutch in their school uniforms, but they froze when they saw him walk out to the curb.

LaNeisha yelled out, "You live here now?" Darren looked over his shoulder. " 'Scuse me?"

"If you move in here," LaQuita said, "you gotta 'bide by our rules. First rule is, you gotta play with us."

LaVita caught on and said: "And the second rule is you gotta buy us something from the ice-cream man every Wednesday and Thursday."

"Okay," Darren said. "Every Wednesday and Thursday. Got it."

"Are you Babysister's new husband?" LaKeisha asked.

It was too late for me to do anything but cover my mouth in embarrassment.

Darren only laughed, though. " 'Fraid not."

LaQuita tossed one of the jump ropes over her shoulder while looking him over. "My momma needs a husband if you don't want Babysister."

Darren started laughing full-out then. I lifted my window all the way up and called down to them, "Why aren't you little busybodies at school?"

"Half day!" they shouted back.

Darren smiled up at me. "It's okay. They were just playing matchmaker." Then he blew me a kiss, sending the girls into a spontaneous squealing frenzy.

I called Rob that night after work and asked if he'd like to meet me at the park near my house on Saturday. "We need to have a talk," I told him. He complained he hadn't seen me in almost a week. Was I trying to avoid him? Didn't I miss him? On our last real date—one where we actually left the apartment, that is—we had gone to a revival theater in Hollywood to see *Psycho* and *The Birds*. That night I remember thinking how lucky I was that Rob was in my life, that I had someone who liked old movies as much as I did and who was such good company.

The little park where we were to meet was about eight blocks away from my apartment. There was more smog than ever that day and the sky was so brown you had to

wonder how it was possible we were all still breathing.
Rob was in an especially good mood and kept telling me
how great I looked, and how much he'd missed me. We
hadn't been at the park too long before he started playing
football with a skinny little boy wearing a T-shirt that
almost went down to his knees. Rob would throw the ball
so that it spiraled smoothly into the boy's arms and then
chase him around the grassy field pretending the boy was
too quick for him to tackle. He played for a good ten
minutes before coming over to the bench where I was
sitting.

"You're going to make someone a great husband and be
a great father someday, Rob."

"Hopefully I'm going to make *you* a great husband and
be a great father to *our* kids someday."

I wished he hadn't said that. It wasn't like I felt good
about what I was about to tell him.

"I don't think that's going to happen," I said.

"Uh-oh." He rubbed his thick fingers against my cheek
as though I were the one who was about to receive the bad
news. "What's wrong, baby?"

"I met someone, Rob."

"You met someone?" There was a hint of laughter in his
voice like he'd just heard a joke.

"Yeah, I met someone else."

He clicked his tongue and the next thing I knew,
he was up on his feet and walking away. I went after him
when I realized he wasn't going to stop. "Don't you think
we should talk about this?"

He kept his gaze straight ahead. "No."

"Rob, come on. We need to talk. Please, don't
ignore me."

"You want to talk? Okay. Let's talk about all the bullshit

you put me through. Let's talk about how sick I am of all your fucking bullshit."

"What bullshit?"

"*What bullshit?* Everything you've put me through! Do you think I'm a fool, is that it?"

"Of course not."

He cracked his neck like a boxer about to go into the ring. "Who is he, Babysister?"

"Someone I met at work."

"Someone you met at work?" He rolled his eyes upward and started shaking his head. "You must think I'm a fool. A chump-ass fool. Well you can have him. I'm through."

"Rob, come on. I didn't mean for this to happen."

"What do you expect from me? How long do you expect me to wait for you?"

"I don't expect you to wait for me, Rob. I've told you that."

"It's always touch-and-go with you. You introduced me to your family, but you act like moving in with me would be the end of the world."

"I don't regret introducing you to my family."

"And now you expect me to wait on you while you fool around with some jackass you met at work? Bullshit." He turned his back and started walking away so I went after him again.

"Where are you going?"

"I'm walking back to my car."

"Well, let me walk with you."

"I want to walk alone. I don't feel like talking anymore."

"Will you call me later at least?"

"No."

I stepped in front of him. "Please, Rob. Let's not end

like this. Let's not end up like those couples who never see each other again."

He looked at me and his eyes softened. Rob would always have it for me. He couldn't help it.

"Okay, I'll call. But not anytime soon. Bye, Babysister." And he put his hands in his front pockets and walked away.

Twenty

DARREN AND I WERE ABLE to see each other at least three times a week. We especially liked to have lunch together because it was convenient for him to get away from the office and allowed for some private time. He'd bring all sorts of take-out food with him: Indian, Ethiopian, large deli sandwiches stuffed with pastrami or roast beef. One afternoon he surprised me by bringing a bottle of wine and a huge basket filled with fruits and cheeses. He brought along a few of his classical CDs as well and we found ourselves on my living room floor lying on one of my mother's quilts in nothing but our underwear, staring up into the ceiling and listening to Chopin. We drove out to Laguna one weekend (he told Deborah he was going to a conference on architecture in the twenty-first century), walked through galleries hand-in-hand, and spent the night in a bed-and-breakfast that overlooked the ocean. We were cool and confident when we were together, talking about our future as though it were a vacation we were planning. I was feeling so happy about the time he was making for us, I didn't pressure him at all about the fact that he was still married. I had no doubt that he would leave Deborah and thought that the best way to show my support would be to be patient and let him handle that problem the way he felt best. The only downside to our relationship—besides the fact that he was married—was that I couldn't talk about him much. Sharice was the only person who knew I was seeing Darren, but to play it safe, I kept our conversations about him short. Daddy knew I was happier, but didn't know why. It would've been nice to tell him that I had met the man I wanted to share my life with.

Work at Medina's didn't change much. The chef created a fall-winter menu and he and Darius held a tasting party. The entire staff was invited. Sharice and I were the only two people there without dates. My jerk of a brother didn't want to go with her so she brought Prophet along—which was a lot better anyway.

About six weeks after my surprise lunch with Darren, I found Darius in the bookkeeper's office, which was next-door to his and about half the size. He was hunched over her desk with his head buried in his arms. Jorge stood behind him, massaging his shoulders.

"What happened?"

"Erica quit," Jorge said.

"Which wouldn't be a problem," Darius added, "if she hadn't quit on the spot and left all the paperwork in such a mess. Look at this!" He lifted bunches and bunches of papers in the air.

Erica was Darius's cousin and handled the bookkeeping at Medina's. I'd usually see her getting ready to leave just as I was coming in. She always had gum in her mouth and a habit of checking her watch every other minute like she was running late for an appointment.

Jorge dug deep into Darius's shoulders. "Baby, please,

you've got to relax. She left this morning. Came in and told us she was leaving. The problem is that the books are a mess, receipts can't be found. She left everything every which way."

"It's entirely my fault," Darius said. "I became too lax this last year. I love the restaurant, you know? I love the food. I love the customers but sometimes I just forget about the backroom stuff: I should've stayed on top of her."

"He's speaking metaphorically of course," Jorge said.

"I told Uncle Travis not to hire her, but did he listen to me?"

"Why did she quit?"

"Who knows?" He picked up a piece of paper and tossed it in the air. "Her excuse is that she's planning a trip to Europe and doesn't want to set a return date. Probably for the best 'cause that girl is a complete flake, not to mention a slob. Look at this!" He held up a piece of yellow paper. "*Paid. January. 52 dollars.* What the hell is that supposed to mean? Who'd she pay? There better not be a penny missing or that girl is going to be in some serious trouble."

"At least you'll know where to find her." I went over and started looking through some of the piles on the desk.

"Everything else is on the computer," Jorge said. "Two months ago she told us she was converting the system—"

"—whatever that means—"

"—and now we can't make heads or tails of what she's done."

"I could kill myself for not checking in with her more, but Uncle Travis said to let her find her own way."

"Well, maybe you should categorize. Say, put purchases here. Move all the payroll stuff over there. If you get some general order going then you can start checking her figures."

"I don't want to start checking figures. I'm horrible at math."

"He really is," Jorge said.

"Give me a problem, Jorge."

"Three twenty-eight times four."

"See, I have no idea."

"Thirteen twelve," I said, "but it's not your fault you couldn't figure out the problem. People haven't been trained to do math in their heads."

Darius moaned.

"I have to get out to the floor in a half hour, but I could get a few categories going for you before then."

"That'd be great, Babysister," Jorge said, clearly relieved. "Darius and I will go out and have a quick drink at the bar. You sure you don't mind?"

"Not at all."

Jorge lifted Darius's limp body from the seat and they went off to have their drink. I made myself comfortable at Erica's desk, then set out to make order of all the confusion she'd left behind—and I'm talking about some serious confusion. I found a stack of time cards in a manila envelope and bills that were due under an old *Ebony* magazine. It's a wonder Medina's hadn't been shut down.

Twenty minutes had passed when Jorge walked in. "How are you doing?"

"Fine." I was pretty proud of the four stacks I had going: receipts, bills, kitchen, staff.

"Can I get you anything?"

"What about my tables?"

"Don't worry about it. I asked Diane to cover for you.

Darius's peace of mind means *my* peace of mind. You sure you don't want anything?"

"Can I take a look at the computer?"

He played with the end of his long black braid then flipped it so that it swung over his shoulder. "Well, as long as everything stays confidential, I guess it won't hurt. Don't let Erica's so-called system put you in a bad mood, though. You sure we can't get you something?"

"Tea would be nice."

"You got it."

The software program that Erica used was far more complicated than it needed to be, but all my years at the bank came in handy and by the time I'd finished my cup of tea, I was finally able to make sense of her madness. It felt good to be working with numbers and money again.

Both Darius and Jorge kissed me on the cheek before I left. I told Darius that things were in no way finished, but at least the next bookkeeper would have an easier time.

The next night, I found Darius in Erica's office again looking as upset as he had the night before.

"So where are last month's figures? I've been looking for the past thirty minutes. I swear, I'm going to kill that girl."

I went over to the computer, moved the mouse around, and clicked. "See. Right here. I couldn't find everything, though." I moved the mouse again and we watched more numbers scroll down the page.

Darius threw up his hands. "Uck! I hate numbers. Hate them. I like words. I was a star student in my English class. You were probably one of those math geniuses, right?"

I laughed. "I don't know about genius, but I probably

got better grades than Erica." I gave him a pat on the back and then turned to leave. I only had five minutes before I was supposed to start work.

"Babysis'," Darius said, "you were my true-life heroine yesterday and I would never take advantage in a million years, but how would you feel about working on the computer again tonight? You can say no of course. You're not obligated in any way, but you're a natural and well we'd really *really* appreciate it."

I loved waitressing, but Darius was my boss, after all. "Sure," I said, "but I missed out on a lot of tips last night and—"

"Oh, don't worry. We'll definitely hook you up for both nights. It will be like the gods of tipping graced your paycheck. So what do you think?"

"Okay," I said. "No problem."

"Really? Terrific!" He shot up from Erica's chair and extended his hand. "Would you like anything? Tea? Mineral water? How about an appetizer?"

"Tea would be fine."

After he left I turned on Erica's portable radio—the only thing she hadn't taken with her—found a classical station, and started right in. I really was curious to see if the figures would balance out. I was the same way with my monthly check statement. I couldn't rest until every last cent was accounted for.

The hours flew by. From time to time Darius would come in to check on me, always with a gift of food: a small piece of fish, a bowl of soup, a slice of cake. Then he'd tiptoe out as though I were performing surgery and needed to concentrate. I finished just before midnight, and while Darius and Jorge sipped at their decaf cappuccinos I explained what I'd done, step by step: the codes, the

logs, the files. When I was through, Darius stood up and
left the room. I looked at Jorge for an explanation but he
only shrugged. A minute later, he was back with his face
lit up and a bottle of champagne in his hand.

"What's that?"

"I wanted to give you something special so you'd know
how grateful I am." He pushed the bottle across the desk.
"Share it with someone you love. Or drink the entire thing
yourself. You deserve it."

They both started applauding. "Speech! Speech!"

"Darius, stop. It was no big deal."

"Well, it was to me. You should be proud of yourself.
You did a good job. Go on and let me hear you say it."

"Say what?"

"That you're proud of yourself."

"Darius . . ."

"Go on."

"I'm proud of myself."

"Good. Now go home and get drunk."

Darren called from his office two days later.

"You're not working tonight, right?"

"No, it's my night off. You know that."

"Got any plans?"

"Mmmm, seeing you would be nice."

"I've got two tickets to August Wilson's *Fences*. It's playing at the Wiltern. How does that sound?"

I'd never heard of August Wilson but told him that I'd
love to go. The last play I'd seen was a production of *The
Wiz* at the Carson Community Center. Deborah and I had
gone one night with my father and Malcolm. Malcolm was
dating the Good Witch of the North at the time and was

able to get us free tickets. Dorothy was played by a woman who looked like she was at least forty. Toto didn't like her at all and kept snapping every time she had to pick him up. He even started to howl during one of her solos. The whole audience cracked up.

Darren arrived at my door wearing a sea-green suit and silk tie. I wore a sage-colored suit with a jacket that fell to my hips and a miniskirt that covered my butt but not much else. When we got to the theater, the lobby was packed, but we walked through the crowd with such ease, you would've thought we were the stars of the play on our way to the stage. We sat in the middle section, ninth row, and while we thumbed through the program I told Darren about the dog in *The Wiz*. He threw back his head and laughed out loud. "That's one of my favorite things about you, Babysister. You're funny as hell. You make me laugh." He took my hand and kissed my palm. "Mmmm . . . Your hands are so soft." He started kissing the tips of my fingers. "Your fingers are as smooth as rose petals," he said. I giggled softly. I knew I was having one of those moments we women dream of. The man of my dreams was kissing my fingers in a beautiful theater. I closed my eyes.

"Oh shit!"

My eyes shot open to see Darren staring over my shoulder as though there was some crazy person waving a gun.

"What? What's wrong?"

"My parents are here," he whispered. He ducked suddenly and waved for me to bend down.

"Your *parents*?" I sat up. "Where? Where are they?"

He grabbed my arm so I bent down again. "Don't let them see you."

"Why not? I doubt if your mother remembers me." That was a lie. She'd remember me all right. I could only imagine what she'd say if she saw us together: "Well, Darren, if it isn't your little friend. What was your name again, sweetheart, Sister Baby? Sister Hussy?"

"It wasn't like the first time we met was all that bad," I said.

"Be serious, Babysister. You know she didn't like you. And whether she liked you or not, the fact of the matter is, I'm here with you and not Deborah."

"Are you sure it's your parents?" I sat up again and I immediately spotted his mother. She and Darren's father were walking arm in arm as they followed the usher to their seats. Her nose was tilted toward the ceiling like there was a bad smell coming up through the floors. She had on a silver dress that sparkled like a disco ball; you wanted to hang her from the ceiling and watch her spin.

"You see them?" Darren was still hunched over in his seat.

"Yeah, I see them."

"Where are they now?"

Darren's father spotted a couple he knew and waved. When the couple saw him, the man put his finger in the air like he was testing the wind and the woman next to him waved her white handkerchief like she was surrendering in a war. His father and mother walked over to the couple and sat down.

"Second row," I whispered, "to our left." Darren's head was practically in my lap. "Well what are you going to do?" I asked. "You can't watch the play from down there."

"Can they see us?"

"No they can't. Besides, they're talking to their friends."

Darren peeked over the shoulders of the people in front of us. "Oh *shit*. My uncle Peter and aunt Ezinda are with them."

"So?"

"So my aunt Ezinda is crazy."

"And so is your mother."

"We're going to have to leave."

"Leave?"

"You're not going to be comfortable watching the play with them here, are you?"

"I'll be fine. They're not going to see us, Darren. They're going to be watching the play."

"They could turn around any second. And what about intermission?"

"Maybe we can just move to the balcony."

"It's too risky. Can you imagine the story I'd have to come up with if they saw me here with *you*?"

"Yeah, the story could go something like, I'm leaving Deborah because I'm with Babysister now. The end."

"I thought you said I had your support? Listen, we'll come back another night, okay? Your next night off. I promise. We can't risk my family seeing us together like this. Not yet anyway."

When the lights went down, Darren grabbed my hand. "I'm sorry, sweetheart. I'll make it up to you. Come on." He gave me a quick conciliatory kiss and we slunk our way out of the theater. I had managed to hear the first line of the play right before we stepped into the lobby. "Troy," the actor yelled, "you ought to stop that lying!" I laughed to myself when I heard it.

I didn't say a word to Darren as we walked to the car. I quietly listened as he begged me to forgive him. I listened as he offered to take me to see a different play that very night. I listened as he explained how difficult it was for him to tell Deborah everything. I listened as he went on about how hard it was for him not to hold me in his arms every night. And when he finally stopped talking I looked him straight in the eye.

"I won't be second best this time and I won't be hurt again. If you really want me in your life, you need to act like it. When we got back together you said you weren't into sneaking around anymore but that's all we've been doing."

"You're right, Babysister. You're absolutely right. What I should do is walk right back into that theater and tell my parents we're together." He got out of the car then, his jaw set with determination.

Suddenly he became my Darren again, not the spineless man I had seen only minutes ago. I knew I didn't want him bursting into the theater to prove his love. I wanted to be reintroduced to his mother after he had left Deborah.

"Come back, Darren," I said. "Let's just go out for a drink or something."

"Are you sure?"

"Yes."

"You're too good for me, Babysister."

"I know," I said. "So why don't you stop acting crazy, baby, and take me somewhere else? And it better be nice. Very nice."

Over the years, I've known many women who've dated married men and have always thought that most of them needed their heads examined. Seems to me they'd fall for any tired excuse the man came up with. I've heard so many lame explanations it's not even funny:

"I know he's going to leave her, but he's afraid that she'll get full custody of their four boys."

"I should just give him an ultimatum: me or her. I mean it's been four years now!"

"He's seeing another lawyer. I have a good feeling about this one. He'll be able to settle on *his* terms and we'll finally move in together."

"He says he can't leave her because he's Catholic."

"He says he can't leave her because he's born again."

"He says he can't leave her because she'll keep the dog."

"He says he can't leave her because she'll have a breakdown."

Up until our night at the theater, I hadn't really acknowledged that I was one of *them,* one of those women who was *having an affair with a married man.* I simply felt that Darren needed to get Deborah out of his life for good, but when *hadn't* he needed to get rid of Deborah?

Even still, I had no doubt he would leave her. I mean, I'd watched him make a vow before God to stay faithful to Deborah and he *still* came back to me. Good or bad, we were connected.

To make up for our ruined evening, on my next night off, Darren showed up at my apartment with front-row tickets to the August Wilson play. And not only that, but we had dinner at Spago's then spent the night at a hotel in Malibu that overlooked the beach. Before we went to sleep he held me in his arms and apologized.

"I'm sorry, Babysister. I swear to you that I'm going to tell her. And you know why?"

"Because if you don't I'm going to kill you?"

"No, I'm going to tell her because I love you, Babysister. I love you with all my heart."

I felt like I'd spent my entire life waiting to hear those words. And because he had waited so long to say them I knew he meant it. I turned into his chest because I.didn't want him to see the tears in my eyes. But it was too late. I cried like a baby.

Twenty-One

THE NEXT MORNING I FOUND a message on my answering machine from Darius. He wanted me to come in an hour early because he had something "special" he wanted to discuss. I immediately assumed I had screwed up all the accounts the previous week and was going to get my ass fired. But when I walked into their office at three that afternoon, he and Jorge were all smiles.

"Darius and I are pretty knocked out by all the work you've done for us," Jorge said. "And, well, we want to know if you'd like to have Erica's job. That will mean a substantial raise, of course, and full benefits."

"We've already cleared it with my uncle," Darius said. "And I know I can get you more bookkeeping work at other restaurants. I mean, after everything is organized here, it's really not a full-time job, and Jorge and I want you to make *beaucoup* bucks."

"But everything is up to you, of course," Jorge added. "We're not trying to force you into anything."

The first thing that came into my head was a picture of me going from restaurant to restaurant and making a mess of everyone's books. What made them think I could be a bookkeeper? "I don't know. . . ."

Darius rolled his eyes. "Oh please. Why are you so worried? You're a mathematical genius."

"Look how you straightened out the mess here," Jorge said. "That was probably the most difficult job you'll face."

I felt anxious about the idea but excited as well. Very excited. I couldn't believe Darius and Jorge would trust me as they did. So many questions had begun to run through my head, but the biggest one was this: What did I have to lose?

"So what do you think, Babysis'?"

"Well, if things don't work out, can I still wait tables here?"

Darius threw up his hands. "Oh, honey, please! Are you kidding? Things are going to work out. Listen. Repeat after me."

"Darius, come on."

"I'm serious. I will make an excellent bookkeeper. Say it."

"I will make an excellent bookkeeper."

"Okay. So do you want the job?"

"We know you can handle this, Babysister," Jorge said. "You get Erica's luxurious office."

"I'll have an office?"

"Of course you will. More than one office really. If you get as much business as I think you will, you'll be driving out to different restaurants to do your work and there'll be a place for you in each one. It'll be the beginning of your very own business."

Damn. My luck had truly turned around: Darren told me he loved me—and now this. I pictured myself as one of those women who came home and threw her briefcase on the couch and complained about all the thinking and planning she had to do all day, but who loved every minute of her job, loved the rush she got from all her *responsibilities*.

I walked over to them and gave them both long, warm hugs. "Thank you so much," I said. "Looks like you've hired a new bookkeeper."

I called Darren right after I accepted the job. I'll admit that he was more surprised than I would've thought.

"I had no idea you were good with numbers."

"Well, I've been told that I am, but I never thought I'd be trusted with people's money like this."

"And you straightened out all their books by yourself, huh?"

"I didn't think it was a big deal at the time. I certainly didn't think I'd get offered Erica's job."

"Yeah, but are you sure you can handle more than one restaurant?"

"I hope so," I said. "They told me I could go back to waiting tables if it doesn't work out."

"Well, that's good. It's always best to have something to fall back on."

I won't deny that his words stung, but I let them slide because I never saw myself as a bookkeeper, and figured I couldn't expect him to.

I don't know if it's possible to fall in love with a job, but that's sure as hell how it felt. I loved my work so much I'd sometimes close my office door and jump and dance until I had to catch my breath. And for those first few weeks, I'd refer to my office as much as I could. "Oh, I'll be in my office if you want me." "Oh, tell her she can reach me in my office." I had the walls painted a soft peach color and put up a huge poster of this fierce-looking African woman staring over her shoulder like she was ready to cuss someone out.

I soon learned that I was basically responsible for making sure everything was on the up and up. I checked the chef's purchases against the monthly budget, handled the payroll, even stayed on top of Darius as far as his spending habits. "You can't buy a three-thousand-dollar painting, Darius. We're not a gallery!"

In my second week on the job, Darius handed me a business card for Basil's, a restaurant in Century City. It was bigger than Medina's and slightly cheaper. There was a man's name scribbled on the back. "Call this guy," Darius said. "His bookkeeper just joined the Hari Krishnas —no I'm not joking. Don't laugh. He's desperate and I already told him about you." By the end of the second month, I had three clients in addition to Medina's and was making the same money as I had waitressing.

I soon started a new schedule, which meant going to work at eight in the morning and getting home at six or seven instead of after eleven. With my nights free, I became impatient with the fact that I couldn't see Darren when I wanted to. I mean, yes, he and I were having wonderful times together, but the man still couldn't spend an entire night with me at home. Usually I'd wake at one a.m. to feel his hand on my bare back: "I have to go, sweetheart." I'd open my eyes and see him standing over me, fully dressed, checking his watch or straightening his shirt. I'd tell him how ridiculous I thought his leaving was, only to hear a variation on one of two lines: I need a way to break this to Deborah so she's not completely crushed. Or: This is tearing me apart too, you know. I need your support. And what's worse is that in the end, I'd believe him. He'd touch me or look at me in a certain way and I'd be as gullible as Rob. He could have told me that he was the king sultan of Alibaba and that he planned to marry me and make me his queen and all I would have said was Whatever you say is fine with me.

I was at my most frustrated while waiting for him one night at a restaurant off of Melrose Avenue. One of those places packed with hip young white couples who own cappuccino makers and pasta machines and pay a lot of money for new clothes that look secondhand. The walls of the place were painted lime green and decorated with all kinds of painted car parts. The table and chairs were made from metal, but at the same time every table had a delicate bouquet of lavender or red tulips. I didn't like the place at all and it certainly didn't help matters that Darren was over forty minutes late. Thing is, I was more pissed off at myself than him. I knew if he had been any other man I would have shown some dignity—given him a polite fifteen minutes, and gone home.

I was finishing my gin and tonic when he finally walked through the door—superstar that he was—a leather trenchcoat draped over his arm, suit, tie. Everyone held their breath. He was making his way toward me when a lanky woman grabbed his arm as he was walking past her table. She had on a mauve-colored pantsuit and was about my color with long black hair cut close to her narrow head. She was as skinny as Sharice with large even teeth and thick cheeks that stuck out of her thin face like lumps. Darren nodded politely while she talked, then said something that made her smile. I would've been jealous if the woman hadn't looked so much like a horse, but Darren didn't seem all that interested anyway and looked as if he was doing his best to cut the conversation short.

"Thank God you're still here," he said after sitting down. "I'm so sorry."

He looked both worried and apologetic. When he leaned forward to kiss me, I put up my hand before he got too close.

"Come on, Babysister. My meeting ran late. I'm sorry." He touched the side of my face, but I kept my eyes straight ahead. "I can only be away for a few hours tonight, baby, you want to spend the little time we have fighting?"

"Who was the woman?"

"She works in the same building as me. I think she's in advertising or something. She's a chattermouth."

"She looks like a horse," I said.

He shook his head, then placed a small white box on the table. "Hey, look what I bought you today," he said, sugarcoating his voice. "Why don't you open it?" When I didn't budge, he slowly lifted the lid of the box as if something might jump out at us. It was a silver bracelet, heavy enough for me to wonder how much it cost. "This bracelet was made in Thailand. It's to remind you of our first date at the Thai restaurant and all the dates we'll share in the future. May I put it on?"

One part of me thought that I was surely being played for a fool. How dare he show up forty minutes late and expect me to fall in his arms because he bought me a bracelet. When was he going to leave Deborah? I thought. I should ask him *that*. The other part of me was thinking how special he made me feel; how thoughtful he was; how he was always sending me flowers and cards.

I felt the hairs from his wrist brush against my skin as he helped me put the bracelet on, then felt his breath next to my ear: "I feel foolish saying this considering the situation I'm in, but while I was buying this bracelet, I imagined what it would feel like to buy you an engagement ring someday."

"Really?"

"Yeah. Will you forgive me for being late?"

I didn't have a choice. I wanted more than anything to give him that chance to buy me a ring. I'd forgive him again and again if it meant that we'd end up as husband and wife. "Of course I forgive you," I said. "I promised that I'd be here for you, Darren, and I meant it. I love you." I raised my arm to have a better look at my bracelet. One day, I thought, I'll be looking at a diamond engagement ring instead.

We were well into eating our dinner when a man with a neatly trimmed goatee and expensive glasses came over and tapped the side of Darren's arm. Everything about the man—from his haircut, to his tailored suit, to his manicured nails, said that he spent a lot of money on trying to look good. "Wilson? What are you doing here, man?"

Darren stood and greeted his friend with a handshake and half a hug. I waited to see if he was going to introduce me. I was curious as hell. I mean, besides good old Thorton and Richard from the preacher's office, I had never met any of Darren's friends. I cleared my throat.

The man peered over Darren's shoulder. "And who do we have here, Wilson? You're always surrounded by the beautiful ladies, aren't you?"

"Babysister's an old friend. Babysister, this is Kevin."

"Babysister, huh? I take it you're not the oldest in the family." Ha ha. "Kevin Hamilton. Nice to meet you."

He took the opportunity to peek down my blouse as we shook hands, even had the nerve to wink when he saw that I knew what he was up to. Where did Darren meet these people? But still, I was curious enough to touch the seat on my left and to ask if he'd like to join us.

"Sure, sure. I'm waiting on a business associate. You don't mind do you Wilson?"

"No have a seat." Darren shot me a look as he sat down. "We were just about finished here anyway."

"So what do you do, Kevin?" I asked. "Are you an architect?"

"No, financial planner. Mutual funds, investments, taxes. Do you have a portfolio? The best thing a person can do for himself is get his financial house in order. You should let me create a portfolio for you."

Normally, I would've told him what was what. I get tired of men assuming women don't know anything about money, but I chose to ignore his comment. "So how did you and Darren meet?"

"I'm lucky enough to get hold of Darren's taxes every year. We discovered our mutual love for skiing and have been friends ever since." He hit Darren's back. "Right, man?"

The waiter came by and Kevin ordered a double martini with a twist and a plate of crabcakes. "I love crabcakes. This place makes a dynamite crabcake." He glanced at my breasts then, like they were ski slopes he'd like to explore. He reminded me of those black Republicans you see on TV during the conventions who stand around like brown spots in a blur of white. You just want to shake your head at them in disbelief.

"Darren's my numero uno skiing partner. Have you told Little Sister here about our last trip? Oh, you should have seen this man on the Double Diamond. You like to ski?"

"I don't think so. I've never tried."

"Well, you can learn. Once you learn, I *promise*, you'll be hooked. Darren's wife just learned how and she loves it."

I pictured Deborah in one of those tight ski outfits flying down some mountain with the wind in her hair, Darren rushing to her side every time she fell. When had Darren taken her skiing? Was it before we had gotten back together? Later?

"Have you met this man's wife?"

I looked over at Darren, but he was suddenly interested in the last pieces of sea bass on his plate.

"No, I haven't met her yet."

"Beautiful woman. Beautiful. This man knows how to attract the beautiful females. You included of course."

"Thank you. Sounds like you all go skiing often."

"Well, actually, me and . . ."

"Don't forget Tammy," Darren said.

"I was going to mention her, man. Tammy is my girl-friend. No ring on my finger yet, though." He shoved a whole crabcake in his mouth and gave me a wink. "Deborah and Tammy get along. They'll usually drag us to a play or something. Did you tell her about the ballet we saw a couple of weeks ago? What *was* that mess? The dancers all had on suits and ties, for christsake. And they hardly did any jumps! I could've been on that stage with them for all their so-called talent. I blame Tammy for convincing me to buy those tickets. I paid close to a hundred dollars a pop for that mess."

Darren said, "It wasn't ballet, Kevin, it was a particular type of modern dance. There's a difference."

I felt suddenly like I was sitting next to two men with nothing to worry about but what to do with their money and free time. I'd never seen two brothers arguing about ballet before.

Kevin wiped grease and crumbs from his goatee with his napkin and grinned over at me. "Whatever it was, it was a mess. Give me Alvin Ailey any day."

I turned to Darren with a bright phony smile on my face. "Deborah must feel very lucky to have a husband who spends so much time with her."

"Oh yeah," Kevin said, "they got a good thing."

I glared at Darren, but kept my voice sweet. "I really can't wait to meet your wife, she must be a very special woman."

Kevin's associate walked up to the table just then and Kevin introduced us before standing. He said goodbye to Darren then had the nerve to kiss the back of my hand with a deep bow as though someone had told him he was a black knight and not a financial planner. "It was a pleasure meeting you," he said. We watched as he and his associate made their way to a table near the front of the restaurant.

"You realize Kevin was flirting with you, don't you?" Darren said.

"No kidding." I folded my arms and fell back against my trendy metal chair. "You told me you and Deborah barely speak to each other, but it sounds to me like you guys are having a grand old time together."

"Kevin exaggerates. If you knew him any better you'd know not to believe everything that comes out of his mouth."

"If you knew *me* any better you'd know I'm getting sick of this, Darren. You're off going to the ballet and shit and

I'm sitting around waiting for you like a fool. How long do you expect me to put up with this crap?"

"Could you lower your voice please?"

"I don't want to lower my voice!"

He sat up in his chair and played with his tie like he needed to look presentable for our argument, then peeked over at Kevin's table. When he saw that they were too busy whooping it up over mutual funds to notice, he took my hand in his and held it there at the table as though we had nothing to hide. "Listen to me, Babysister. Listen."

I waited.

"I know I need to tell Deborah. I know I need to put an end to that situation, but please be patient a little longer, baby. I fell into marrying Deborah because I thought she gave me what I wanted, but *you* are what I want. You have to believe that. All Deborah offered was a false sense of security, but you bring joy into my life. Kevin doesn't see all the fighting that goes on between me and Deborah when no one's around. That ski trip was months ago, before you and me were even together. Kevin doesn't know how separate Deborah and I are, no one does. But you know what's going on. You know what it's like when *we're* together. You know when we're together we create magic. We have something special, Babysister." He brought my hand to his cheek and held it there. When he finally looked up I saw there were tears pooling in his eyes. "I couldn't stand to lose you right now, Babysister. It would crush me."

I watched as two tears fell. One from each eye.

You know when Dorothy throws that pail of water on the Wicked Witch of the West and the witch melts right into the floor? Well, that was me. I melted on the spot, turned into a harmless puddle of water at Darren's feet.

Two nights later he was at my door. I was in my pajamas watching *Love Affair* and eating a bowl of popcorn. He looked disheveled and tired as if he had been out all night wandering the streets of L.A., and who knows, maybe he had, because when I asked what happened, all he said was, "I'd like to stay here tonight, if you'll have me. Deborah and I had a fight. I say, let her think what she wants to think. I told her I was going out and that was that." Then he said he didn't want to talk about it, which was fine with me. I could care less about the details. The fact that he was staying with me for the night was all I needed to hear. There was nothing better than waking up next to him. How much longer could his marriage last if he was staying out all night? Surely Deborah would catch on to the fact that there were only so many conferences he could be going to. Surely she'd catch on to the fact that he had met someone.

I had breakfast made for him when he woke up the next day: pancakes made from scratch, bacon, eggs. I even ironed his clothes so they'd still look neat. He pulled me down onto his lap when he saw what I had done. "You're a sweetheart, you know that?"

"Yeah, I know."

He played with the button on my pajama top. "I want to do something special for you because of how patient you've been."

I touched my nose to his. "All you have to do is leave Deborah and we'll consider it even."

"I will, baby, I will."

Twenty-Two

TEN DAYS AFTER Darren had spent the night, *Lisette* of all people helped prove that his marriage was indeed coming to a once-and-for-all final end. She showed up at my apartment the following Saturday morning. I was cleaning my bathroom and met her at the door with rubber gloves on my hands and a scarf over my head. She walked into my apartment rambling about the meaning of sisterhood, not bothering at all to bring up our last argument—except to say that she had been angry that I could do something so mean, but Hey, she needed to talk and Oooh, she needed a new pair of dress shoes and how would I feel about running over to Fox Hills Mall? I realized how much I'd missed her as I listened to her ramble and gave her a hug as she helped herself to a soda.

"You're crazy," I said.

"No," she said smiling. "You're crazy. Crazy as they come."

We drove to the mall in Lisette's sky-blue VW Rabbit which had been buried beneath feminist bumper stickers over the years: *A Woman Without a Man Is Like a Fish Without a Bicycle*; *I Believe You, Anita Hill*; *The Goddess Is*

Alive and Magic Is Afoot. You get the picture. Thing is, there was no way you could read them all unless the car was parked or stuck in traffic and that's because Lisette drove like a madwoman. She was one of those people who let out all her aggression when she was behind the wheel. She'd put on a tape, start singing along, and off she went, weaving in and out of traffic, giving people the finger, honking her horn at anyone who had the nerve to wait longer than a second after the light turned green. All you could do was fasten your seat belt and join in when she made the sign of the cross before starting the engine.

Once we were at the mall, Lisette headed to the first shoe store she saw. "Oooh, Babysister, look at these. Aren't they beautiful?" She held up a pair of purple velvet pumps with a mile-high heel.

Yeah, Lisette was a diehard feminist, but the girl liked her high heels and tight clothes. The tighter, the brighter, the better.

"Oooh, I want to try on these." She called over a saleswoman, a tiny woman with hair to her butt, and started talking and laughing in Spanish as if they were old friends.

The first pair was a size too small, but that didn't stop Lisette from hobbling around in them anyway.

"They're too small, Lisette," I said.

"No, I don't think so. Besides, I have a stretcher at home." Only when the saleswoman said something to her in Spanish did Lisette pull them off. "Well, okay, since everyone is ganging up on me. I'll try a seven and a half . . . and maybe an eight."

She sat down next to me while the saleswoman went to

get the other sizes. "Babysister." She moved in close to my face, lips puckering. "They are all dogs. Every one. I cannot get myself to believe otherwise and now Deborah is learning the truth the hard way." She mumbled something in Spanish and started running her hands through all the tight curls on her head as if they were giving her a headache.

"What are you talking about, Lisette?"

She pointed to the scar on her face. "When this happened here, I lost hope in men. But let me tell you, I see a few of my friends meet nice good-looking men and I think all men can't be that bad. I even date one or two who seem okay—they don't want to make me give up my fucking freedom, but they're okay."

"Lisette—"

"Hold on. Hold on. Let me try on my shoes."

After the saleswoman came out and helped her with the new pair of heels, Lisette started dancing around the shoe store in her tight jeans and velvet pumps like a salsa dancer, singing in Spanish and admiring her feet. She went on and on in Spanish and English about how cute the shoes were. "I'll take these," she said, but as soon as the words were out of her mouth, another pair caught her eye. They were a homely-looking pair too, like the shoes flamenco dancers wear. "Oooh, these are cute. Let me see them in a *seven*." The saleswoman shook her head then disappeared into the back of the store.

She sat down again. "So I see one of my best friends, one of the nicest people I know, fall in love and have this big fucking Cinderella wedding, okay? And then I hear how her Prince Charming is never around and stops paying her any attention at all, and I watch with these two eyes as my friend falls to pieces. The cruelty of men to women has gone on for centuries, but sometimes we get it in our heads that we deserve it. We lose all sense of our divine power and we expect to be treated like shit. Deborah has lost all sense of her gifts. Her eyes are red and bloodshot; she's got no color. Let me tell you, Babysister, I have lost hope all over again. Men are dogs, you know what I'm saying? I'm sorry, but they are."

My voice might have been full of concern, but inside I was smiling. Darren was finally going to be mine, all mine.

"So you're saying Deborah and Darren aren't doing well? Is Deborah unhappy or something?"

Of course the saleswoman would have to show up right then. Talk about ready to scream. The sevens didn't fit, surprise surprise, but the saleswoman had been smart enough to bring out a pair of eights. Lisette put them on and walked around and around. "What do you think, Babysister? They look good, huh?"

"Yeah, Lisette, they look fine."

"Okay. I'll take both pairs, *por favor*."

I somehow managed to remain patient until Lisette bought her shoes and I was able to lead her over to the fountain out in the mall so she could concentrate on telling me about Deborah and Darren. "So what's going on Lisette? You're not making any sense."

"I knew when I saw what happened with you and him that that man could not be trusted, but I hoped for Deborah's sake that that bastard would appreciate her. But now she calls me crying all the time. And I'm like, *Why don't you leave his fucking ass? Leave his ass at the door!* But she keeps saying how God is going to help her save her marriage. Like God has anything to do with this. This is about *her* and how she can do better than that dog, okay? What does she think? God is going to strike him with lightning 'cause he's an asshole? Half the planet would be dead by now. But she thinks she made a vow she can't break." She twirled her finger in the air. "You know death do us part and all that mess."

"What exactly is he doing, Lisette?"

"He's never home. Never. He likes to show her off to his la-la rich friends and have her give la-la dinner parties and have her on his arm so he'll look like a la-la hot shit. But when they're alone, all they do is fight. She wants him around the house more, but he's out all the time. You know what I call him? I call him Mr. Manipulative. I talk to her on the phone and I say, so how's Mr. Manipulative doing? He's out almost all the time and then he makes her feel like *she's* doing something wrong."

"Do you think he's seeing someone else?"

"Of course he's seeing someone else! What you think, he's out late at night 'cause he's going to mass?"

"And there's no way you can convince her to leave, huh? You can't try any harder? Sometimes all Deborah needs is an extra push."

She shook her head. "I've tried. She says that deep down inside he's a good man. I say deep down inside a dog is a dog. My only hope is that he leaves her first so she's able to get him out of her system.

"Not all men are dogs, Lisette. I'm not trying to defend him, but it takes two people to make a marriage work."

Lisette looked at me and rolled her eyes. "I don't know. What do I know? I needed to talk about it, though. I get so mad sometimes and no one knows her like you and me. And you know what else I need? I need me some panty hose. Let's go look at some panty hose. I like the ones with the seams down the back, don't you?"

At the top of the escalator I said, "I'd help out with Deborah, but I'm sure I'm the last person she wants to hear from."

"She doesn't speak bad of you anymore, but you're probably right. She'd sooner forgive that dog over and over. But who knows, Babysister? Maybe she'll come around and dump him. How much bad treatment can she take? The dog doesn't even come home some nights. Stays out catching filthy diseases. I told her to start making him use a condom."

"Let's hope that the marriage ends soon."

"It better or I'm going to have to go kidnap her and deprogram her like they do those cult people." She tapped my stomach lightly. "You like Cuban food? We should go get some lunch after I buy my panty hose. I'm hungry. I know a good Cuban restaurant on Sepulveda. I'm craving some black beans." She studied me then like I had suddenly appeared from nowhere. "You look good, woman. You look happy. Life treating you well or something? You finally learn you don't need a man to make you happy?"

"Oh you know me Lisette. I like to have a man in my life, but that doesn't mean I'm man crazy." And then I went on to tell her about Medina's and how I got promoted and was starting to build my own bookkeeping business.

"I always knew you had the brains girl. Always. I saw it at the bank. I saw how quick you were with everything. You got looks, but you also have brains. And let me tell you, when your tits start falling and your ass gets heavy, you're going to be glad you learned how to rely on your smarts, you know. We aren't our bodies." And then she wrapped her arm in mine and started telling me about the history of high heels and how they were created as torture devices, but they made her legs look good so what can you do?

Twenty-Three

DARIUS STAYED TRUE to his word about helping me find clients. He had a large network of friends and word of mouth got around so fast, I was soon able to pick and choose who I wanted to work with. I bought a cellular phone and had business cards made up. I was feeling just too proud of myself. Like I said, not finishing college was one of my biggest regrets so I was grateful that I had managed to find a career for myself. Lisette and I started hanging out again. She loved gossiping about Deborah and Darren so I had a perfect way to spy without having to do any work.

Things started happening for Sharice as well. She and Darius began to meet seriously about starting a vegetarian restaurant, and as a result she began checking out whatever potential competition she could locate within a radius of fifty miles. One afternoon she called to see if I wanted to have dinner with her at a place called Winter Sun in Sherman Oaks. She wanted to car-pool, of course, so I told her I'd pick her up at six.

Malcolm met me at the door in his UPS uniform. "I'll say. Look what the cat dragged in."

"So Sharice hasn't kicked you out yet, huh?" I hadn't seen Malcolm since the night of the dinner party. I had to wonder if he fell from the face of the Earth if I'd miss him or not.

"On the contrary. She's the first woman to really appreciate what I'm about."

"If Sharice knew what you were about, you wouldn't be here right now."

"With an attitude like that, I don't see why I should let you in at all."

I pushed my way past him. "Would you let her know I'm here, please?"

"She went to the store, but she should be back any minute."

Prophet was playing the piano. As soon as he saw me he started in with the Swahili. "Yeah, yeah," I said. "You can save all the African stuff for someone else." I gave him a kiss on the top of his forehead. "You can be real with Babysister, Prophet. Why don't you start giving me a high five or something." We hit our hands together and he started playing the piano again. Somewhere buried beneath those clashing notes was a song, but you'd have to dig pretty deep to find it.

Malcolm shifted on his feet a little. "Prophet, why don't you go on out back. You can worry about practicing later."

Prophet gave me a high five on his way out and just about the sweetest hug ever.

When he was gone, I made myself comfortable on the couch. Malcolm sat down on the piano bench. "I don't appreciate you teaching Prophet high fives and all that mess, Babysister. I don't want him learning to be a hoodlum. I'm trying to raise him to be a respectable young black man."

"Fine, but even respectable young black men need to have fun once in a while."

We sat for a while trying simultaneously to make small talk while avoiding eye contact. I couldn't remember the last time we were alone in the same house. It felt strange that Daddy or Sharice weren't around. I had to wonder if we could make it until Sharice came home without killing each other.

"So how's that new job of yours? Made any major mistakes yet?"

"As a matter of fact, I'm doing very well. I'm handling books for more than one restaurant, thank you very much."

"Well at least we know you didn't get the promotion 'cause you slept with your boss." He gave his thigh a good slap and started laughing.

"You are so stupid."

"So do you like it or are you gonna quit like you did at the bank?"

"I won't be quitting anytime soon. I love it."

"Well, don't become one of those ball-bustin' sisters with nothin' to do but complain about us hardworking brothers."

I shook my weary head. "Did Sharice say exactly when she'd be back?"

"She should be here any minute. Now *she's* someone I worry about. That Darius dude has been feeding her head with pipe dreams, and if this restaurant idea doesn't work, she's going to be hurt, big time. And who's going to have to help her through it?"

"I don't know. Who?"

"*Me*, that's who. I don't want to see her get hurt." He

licked his lips and unbuttoned the top button of his uniform. "Speaking of getting hurt, Sharice told me you dumped my man Rob and started seeing that white-collar dude again. What's up with that? Rob not good enough for you?"

"Since when do you care about Rob? You only met him once."

"I liked Rob. He was a little on the quiet side, but he was cool. This other brother is an architect right?"

"Yeah."

"And didn't Deborah marry an architect?"

I crossed my legs and straightened out the jacket I was wearing. "What's with all the questions?"

"I'd never even heard of black architects. Now Deborah is married to one and you're seeing one. That's some funny shit, don't you think?"

"No. There are thousands of black architects. Millions. What do you care anyway?"

"I don't. I just think it's interesting." He leaned back but jumped when the keys from the piano all sounded at once. "I keep telling Prophet to close this damn thing." He pulled the cover down and crossed his legs. "So I was talking to Pop last week and he said he hasn't seen Deborah one time since she got married. You two must've had a falling out, huh?"

"We didn't have a falling out, we just grew apart, that's all. You sure are asking me a lot of questions."

"I like to know how my little sister is doing in life. And if you want some friendly advice from your older brother, remember to check the attitude at the door 'cause like I said, those white-collar dudes don't put up with too much mess. He gets rid of you and there will be a thousand white girls waiting to take your place and about a million sisters."

"You know, it truly amazes me that you and I were raised by the same person."

"So are you going after this architect 'cause you really like him or 'cause you want to get your hands on his money?"

"I don't need a man for his money. I make my own money. Good money."

"Don't go getting all stuck-up on me just 'cause you've got a new job."

"You know what's funny, Malcolm? You're always talking about *my* attitude, but have you ever noticed how everything—*everything*—out of your mouth is negative?"

"I only get negative when I'm talking to you and that's because I have to deal with *your* attitude."

"God, Malcolm, would you change your song please?"

"It's the truth. Things might've been different if you weren't so spoiled. But you grew up thinking you were the Queen of Sheeba and now you're too stuck-up for your own good. I spent my whole life watching Daddy spoil you. And you know what I think? I bet if Momma were here you'd be more of a lady."

"Fuck you, Malcolm."

"What?" He stood up and in just two steps was towering over me.

"Fuck you, Malcolm." He moved his hand up the side of his leg as if it were being pulled by a string. I knew he wouldn't hit me, not even Malcolm was that crazy, but he wanted to scare me into thinking that he might, which was ridiculous. I wasn't a little girl anymore. I stood up so that my chest touched his uniform. I watched as his nostrils flared and tiny bubbles of sweat formed under his nose.

"You know what?" he said finally. "I refuse to waste my energy arguing with you."

"Fine."

"I am your only brother you know."

"Yeah, it's unfortunate isn't it?"

Sharice walked through the door then, two shopping bags in her arms. "You're early, Babysister. I hope you haven't been waiting too long."

"Not too long."

"You get a chance to have a chat with your big brother?"

"Yeah," Malcolm said, his expression suddenly light and friendly. "She's been telling me about her job. Let me help you with those bags, baby."

"Aren't you proud of your little sister, Malcolm?"

"Oh yeah. Course I am."

Sharice came over and gave me a hug, bracelets tinkling, hair smelling like jasmine incense. "I'm going to change and I'll be right out."

After she was gone Malcolm said, "I feel it's my responsibility to look after you. You need to be careful with that mouth of yours, and be more respectful, that's all I was trying to say."

I rolled my eyes and started walking toward the hallway.

"Where are you going? We're having a conversation here."

"Actually I was thinking that I'd go find Prophet. I'm in the mood for some intelligent conversation."

"When Pop dies, we're all we have. Better think about that."

"Leave me alone, Malcolm," I said halfheartedly. But he was right, of course. We would be all we had after Daddy died. The idea of being left behind with Malcolm made me feel lonely and afraid, not so much because I couldn't stand my brother but because I couldn't imagine my life without my father. He was my one constant in life. I knew he loved me unconditionally. I felt a chill then and like other times when I thought about my father not being around anymore, forced myself to think of something else, which wasn't a problem at all with Malcolm standing right there. "Some things are too scary to think about," I said. "Sort of like the idea that Sharice thinks she's in love with you and is practically letting you raise her son."

"Hey, there, watch it. Prophet needs a man in his life."

"I'm going to leave that little comment alone," I said walking out of the room. "It's too easy."

Twenty-Four

Two months later I received a call from Lisette. I was pouring myself a bowl of cereal for a snack when she called. Darren and I were going out to eat that night, but I had skipped lunch because a client had just opened another restaurant and I was still trying to get the accounting set up.

"You won't believe this one, honey."

"What?"

"She finally did it, that's what."

"What are you talking about, Lisette? Who did what?"

"Deborah kicked out the dog! Our girl finally kicked his ass to the door. Hold on." I listened as she mumbled something to someone. "I'm at work so I can't talk too long. We're handling two sexual discrimination cases at once so it's extra busy here. You know what I think? I think if we get beyond our problems with gender then we can get beyond our problems with race. Look at the world, Babysister, who has it the worst? The women and children, no matter what their race."

"What happened with Deborah, Lisette?"

"She kicked him out. She already changed the locks.

That was my idea. The locks, I mean. He can't get back in the house if he wanted. I'm so proud of her."

"When did she kick him out?"

"Two days ago. He's staying in a hotel."

I tossed my mail in the air and started dancing around my kitchen. Darren was out of the house! All the waiting was finally over.

"Good for Deborah," I said, a little out of breath. "What finally made her do it?"

"She discovered a bunch of old credit card bills in his briefcase. Well, okay, I told her to go through his briefcase. I told her it wouldn't hurt to look, okay? And see what happens. Deborah found all kinds of charges to all kinds of restaurants and for flowers and jewelry. I want to know who this woman is that he's seeing that she can't pay her own way. We can't demand equality if we don't pay our own way."

"So what's going to happen? Is Deborah going to divorce him?"

"She better. Let me tell you, I'll drag her to a lawyer myself if I have to. She says there's no way in hell she's taking him back. She says there's only so much praying she can do and that God meant for her to find those credit card bills. But God had nothing to do with it. That dog meant for her to find the bills. He *wanted* to get caught. Let me tell you something, Babysister, they all want to get caught. They are all proud of the way they sneak around." She covered the phone and I listened to her mumble. "I gotta get going."

"Well, keep me posted okay?"

"Promise."

I fell into my chair and stared up at my ceiling. I saw rainbows and hearts and Darren and me running into each other's arms. "I'm free, Babysister! We're going to live happily ever after." I started to dial Darren's work number but decided against it. If he had wanted me to know what had happened he would've called first. He was probably trying to get his life in order the best he could. We were meeting for dinner after all and he probably wanted to tell me everything in person. He was probably going to ask if he could stay with me. Greet me with a bottle of champagne at dinner. "We can finally be together, sweetheart. I'm so sorry all this mess took so long."

We were meeting at a restaurant in Brentwood. In honor of the occasion, I wore a dress he'd given me for our three-month anniversary. It was one of those Chinese dresses with a high collar, sky blue and gold, tight as hell, and very classy. I put my hair up in a bun and put on my eyeliner so that my eyes looked more almond-shaped. While driving to the restaurant, I started planning out our future. Darren would stay with me until we found a new place to live. Maybe we'd find something fairly reasonable so we could save up for a house. Daddy would probably want to help us with a down payment, I thought, and Lord knows Darren's parents had money. We'd probably wait a year or so before we got married because he and Deborah would have to file for a divorce. I wouldn't mind waiting though, I'd grown used to it, and besides, I was finally getting my way.

Darren was already at the restaurant when I arrived. I had to wonder how long he'd been there because his tie was loose and he had two empty shot glasses in front of him.

I greeted him with a long kiss. You're free, I thought. Free!

"Hey, baby. You look great." He kissed me and then

stared down into his glass as if he were reading tea leaves. The waiter came and he ordered another whiskey. I ordered a glass of wine. We sat with our drinks for a while without talking much. I guessed that he was being quiet because he was trying to come up with the right way of telling me what had happened. He had been kicked out of his home, after all, and was probably feeling a little upset. Maybe he was embarrassed about asking to stay with me.

I reached over and began stroking his hand. "You okay, sweetheart? You don't look so good."

"Shitty day at work."

"Work?"

"Yeah, they changed the date for a project I'm in charge of so it's been busy as hell."

Okay, I thought, if he needed to talk about work before getting into what happened with Deborah I could wait. There was no rush really.

We ordered dinner then I told him about my day and he told me about his. Meanwhile, I waited for him to say something. I waited through dinner. I waited through dessert. When he paid the bill and reached for his jacket I realized that maybe waiting for him to tell me was a mistake. Maybe he needed a little help.

"Darren, is there anything you want to talk about? You seem distracted tonight. You know if you need to talk about something I'm hear to listen, right?"

"You know me so well," he said. He put his jacket in his lap and folded his hands. "There is something I have to tell you. See, I know I told you I was going to stay with you tonight, but I should probably head on home. This project is kicking my ass and I need a good night's sleep."

"Home?"

"Yeah, I know I promised. I'm sorry. I'll make it up to you, okay? I know how limited our time is together."

"That's all you have to tell me? You're going *home*?"

"Yeah, I need some sleep. I'm exhausted."

He stood and put on his jacket while I sat staring at our empty coffee cups. What the hell was going on?

He walked me out to my car and gave me a kiss. "I love you. Thanks for being so patient and supportive. I'd be a wreck without you in my life."

"Sure," I said, stunned. I knew I could've told him about what I'd heard but I began to wonder if Lisette had messed up the story—which wasn't likely, but that was all I could think had happened. I gave him a hug. "Call me if you need anything. Anything at all."

I drove straight to Lisette's house. I didn't care that it was after ten. I didn't care that she lived on the other side of Inglewood in a neighborhood that was more dangerous than mine. I needed to know what the hell was going on.

I'd stood knocking at her door for a good minute when she suddenly swung open her door and stood there with a crowbar raised high above her head. *"What do you want?"*

I pointed to the crowbar. "What the hell is that?"

She looked from me to the crowbar then shrugged. "I didn't know it was you. What you expect? You want me to open the door with a fucking smile on my face?"

"Why don't you just ask who it is before you open the door?"

"I like the idea of catching some bastard who's up to no good and smashing his face in. What are you doing here? You know what time it is?" Her curly hair was uncombed and wild-looking. She had on sweats and an old T-shirt that said *Never Another Battered Woman*.

"I was on my way back from a date and thought I'd stop by."

"Well, get inside. In. In. You look too good for that filthy hallway."

Lisette's apartment was decorated with furniture she bought at Goodwill. She bought the entire set they had displayed in the front window when she first moved to L.A. She was proud of her furniture even though it looked like it had belonged to an old white couple from Idaho. The couch was a dull moss green and took up most of the space in her living room. There was also the brown-and-green-plaid swivel chair and the tall lamps with lacy white lampshades and the porcelain cat with creepy glass eyes on the coffee table. Except for all the pictures of her family back in New York and all the political posters, you'd never know an Afro–Puerto Rican feminist lived there.

The television was turned to a Spanish-speaking channel. A woman with green eyes and big tits was crying on some man's shoulder. "The *telenovelas* are my weakness," Lisette said while moving all her magazines and newspapers from the green couch so I could sit down. "Let me tell you, I get hooked every time." She found her remote and turned the TV off.

I didn't bother with small talk. "So what's going on with Deborah and Darren? You heard anything else?"

"I went by her house after work today. We had dinner together. Oh can I get you something to drink? We can make some rum and Cokes and celebrate the impending divorce."

"Divorce?"

"Mr. Manipulative confessed everything, girlfriend. He's been having an affair."

For a quick second I thought she was testing me, but I

knew Lisette didn't operate that way so I took a deep breath. "With who?" I asked.

"A woman who works in his building. Second floor. She's in advertising. Her name is Fumani. Can you believe that name?"

"Fumani?"

"Yeah, I don't like it either. Have you seen the commercial where the three women are on a hike and talking about their tampons? That's her commercial. Pretty silly if you ask me. Have you ever been on a hike and talked about your tampons? Know what I'm saying? I thought men wrote those commercials, okay?"

I couldn't bring myself to believe what she was saying. Maybe she was thinking of another friend whose husband was cheating. Maybe she had confused one of her feminist friend's husbands: David or Doug. Or maybe Deborah had told her Darren had a new friend named Fumani and there was nothing more to the story than that.

"He's seeing someone named Fumani? Are you sure, Lisette?"

"Of course I'm sure. Deborah has even met the woman! Deborah said the woman showed up at one of the dog's la-la parties he gave at the house. The dog invited her because she just moved from New York and said she was having a hard time meeting people in L.A. Let me tell you something, I'm from New York too and I met people just fine when I moved here. People who weren't *married*, okay? Deborah says she's one of those tall, skinny types. So the dog is out of the house and poor Deborah is at home with the new locks on her doors crying her eyes out."

"Are you *sure* about all this, Lisette?"

"What? You trying to say I got my facts wrong? Have I ever gotten the facts wrong? Huh?"

No, that was one thing about Lisette. She never got her facts wrong. Never. My heart shrank.

"Do you know how long they've been seeing each other?"

"He told Deborah it's been over a month. That's what he says, but he's a dog so he's not telling the truth."

I couldn't stop my head from shaking back and forth. No no, this can't be happening. *This can't be true.*

Lisette nudged me then and tilted her head. A wave of curls went falling from the right side of her head to the left. "And why you seem so surprised anyway? What did you think? He was a faithful husband? You know him yourself, Babysister. Look what he did with you."

"You're right," I said softly.

"Once a dog, always a dog. That's what I say."

I felt like all the blood was leaving my body, not gushing like a river, but slow and heavy. "You're right," I said again. I felt sick, too weak to do anything but lie on the old moss-green couch and close my eyes. And *that's* when I remembered her. The woman I'd seen him with at the restaurant on Melrose. The woman who looked like a horse.

She works in the same building as me. I think she's in advertising or something. She's a chattermouth.

My body started to shiver.

"Hey, what's wrong? You cold or something?"

I held myself as tightly as possible. I wanted to be a wall. A wall made of bricks and steel and iron. I wanted to be something that shut things out, but it was too late for that. The truth had made itself known and was standing in my face with a hand on one hip. You've been *played*, girl. That man played you for a *fool*.

"Ohhh, Babysister? Honey what's wrong? Why are you crying, huh? Is it because of Deborah's husband? You thinking about the pain he caused you?"

I nodded.

"And you're thinking of poor Deborah now and all the pain he's causing her? I know it's upsetting, but Deborah will be all right. Everything will be fine."

I had no choice but to calm down and stop crying. I didn't want Lisette to realize there was more going on than she thought. "Can I take you up on that drink, Lisette?"

"Sure, sure." She left and came back with two tall glasses filled with rum and Coke.

I took a long drink.

"You going to be okay?"

"Yeah, I'll be fine. It's just . . . it's hard to hear that he's so cruel."

"Yeah, well at least she's leaving him. Let's make a toast to Deborah, okay? Our girl did good, didn't she?"

"Yeah," I said, "that Darren is a motherfuckin' goddamn shitty bastard of a dog and I hope he rots in hell."

"Whoa, girl. Listen at you getting all poetic and shit. You should apply for one of those grants and write a book or something."

"Yeah," I said, clinking my glass to hers. "I just might."

Twenty-Five

I WOKE UP the next morning on Lisette's moss-green couch. I was still in my dress, but at some point Lisette must have slipped a pillow under my head and thrown a blanket over me. At first I thought I was home—I heard a guitar and a man singing in Spanish and figured it was my neighbor blasting his stereo again. But then I heard Lisette's voice rise above the music—very loud and very off-key—and remembered all the rum we drank the night before and why I had gotten drunk in the first place. I pulled the blanket over my head. Goddamn motherfuckin' shitty bastard of a dog. *How could he do this to me?*

"Hey, sleeping beauty. Time to get up." I felt Lisette pushing at my shoulder. "What you think? You on vacation? You on some Caribbean cruise ship?"

She yanked the blanket back. When I looked up I saw she was already dressed. She had on a tight pair of jeans and a white blouse with ruffles around the neck and chest, hot-pink lipstick, and blue-black mascara. She held a glass of water in one hand and two aspirin in the other. "I'm making some breakfast. Eggs, coffee, toast. Sound good?"

She handed me the water and aspirin and sat on the

edge of the couch. "You got pretty wasted last night, huh? You kept saying how you were a fool."

"Me?"

"Yeah, after I tucked you in, you said you were a fool for believing him and a fool for ever being with him."

"I did?"

"Let me tell you something, Babysister. You have to realize that what happened between you and that dog was a long time ago and neither you nor Deborah knew how evil he really was. He's Mr. Manipulative. Mr. Deceptive, okay? He's like Satan. You didn't marry him, at least. Think how poor Deborah must feel."

I tried to sit up without causing too much pain. My head was pounding. "What time is it?"

"A little after seven. What time do you have to be at work?"

"I can't go to work, Lisette, my head is killing me."

"You're going to work, okay? You're going to work if I have to drive you myself. It's not like you're still working at the bank and no one cares if you miss a day. There's a difference, okay? People depend on you. What about that man who opened the new restaurant? You told me last night you had to be at his place today by nine o'clock."

She was right. Even if Darren had played my ass and I had every right to stay at home and nurse my hangover, my name was at stake now. I couldn't let my clients down.

"Okay okay."

She pulled me up by the arms. "You can borrow one of my dresses. That way you won't have to go home and change. That way you can take your time and eat my eggs. Have I ever made my eggs for you? Lots of Tabasco and chili. Let me tell you, my eggs will get rid of that hangover in no time."

Wearing one of Lisette's outfits was about the last thing I wanted to do. If her clothes didn't look glued on to her skin, they were from the Goodwill or some vintage clothing store—which was fine for her, but not my style at all. She wouldn't take no for an answer, of course, and before I could say anything, ran off to find something "extra special."

I decided, while taking my shower, that I would have to kill Darren. I mean there was no other way really. Besides, I'd be doing womankind a favor. I would get support from all the women he had lied to, cheated, and betrayed. Lisette and all her feminist friends would write folk songs about me. They'd sing while waving their hands in the air, showing off their hairy armpits in my honor, praising me for killing off another dog.

Still dripping, I walked to the living room and saw Lisette had two dresses draped over the couch for me to choose from. The first was a skintight blue-jean dress with no back and a hole in the front ready to make visible any amount of cleavage. The second looked straight out of the fifties, complete with white collar and a pattern that consisted of hundreds of bright red cherries.

I chose the cherry dress.

"Ohh, you look beautiful."

"Lisette, I look like a black June Cleaver."

"What do you mean? That dress is beautiful, okay? That dress is forty years old and look at the condition it's in. I have the perfect purse for it too. Two plastic cherries at the top. Oh and wait till you see the earrings."

"I'll pass on the earrings, Lisette."

"Well, it's your life, but they're really cute. They look like cherries."

"Where'd you get your taste in clothes anyway?"

"What you trying to say? I got style. I got plenty of style. I like my clothes like I like my men: classic, okay?"

"Lisette, you haven't been with a man since I've known you."

"That's because I got patience. Let me tell you, I got patience and I've got a life. I know I don't need a man to make me happy. Now let me go get those earrings for you. I won't take no for an answer so stop rolling those big ol' eyes at me."

I went straight to work after eating Lisette's outrageously spicy eggs. I figured it was a good thing I looked like a fifties housewife, otherwise I would've driven straight to Darren's office and made a huge scene, embarrassing no one but myself, maybe even getting my butt put in jail.

I didn't get much done that first hour of work because I was too busy plotting ways I could murder Darren. I mean, if you think about it, there are hundreds of ways to kill a person. I did get as far as deciding that he had to be tortured—with a butcher knife. But after I made that decision, I had to figure out what to do with the body. Where would I hide it? How would I lift it? Not to mention the hassle of finding an alibi, destroying all evidence that linked the two of us together. I mean, murder is some complicated shit.

I wouldn't have gotten any work done if I hadn't lied to Mr. Fontina, the owner of the restaurant where I was working that day. It was an Italian place set to open in four days and Mr. Fontina was nervous as hell about everything. While I was typing out one of my many plans for killing Darren, he stuck his head in the office and went on about how important it was for the books to be finished. Just to get him to leave me alone, I lied and told him not to worry. "I'm making great progress," I said. "I'll definitely be finished on time." He seemed reassured then and told me how nice I looked in my "cheerful cherry dress." When I snarled, he said that he could see I was busy and closed the office door.

After such a big lie, I had no other choice but to get some work done. I worked my ass off too, but by four o'clock I felt thoroughly drained. I remember typing a name into the computer and suddenly being struck by an overwhelming feeling of fatigue mixed with grief. I had loved Darren with all of my heart, had wanted to have children with him, grow old with him. I believed he had discovered the true meaning of love and friendship just as I had, but all the while he had been playing me for a fool. I completely lost it. I closed the office door and broke down over my desk. I cried because everything I had dreamed of had come to an end. I cried because the love we shared meant nothing to him. And just when I thought I couldn't cry any more, I stared down at Lisette's cherry dress and realized what a complete fool I looked like. I mean, just three days ago I had been scanning the classifieds for apartments and thinking about where Darren and I might live, and now here I was in a fifties dress wearing plastic cherry earrings, mourning my relationship to a man who was cheating on me with a woman who looked like a horse. It doesn't get any worse.

By five I had decided that all I needed was an explanation. All I wanted was an explanation. I deserved an explanation. And after I got it, *then* I'd kill the bastard. I dialed his office from my cellular phone after work, but his secretary told me that he had called in sick. "He has that terrible cold that's going around," she said. "He won't be in until Friday." I almost asked her if she had slept with him too, but Darren had told me she was in her sixties and like a grandmother to everyone in his office. I tried his condo next. I knew good and well that Deborah had locked him out, and figured if she answered, I'd hang up. But after four rings the answering machine clicked on. There was nobody home.

He's with Fumani, I thought suddenly.

Fumani the advertising woman who didn't have sense enough to know that women don't talk about tampons while they're hiking. I turned on the radio. I needed to start training my mind to think about something besides Darren. He was like a virus that I needed to get out of my system once and for all.

The four little sisters were sitting on the porch when I got home, arguing over a bag of sunflower seeds LaQuita held close to her chest. The bag was supersize and took up her entire lap.

"You can't hold that bag forever," LaNeisha said. "Momma said to share!"

"It's my turn to hold it," LaKeisha yelled. "I'mma tell!"

The barrettes had been taken out of their hair and replaced with two big puff balls near each ear. You would've thought those girls were nothing but sweet if you didn't know they could be such smart alecks.

LaQuita passed the bag of sunflower seeds to LaNeisha when she saw me. "Why you wearing that dress? You look like 'I Love Lucy.'"

"Thanks."

"Where your boyfriend at?"

"We broke up."

All four girls moaned at once.

LaNeisha said, "We ain't never going to your wedding, Babysister. You too picky."

LaNita spat a mouthful of shells onto the sidewalk. "Why don't your kids live here? They stay with they daddy?"

"I don't have any kids. You all know I don't have any kids."

LaKeisha's eyes grew wide. "You don't have no boyfriend? And you don't have no kids? And you live all by yourself?"

LaQuita cracked open a seed with her back teeth. "I ain't *never* heard of that," she said.

I started up the steps. "You girls need to learn that women were put on this earth to do more than meet men and have babies."

"You fixin' to go stare out your window 'cause you depressed?" LaKeisha asked.

"I just might," I said. "So don't be surprised if you see me."

My apartment felt different somehow, not at all like home. I thought, for a moment, that I should turn it into a museum. Label all the furniture so that everyone could see what Darren and I once had together. Everything I owned had a story to tell. I looked over at my blender and thought about the afternoon when we made margaritas and ate quesadillas. I leaned against my couch and thought about how we liked to snuggle there while reading. With each memory I'd begin to feel myself warming toward him and then have to remind myself of what he had done. Lord only knew how many other blenders he had used or how many other couches he had snuggled on.

I went to check my answering machine. I had three messages.

"Babysister, it's your father. I'm making pork chops and

mashed potatoes for dinner. Haven't seen you in a while. Come on over if you want."

Lisette's message came afterward:

"Hey, you okay? I was calling to see how your day went. I don't care what you say either: You looked cute in my dress, girlfriend. Oh! I talked to Deborah. She says the dog is staying with that Fumani woman and had the nerve to ask her to be his *friend* because he's going through a tough time. Can you believe that shit? Didn't I tell you he was Satan? Call me."

And then Darren's voice:

"Hey baby, I was wondering if I could see you tomorrow. I miss you. I would've called earlier but I had to drive out to La Jolla of all places. I'll tell you, work has been a nightmare lately. But don't worry, I'm fine. I'm still here in La Jolla, but I'd like to see you tomorrow. Think you can schedule your appointments so we can meet for lunch? I'd love to hang out at your place—if you know what I mean. I'll call you tonight so we can confirm. I miss you baby."

"La Jolla my ass!" I yelled at my machine. Goddamn liar. I was crazy to think he'd have an explanation. An explanation for what? Being a no-good shameless *dog*? I found a cigarette and, yes, went to my living room window. The little girls were arguing over the bag of sunflower seeds, shells covered the sidewalk and porch like hundreds of black ants. Staring down at them, I thought about how great things were when I was a little girl. I didn't have a care in the world. Suddenly I realized that I wanted to see my father. He was the one man whose love I could always count on.

Twenty-Six

Daddy was still fussing around the kitchen when I got there. He said he didn't want any help so I sat at the table and watched as he took out the last pork chop from the cast-iron skillet and put the mashed potatoes in a large bowl. I didn't eat much during dinner. I played with my food while listening to Daddy go on about how he was trying to cut back on his salt. We had just about finished eating when he cleared his throat in a way that said he wanted my attention.

"I ran into Mrs. Moore at the store the other day," he said. "She told me you stopped going over there and she hasn't seen you in months. I told her the same was true about me and Deborah. I can't remember the last time I saw that girl. Wouldn't know her if I saw her on the street it's been so long."

My friendship with Deborah was the absolute last thing I wanted to talk about. "Well, you know since I stopped working at the bank, we've grown apart. I hardly see her myself anymore."

"Sad thing to lose a friend you've known most of your life."

"Yeah, but I'm sure it's just a phase we're going through."

"You seem a little tired tonight. You're not working too hard with that new job are you?"

"No, no. I love it. I never would've thought of myself as a bookkeeper of all things, but I really do love it."

"Well, you were always good at math, makes sense you'd be doing something with figures." He looked at me while folding his napkin. "You know," he said, "Deborah's mother mentioned that you weren't in Deborah's wedding like you said you were."

I sat my fork down and swallowed.

"She said she didn't see you at all that day."

Shit. I didn't have a choice but to lie. What was I going to do? Tell him the truth?

"I'm sorry I didn't say anything about not being in the wedding when you asked. Deborah and I had an argument a couple of weeks before the ceremony and I just didn't see the point in telling you about it."

"And that's why you weren't in the wedding? Because you had an argument with her?"

"What we were arguing about seems silly now. I did go to the ceremony, though."

"Must have been some argument."

"Well, I just thought Deborah was going on too much about her wedding and we got in this silly disagreement about whether I supported her or not and then we both just sort of exploded. She was the one who told me I shouldn't be a bridesmaid."

"Now that there is a surprise. Doesn't seem like Deborah would say something like that. That doesn't sound like her at all."

"Yeah, I know, but things are better now. I think we

both realized that we were being immature. Deborah was under a lot of pressure with the wedding and all."

Daddy seemed satisfied with my answer. I felt my body relax and watched as he pushed the last bit of his mashed potatoes from one side of his plate to the other. But then he lifted his head and looked me straight in the eye. "Malcolm told me this new boyfriend of yours is an architect. It would be something if he knew Deborah's husband, now wouldn't it? Can't be too many black architects floating around."

Could this conversation get any worse?

"Yeah, not too many, I suppose."

"I think we should have Deborah and her husband over for dinner, don't you? You can both bring your architects along. I'm interested in meeting this new friend of yours. Very interested, in fact."

I realized right then and there that my father had somehow found out about me and Darren. I looked around the kitchen like maybe there was a good lie somewhere—hiding under the toaster or taped to the fridge like a grocery list. But no. It was too late and I knew it. I took a deep breath.

"We can't," I said quietly.

"Can't what?"

"We can't have dinner together."

"And why is that?"

I stared down at my hands. I knew he'd be upset, but hoped that after I told him what a dog Darren was—how he'd played me *and* Deborah—Daddy would understand. He would see how hurt I felt and try to comfort me.

"They're the same person," I said finally. "Deborah's husband and my boyfriend are the same person."

My father tossed down his napkin. "I was wondering how long it was going to take for you to stop all that lying."

"I'm sorry about lying, Daddy, but—"

"All the men you go out with and you have to mess around with Deborah's *husband*?" He looked at me then like he couldn't fathom the idea that I could do something so awful. Not *his* daughter. Not *his* baby girl.

"They weren't married when we—"

"*Hush up, Babysister!* He's her husband. I thought I taught you better than that."

"I fell in love with him, Daddy. We had more in common—"

He slammed his hand against the table so hard the plates jumped. "Hush up! I mean it. I don't want to hear another word out of that lying mouth of yours! You ought to be 'shamed of yourself, girl."

"Daddy!"

He stared at me then. I saw nothing but disappointment and anger in his eyes.

"I never would've thought you could do something like this. You've known Deborah most of your life. She was like a *sister* to you."

I was actually afraid. I'd never seen my father so pissed off. I'd seen him upset with Malcolm, but that was different, that was *Malcolm*.

"But it's over between me and him, Daddy. I found out that he was cheating on me with another woman. I thought he loved me but he didn't. He two-timed us both."

"I don't give a damn about him or what he was doing or who the hell he was two-timing. You think I care about

him? You're just as bad. I did not raise you to be like this.
You had no business whatsoever going near that man, you
hear me? Does Deborah know about you?"

"I don't think so. She just found out about this other
woman and kicked him out."

"Serves him right."

"I know. He's—"

"No matter what he is, you are no better—*no better*."
He sat there for a moment wiping his fingers on his napkin. His voice was quieter, but the anger was still there. "I
know I spoiled you, Babysister, spoiled you something
terrible. And things might have been different if you
hadn't seen your mother that day. That's something a
child just shouldn't see. I thought I was doing right by
spoiling you, but I was wrong. I was wrong for how I let
you get away with so much. All those lies you been telling
me over the years, all those games you used to pull when
you was a girl."

My mouth dropped.

"That's right. I knew what was going on. I knew exactly
what you were up to. You think you can get over on
anybody, don't you? Even your own damn father. Your
behavior has been disgusting, you know that? And I won't
say I haven't played a part in it either. I chose to let everything slide. But no more. The days of me spoiling you
have come to an end. You hear me? All that mess is over.
You went too far this time."

"I'm sorry, Da—"

"You need to apologize to Deborah, not me. And don't
come back lying to me about how the two of you made
up. You lie to me so much, I don't know when to believe
you anymore." He stood then and leaned forward so that

his face was close to mine. "Your mother is probably rolling over in her grave, probably completely ashamed of you right now."

Nothing could've hurt me more and he knew it. My eyes welled up, and while he saw that he had made me cry, he did absolutely nothing. He simply turned and left the kitchen. After a minute or two I heard his bedroom door close. I was stunned that he could be so cold. He'll come back out, I thought. He's thinking of a way to apologize. I listened for his footsteps, but all I could hear was the clock over the refrigerator and my own breathing. I waited in that kitchen for a good thirty minutes before I realized he wasn't coming out.

Back at my apartment, I listened to *James Brown Live at the Apollo* from beginning to end. I sat on my couch, crying one minute, mumbling the words to "Lost Someone" or "I Love You Yes I Do" the next. Lord knows I had experienced my share of pain with Darren, but nothing that dog had done had hurt me as much as what my father had said that evening. And worse, I knew he was right. I needed to get my shit together, needed to somehow, some way, turn things around with him—*and* myself.

Darren called again a few minutes after ten. How I was able to talk to that man without going off on him was beyond me, but I managed to keep my cool.

"It sure is nice to hear your voice," he said. "I missed you."

"So how was La Jolla?"

"Exhausting. I'll tell you, I'd much rather be in your arms. Did you have a chance to think about lunch tomorrow?"

"Yeah, lunch would be nice."

"How about if I bring some Indian food. I'm in the mood for something as hot and spicy as you are. Twelve okay?"

"Twelve is fine." You fucking bastard.

After we said goodbye, I slammed the receiver down in its cradle, took a grocery bag from under the sink, and threw all the gifts he'd given me inside: the dress from China, a pair of gold hoop earrings he bought while on one of his "business trips"; the bracelet from Thailand; an antique candleholder with a small angel at the base; a lace teddy; a silk chemise. Once the bag was packed, I sat it by the door within easy reach—I planned on throwing it in Darren's face when he arrived, cussing that man out something good.

But there was one small problem. When I saw him standing in the hallway with a bag of Indian food in one hand and a bouquet of lilies in the other, my entire body went weak. I mean, it's easy to forget you love somebody when you want to kill him. It's easy to forget your dreams of sharing the future with someone when all you want to do is wrap your hands around his neck and choke him to death. So when Darren smiled and handed me the flowers —"These are for the woman I love, the woman I can't stop thinking about"—everything I had practiced saying the night before went flying out the window. You're a goddamn cheating bastard of a dog and I hope you rot in hell turned into "You're so sweet, baby. Why don't you come inside."

I couldn't break up with him. I *loved* him. And I knew he loved me. We just needed to have a long talk, that's all. He'd explain everything and then we'd make up and be together forever.

I put the flowers in a vase and sat them on the table along with our food.

"I know I must be in love," he said. "I feel like I haven't seen you for weeks."

He picked up his fork, but I touched him on the wrist. "I love you too, Darren. I know we can work through any problem that might come our way. *Any* problem. I'm here for you."

"You're too good for me, Babysister. I know I always say that, but it's the truth."

Thing is, instead of confessing, he started eating again, started talking about La Jolla as though La Jolla was the only thing on his mind. "It's a pain driving down there, but this project could mean big things as far as my career goes. If this job goes as well as I think it will, I'm going to get better assignments, which means you and me are on the road to getting a house. The downside is that I'll probably have to start spending more time in La Jolla. We'll probably have to cool things down for a while, baby."

"Cool things *down* for a while?"

"Yeah, at least for a few weeks."

I couldn't believe what I was hearing. He wasn't going to confess a damn thing.

"And I suppose you're going to ask me to be patient."

"Well, yeah. Only for a few weeks."

He was such a dog.

Without thinking I grabbed the lilies, walked to the door, and picked up the bag. I glared at him as I shoved the flowers inside.

"What the hell are you doing?"

"Fumani," I said.

"What?"

"Foo-MAN-eee!"

He lifted his hands like I was holding a gun to his chest. "Hold on now, Babysister. I don't know what you're thinking but I can explain."

"Explain what? How you became such a dog? How you're two-timing me and Deborah and Fumani and God knows who else?"

I flung the bag at him. His tandoori chicken fell in his lap. "Take your shit. Don't call. Don't write. Keep the fuck away from me. Understand?"

He looked from me to his lap, completely stunned.

"Babysister—"

"Get out."

"But I—"

"I don't want to hear it, Darren. I've had enough of your lame excuses. Get the fuck out of my house."

He saw something in my face that told him he'd better listen. He kept his eyes on me as he picked up the chicken leg from his lap then took the bag and stepped into the hallway. I slammed the door just as a hurt look was making its way across his face.

He hit his fist against the door. "Babysister, we need to talk about this!"

"We don't need to talk about jack shit!" I yelled. "It's over!"

I could hear him pacing outside, could hear the sound of his boots against the floor.

"Babysister, are you there? Listen, I can explain. I can explain everything. I don't know what you think is going on, but I'll bet you've got it all wrong. Let me come inside so we can talk about this. We need to talk."

Silence.

"Things have been so hard for me lately. I can't lose you, Babysister. I can't. I don't know what I'd do without you. You mean everything to me. Fumani is a friend, Babysister. Nothing more. I know how jealous you can get. Look how you're acting now. This is ridiculous!"

I didn't want to hear any more of his crap so I walked into my bedroom and closed the door. I sat on my bed wondering how long he'd stay out in the hallway then told myself I should try not to think about him. A dog is a dog is a dog. My neighbor downstairs turned on his stereo. Mariachi music. Lots of horns and violins. Perfect. I hugged one of my mother's pillows to my chest. The pillow was red and shaped like an apple. She'd made it for me for my third birthday. I tried to relax by using Darius's breathing exercises. Inhale: I will not open the door. Exhale: Darren is a dog.

I don't know how long I stayed in my bedroom, but I know I'd heard enough mariachi music to last a lifetime. It was quiet by the time I went out into the living room. I opened the door as slowly as possible. He was gone all right. The hallway was completely empty except for a bouquet of bright-pink lilies.

Four days later I was sitting in my office at Medina's, trying to get up the courage to call Deborah. I'm no fool. I knew that if I was going to make things right, I needed to talk to her. The only problem was that I had no idea what I would say. Listen Deborah, I really didn't mean to mess around with your husband, but I couldn't resist? Or: Hey, Deborah, guess what? Not only was the dog sleeping with Fumani, he was sleeping with me too! I was going crazy trying to think of the right thing to say, but I told myself if I didn't pick up the phone that very minute, I'd never call her and my father would never speak to me again and I'd end up miserable and lonely.

That's what I was thinking when I dialed Darren's condo anyway. I thought I'd leave her a message while she was at work. I mean, I wasn't so confident that I wanted to actually talk to her right then.

The phone rang three times and then Deborah's recording came on. "You have reached the Wilsons' residence. . . ."

I started to leave a message—actually I barely got out a nervous hello—when the next thing I knew there was a click and suddenly Deborah was on the line.

"Hey Babysister," she said, without a hint of surprise in her voice. "Lisette told me you'd probably call."

"She did?"

"Yeah, I talked to her last night and she said, 'I give that girl a week. She's going to call okay? Let me tell you, I know these things.'"

She started laughing then and I remember thinking, Damn, she's doing better than I am.

There was a second or two of silence, when we were both probably wondering who'd talk first. Then I heard Deborah take a deep breath. "So," she said, "where do we begin?"

Epilogue

IT'S BEEN ALMOST TWO YEARS since that phone call. Deborah and I ended up meeting for lunch the day after we spoke. Her hair was in a single braid down her back. No makeup. She had on jeans and a white T-shirt. My first thought when I saw her walking through the door of the restaurant was that she looked the same as she had in high school, like all the mess she was going through with Darren was making her look younger. I did apologize that day, but I also figured there was no reason she needed to know about *everything* I'd done. I mean think about it. What was the harm with letting her assume I'd only fooled around with Darren *before* they got married? Did she really need to know I'd messed around with him *again*? I don't think so. At any rate, she lives in Venice now. She got the condo and the BMW in the divorce and sold them both right away and bought a house off Main Street. Now she's obsessed with her garden and her new Rottweiler, Aretha. And she got promoted too. Mrs. Hodges got transferred and Deborah took her position. She doesn't put up with any of the evil stepsisters' games, told them if they started any mess with anyone, they'd lose their jobs. She gave silent Marsha her old position as loan officer. I love when shit like that happens.

Darren wrote me a total of five letters—no return address—during the first few weeks after I shoved him out the door, but I didn't read them. Every time I saw his handwriting on the envelope, I'd force myself to throw it in the trash along with all the other junk mail. But I won't lie, I still think about him. Still think about the day he came into the bank and how he flipped his keys around in his hand as he walked toward me. And sometimes when I least expect it, an image will come to mind: how he'd give his boots an extra tug after putting them on, or how the hairs swirled around his belly button like a seashell. I'll think about how nice it was to sit on his balcony and share a beer, walk through a bookstore or gallery holding hands, how good it felt to be in love. But I've learned that once you discover a man is a jerk, there's no going back. After Darren, my heart put out one of those signs you see in restaurant windows: *Closed/Cerrado*. At the time I thought that sign would be up forever.

I've only seen Rob a few times since that day in the park. The first time I saw him was close to a year after our breakup. He took me out to dinner and kept staring at me like he couldn't figure me out. I got the feeling that he'd been reading a lot of self-help books because he'd say things like, "You choose partners who need to teach you something, like it or not" or "Life is too short to settle for mediocrity." He's seeing someone else now—a nurse. Two things I know about Rob: One is that he's a good man—not my dream man, but good. And two: He'll always have it for me.

I stayed single for a record year and a half. A year and a half! That's not to say that after about six months post-Darren I refused to get some when I wanted—I didn't pull a Lisette, but I didn't jump into another relationship either. I stayed focused on my job and having a good time. I even went back to junior college. I have a 3.8 grade point average and I'm two classes away from finally getting my A.A. degree. After I graduate, I plan on transferring to UCLA. That's UUUU . . . SEEE . . . LLLL . . . AAEEE. Hell, I've become my own superstar, and take it from me, once you become your own star, you don't put up with any man's mess. I don't care how good he is in bed or where he went to school or how much money he has. Nowadays I can smell that pretentious bullshit a mile away.

Lisette got accepted to Long Beach State. She takes classes at night while working at the law firm. She's majoring in Women's Studies, of course. After she graduates she plans on going to law school. I can just imagine her cussing out some judge who has the nerve to disagree with her. I object okay? That man is guilty. I know these things okay?

Sharice and Darius opened that new restaurant, by the way. It's on LaCienega near Pico and draws in a young thirtysomething crowd, the kind that has money and wants nothing to do with meat or fat. It's called Gaia, and Sharice tells me the name has something to do with a theory about earth and organisms and all that other hippie mess. They had a huge party the week before the restaurant was scheduled to open. Everybody was there. Lisette, Deborah. Malcolm had a scowl on his face for most of the night, but he gave a nice toast and told everyone how much he loved Sharice and how proud he was of her. I almost believed him. Prophet read a poem about the importance of following your dreams. Daddy was there too—with his girlfriend, Melvina. Soon after he went off on me in the kitchen, she started coming around the house all the time, throwing up her hands and showing off her bowling pin calves. I still don't like her. That annoying baby voice she uses when she talks drives me crazy, but who am I to say anything? Besides, you can't help but notice how she makes Daddy smile whenever she's around, how he loves to grab her around her thick waist and pull her in close.

I met Michael the night of the party. He's the man I'm seeing now. He has skin the color of dark-brown sugar after you've melted it in a pot, soft brown eyes, and a strong jawline. It was just like in the movies when we met, except I saw his boots before I saw his face. I'd dropped the napkin I was holding and when I bent down to pick it up—there, through a crowd of legs and shoes—I spotted a great pair of black boots. I let my eyes travel up his gray pants and saw how those same boots gave a subtle lift to his perfectly shaped ass. I stood up and stared, just waiting for him to turn my way. And when he did, I mouthed the words *Nice boots.*

Then I gave him my wide, gorgeous smile.

Acknowledgments

A HUGE THANKS to my agent, BJ Robbins. Thank you for never giving up, for saving the title, for your undying enthusiasm and belief in this book. I am greatly indebted to my editor, Susan Kamil. Thank you for the gift of time. Thank you for helping me to remain true to Babysister's spirit. Thank you for reminding me to have fun. You are a *phenomenal* woman, Susan. Thanks to Carla Riccio of Dial Press for her invaluable suggestions. Thanks also to Kathy MacDonald for her help with saving the title. Thanks to La Liz Gonzales. Two of Babysister's funnier comments come from you. Thank you for sharing. I look forward to reading *your* book someday. Stefani Barber, the little sister I've always wanted. Thank you for your wonderful friendship. Tim Henry for friendship, jokes, and for being such a great stepdad to my dog Rufus. Thanks to Susan Carpendale for taking my photo and for being such a generous friend. Jamex de la Torre, Einar de la Torre, and Nora Moore for an open-door policy at their ranch and for so many great times over the years. My sisterfriends. Michelle T. Clinton and G. Colette Jackson for their friendship and support. Thanks to those who read earlier drafts of the novel, especially Linda Lenhoff, Laurie Edson, Susan Conley, and Linda Koolish. Ivory Broadway —told you I wouldn't forget. Thanks also to Nicole Word-law, Laura Zweckbronner, Susan Sekler, Luna Calderon, and Alexis Adorador. The Guikemas—Barb, Henry, Marcy, Tom, Susan, Josh, and Amanda—for welcoming me into the family. Kathy White, my angel. Thanks for always believing in me. Charlyne Bryant for knowing what would happen and for being right.

I owe so much to those teachers who I was fortunate enough to study with over the years. I especially wish to thank Dr. Robert Folkenflik, Dr. Ephriam Sando, Dr. Dickerson Bruce, Sandra Christenson, and Jerry Bumpus —each of you inspired and supported me, and for that I will always be grateful.

About the Author

RENÉE SWINDLE RECEIVED her MFA in creative writing from San Diego State University. She lives in Oakland, California. This is her first novel.